VELOCITY

What Reviewers Say About
Gun Brooke's Work

Treason

"The adventure was edge-of-your-seat levels of gripping and exciting…I really enjoyed this final addition to the Exodus series and particularly liked the ending. As always it was a very well written book."—Melina Bickard, Librarian, Waterloo Library (UK)

Insult to Injury

"This novel tugged at my heart all the way, much the same way as *Coffee Sonata*. It's a story of new beginnings, of rediscovering oneself, of trusting again (both others and oneself)."—*Jude in the Stars*

"If you love a good, slow-burn romantic novel, then grab this book."
—*Rainbow Reflections*

"[A] light romance that left me with just the right amount of 'aw shucks' at the end."—*C-Spot Reviews*

"I was glad to see a disabled lead for a change, and I enjoyed the author's style—the book was written in the first person alternating between the main characters and I felt that gave me more insight into each character and their motivations."—Melina Bickard, Librarian, Waterloo Library (UK)

Wayworn Lovers

"*Wayworn Lovers* is a super dramatic, angsty read, very much in line with Brooke's other contemporary romances. …I'm definitely in the 'love them' camp."—*Lesbian Review*

Thorns of the Past

"What I really liked from the offset is that Brooke steered clear of the typical butch PI with femme damsel in distress trope. Both main characters are what I would call ordinary women—they both wear suits for work, they both dress down in sweatpants and sweatshirts in the evening. As a result, I instantly found it a lot easier to relate, and connect with both. Each of their pasts hold dreadful memories and pain, and the passages where they opened up to each other about those events were very moving."—*Rainbow Reviews*

"I loved the romance between Darcy and Sabrina and the story really carried it well, with each of them learning that they have a safe haven with the other."—*Lesbian Review*

Escape: Exodus Book Three

"I've been a keen follower of the Exodus series for a while now and I was looking forward to the latest installment. It didn't disappoint. The action was edge-of-your-seat thrilling, especially towards the end, with several threats facing the Exodus mission. Some very intriguing subplots were introduced, and I look forward to reading more about these in the next book."—Melina Bickard, Librarian, Waterloo Library, London (UK)

Pathfinder

"I love Gun Brooke. She has successfully merged two of my reading loves: lesfic and sci-fi."—*Inked Rainbow Reads*

"I found the characters very likable and the plot compelling. I loved watching their relationship grow. From their first meeting, they're impressed and intrigued by each other. This matures into an easy friendship, and from there into dancing, kisses, and more. ...I'm looking forward to seeing the rest of the series!"—*All Our Worlds: Diverse Fantastic Fiction*

Soul Unique

"This is the first book that Gun Brooke has written in a first person perspective, and that was 100% the correct choice. She avoids the pitfalls of trying to tell a story about living with an autism spectrum disorder that she's never experienced, instead making it the story of someone who falls in love with a person living with Asperger's. ...*Soul Unique* is her best. It was an ambitious project that turned out beautifully. I highly recommend it."—*Lesbian Review*

"Yet another success from Gun Brooke. The premise is interesting, the leads are likeable and the supporting characters are well-developed. The first person narrative works well, and I really enjoyed reading about a character with Asperger's."—Melina Bickard, Librarian, Waterloo Library (London)

Advance: Exodus Book One

"*Advance* is an exciting space adventure, hopeful even through times of darkness. The romance and action are balanced perfectly, interesting the audience as much in the fleet's mission as in Dael and Spinner's romance. I'm looking forward to the next book in the series!"—*All Our Worlds: Diverse Fantastic Fiction*

The Blush Factor

"Gun Brooke captures very well the two different 'worlds' the two main characters live in and folds this setting neatly into the story. So, if you are looking for a well-edited, multi-layered romance with engaging characters this is a great read and maybe a re-read for those days when comfort food is a must."—*Lesbians on the Loose*

"That was fantastic. It's so sweet and romantic. Both women had their own 'demons' and they didn't let anyone be close to them. But from the moment they met each other everything felt so natural between them. Their love became so strong in a short time. Addie's thoughts threatened her relationship with Ellie but with her sister's help she managed to avoid a real catastrophe…"—*Nana's Book Reviews*

Coffee Sonata

"If you enjoy a good love story, a great setting, and wonderful characters, look for *Coffee Sonata* at your favorite gay and lesbian bookstore."—*MegaScene*

"Award-winning author Gun Brooke has given us another delightful romance with *Coffee Sonata*. I was so totally immersed in this story that I read it in one sitting."—*Just About Write*

Course of Action

"Brooke's words capture the intensity of their growing relationship. Her prose throughout the book is breathtaking and heart-stopping. Where have you been hiding, Gun Brooke? I, for one, would like to see more romances from this author."—*Independent Gay Writer*

"The setting created by Brooke is a glimpse into that fantasy world of celebrity and high rollers, escapist to be sure, but witnessing the relationship develop between Carolyn and Annelie is well worth the trip. As the reader progresses, the trappings become secondary to the characters' desire to reach goals both professional and personal."—*Midwest Book Review*

Visit us at www.boldstrokesbooks.com

By the Author

Romances:
Course of Action
Coffee Sonata
Sheridan's Fate
September Canvas
Fierce Overture
Speed Demons
The Blush Factor
Soul Unique
A Reluctant Enterprise
Piece of Cake
Thorns of the Past
Wayworn Lovers
Insult to Injury
Ice Queen

Science Fiction

Supreme Constellations series:
Protector of the Realm
Rebel's Quest
Warrior's Valor
Pirate's Fortune

Exodus series:
Advance
Pathfinder
Escape
Arrival
Treason

The Dennamore Scrolls
Yearning
Velocity

Lunar Eclipse
Renegade's War

Novella Anthology:
Change Horizons

VELOCITY

by

Gun Brooke

2022

VELOCITY

ISBN 13: 978-1-63555-983-5

THIS TRADE PAPERBACK ORIGINAL IS PUBLISHED BY
BOLD STROKES BOOKS, INC.
P.O. BOX 249
VALLEY FALLS, NY 12185

FIRST EDITION: JANUARY 2022

CREDITS
EDITOR: SHELLEY THRASHER
PRODUCTION DESIGN: SUSAN RAMUNDO
COVER DESIGN BY GUN BROOKE

Acknowledgments

Thank you to my readers who buy my books and who have, many of them, stayed so loyal to my stories. I'm always humbled and awestruck by that—and that you take the time to drop me a line every now and then.

My editor, Dr. Shelley Thrasher, you are my wing-woman when it comes to the editing and helping shape the story to the best it can be. I'm grateful to have you as you know my writing style so well and know just where to push me, and what to say to make me feel great about my writing. It's a gift, dear friend!

Thank you to Len Barot (aka Radclyffe), Sandy, Cindy, Carsen, Toni, Ruth, Stacia, Susan, Lee, Victoria, proofers, and all the other lovely people involved with BSB—you all rock and I'm thankful for every single one of you.

My first readers, Annika and Sam, thank you for helping me iron out the worst of the mistakes and logical gaps (the size of Texas) and for being there to encourage me when I go home-blind and don't know if what I've written is even readable. ☺

My family, Malin, Henrik, Pentti, grandchildren, Ove, and Monica—you all know how much you mean to me and how blessed I feel to have you in my life.

My friends…online, in "real life," and the girls in my art class, you are amazing and the way you care and take time to be encouraging, I'll never take for granted.

Dedication

For Elon
I miss you

PROLOGUE

The hedge provided enough cover as Holly Crowe made her way along the dark residential street of Dennamore, where she had grown up after she was adopted as a baby. The houses on both sides of the street were dark, which suited her fine. This was her guilty pleasure, and she wasn't about to share it with anyone or, God forbid, answer questions about why she was out in the middle of the night, carrying a large backpack and an even bigger bag.

Heading north toward the meadows, the large open area between two mountains, she had to switch on her flashlight. She kept it on low and turned to the ground, secure in the knowledge that no one else up this late would spot her. She passed the deep lake before she reached the beginning of the meadows. She had stood by the lake and watched the yearly light phenomenon. Now it was still and black, like a dark eye among the tall pine trees.

Holly glanced up at the sky, grinning because it was the clearest night in a long time. With not a cloud in sight, the stars literally twinkled at her. Reaching the perfect perch between the lake and the meadows, she found her favorite level spot and began setting up her state-of-the-art telescope. She hummed just under her breath as she attached her DSLR camera to the telescope and fiddled with the settings. She hoped to snap some beautiful space photos for the web store she owned, which had become quite successful over the past years. It was a welcome change from her work as a published author and researcher. Social and political science was her other love, and she had become famous among her peers after publishing five award-winning books. No one, however, knew the esteemed Holly Crowe spent at least one night outside every week to secretly photograph the vastness of space.

Unfolding the camping stool she used when sitting at her telescope, she began scanning the sky. She kept away from the new moon, so its light wouldn't disturb her photos. She would of course photograph the moon as well, as the people who frequented her online store always enjoyed images of the lunar cycle.

A faint sound made her stop humming. What was that? She looked behind her at the distant muted lights from Dennamore, but no. The sound didn't come from the town. She turned her head from side to side, and as the noise grew louder, she could tell it was originating from the north, from that part of the meadows—until it changed direction.

She stood so fast, her back smarted. Thundering, her heart picked up speed. What *was* that? A hum so low in frequency she felt it rather than heard it made her skin tingle. Another sound, more like a reverberating tone than anything else, erupted behind her and seemed to impossibly come from the lake.

"What the fu—" The lake went from black and reflecting the distant stars to being filled with bright green and yellow flickering lights. This was impossible. Nothing like this had ever been reported. The Lake Lights happened in August each year on the same exact days, even, which somehow no one in Dennamore questioned. And now—here they were, more ablaze than she had ever seen them before.

She was so shocked, it took a few moments to react. Tearing her camera off the telescope, she changed the settings and began photographing. As the lights began to fade, she merely stood there, trying to wrap her mind around what had just happened. Had this taken place before? What were the odds of it happening without anyone noticing? She couldn't be the first late-night wanderer to roam these parts.

The low hum reached her once more, this time from the northeast. She glanced at the lake, but it was dark and still again. Turning back, she drew a deep breath that didn't seem to reach her lungs. Below her, about seventy yards out on the meadow, a glowing rectangle had appeared. The hum rose to a low growl, and the air above it seemed to flicker. Raising her camera, she zoomed in and set it to video mode. She had the presence of mind to rest her hands against the top of the telescope to steady herself, which was necessary, as she was shaking.

The air stilled—and there it was. An elongated triangular vessel hovered above the glowing surface beneath it. Made from what looked like metal, it boasted small glowing lights that emphasized an intricate pattern. Slowly it began to descend, and the rectangle, which she now realized was an opening in the ground eventually swallowed it. The opening began to close, and soon she was alone with the stars again.

Slowly, she sat down on the camping stool, switching off her camera's video function. Pulling up the menu, she played back what she'd captured. No. She hadn't imagined it. A sort of ship, or aircraft, had landed on the meadow in Dennamore or, rather, been swallowed up by it. What was going on? Some secret military facility? Or an equally secret civilian research?

Snorting, she knew she wouldn't take any more photos of the stars and the moon this particular night. She packed up her telescope but hooked the camera strap around her neck. If something else showed up in the sky as she walked back to her house, she wanted to be prepared. Tomorrow she planned to return and explore the area on the meadow.

CHAPTER ONE

Samantha Pike maneuvered *Speeder One* as if it were second nature to her by now. The massive alien shuttle was immensely graceful as it glided over the Adirondack treetops, dipped, and kept an altitude of forty feet while crossing the meadows. She navigated to the concealed hatch in the ground that opened only after she gave the command, making it possible to hover for a moment and then descend into the chute that led to the tunnel hidden beneath the town, excavated by the aliens who founded Dennamore in the late 1700s.

Samantha still marveled that she knew exactly how to operate the complex computer system and the physical levers. *Speeder One* obeyed her every command seamlessly, as if the shuttle were an extension of her body and mind.

"That has to be the smoothest landing yet," Darian Tennen, former LA cop, said from behind her. "Your hands literally danced over the controls."

"I know. It's as if my body just knows." Samantha turned and smiled toward Darian. As amazing as locating ancient, fully functioning alien space shuttles in her hometown of Dennamore was, on a personal level, meeting Darian back in the late summer seemed even more incredible.

"Muscle memory, combined with your neural interface." Darian bent and kissed Samantha's cheek. "We wouldn't even be here if they hadn't given us a crash course in being aliens."

Samantha raised her hand and felt under her hair, just at the nape of her neck, where the NIEC—the Neural Interface Expertise Connector—a small metal disk, was attached. Its filament tentacles had woven into her hair and painlessly fused with her scalp. How they managed to lock on to their user yet were so easy to remove was still a mystery.

Samantha would never forget when she, as the head librarian in Dennamore, found them in the basement archives of the old library: seventy-six metal boxes, all with attached scrolls containing writings in what looked like code but turned out to be an alien language. The boxes held the NIECs, and eventually Samantha and the people she and Darian had invited to help them all had one. The way the NIECs stimulated their brains baffled her, and in her case, it allowed her to read the alien language, pilot the large shuttles, and understand the navigational console. The NIEC had for some reason decided she was pilot material.

Darian's NIEC had in turn homed in on her propensity for law-enforcement work and provided her with everything she needed to know to function as their chief security officer. Their youngest member, Carl Hoskins, eighteen, had offered his opinion that the NIECs operated much like the sorting hat in the famous Harry Potter books, and Samantha considered it an accurate assessment. The NIECs tapped into their brains, figured out where they'd be the most useful, and began infusing them with the suitable information. It took Samantha a while to realize what was happening, but now she had accepted that the transfer of knowledge was becoming permanent over time. Why this obvious manipulation on a neurological level didn't freak out her, the born control freak, was anyone's guess.

She unbuckled her harness and stood, squeezing Darian's hand in passing as she left the helm and walked to the door. "I have to get quicker when it comes to entering the hatch. We hovered too long."

"Too long?" Geoff Walker, the former Dennamore Chief of Police, now retired, huffed behind her. "You set this baby down in seconds." He towered next to her and Darian as they walked out the door, down the steps, and onto the smooth floor of the tunnel.

"I just need to do better with each attempt. Once we find the way into the mothership, I need to be able to fly it. Aiming for perfection with the speeders is the only way I can practice." Samantha frowned, her fear of failure making her irritated at their attempt at reassurance. "It's that or my killing the lot of you if I don't get it right. It has to be perfect."

"I know," Darian said. "So does Walker." She shot Walker a look.

Samantha sighed, uncomfortable that Darian felt she had to smooth things out between her and Walker. She forced herself to relax. "Of course. And I know you all mean well. It's just that... we have pushed back the day when we have to involve more people from Dennamore in our findings. Not discovering the entrance to the *Velocity*, the mothership, is part of it, but also, I haven't felt ready. Perhaps those things are connected? Maybe I can't feel ready before I've learned to master the controls of the *Velocity*?"

"Samantha, it's not all on you. Once we have a full crew, when more people are connected to the NIECs, more pilots will be available, and you'll be their chief. Don't ask me how I know—I just do." Darian's grandmother, the regal-looking Camilla Tennen, wheeled up to Samantha in her new electric wheelchair. Her rheumatoid arthritis had acted up since winter was on its way, and the new wheelchair allowed her more independence. She and her personal assistant, Brandon, were the only ones not using the NIECs, Camilla because of health reasons and Brandon because the NIECs didn't work on him. The consensus was that you needed to be a descendant of the aliens that once settled in the Adirondacks, and Brandon wasn't.

"You have a point," Samantha said while she pushed the flight suit off her upper body and tied the sleeves around her waist. "So much has to fall into place before then though."

"Why don't we return to Brynden 4 and heat some of Brandon's casserole?" Geoff suggested.

Another man his age turned around from where he was attaching a computer to a sensor on the belly of *Speeder One*. Phileas Beresford, who went by Philber, a renowned social anthropologist, shook his head. "Not yet for me. I need to gather the information from the flight-computer core and run it through the diagnostic system. That way, we might just end up with the information we need to unlock the secret to reaching the *Velocity*."

Darian patted Philber's shoulder. "We'll save you a plate. Don't worry."

The rest of them began walking to the vehicle, called a hauler, which sat in the center of the massive, smoothly chiseled tunnel that was thirty yards wide and approximately three miles long. At the far end of it, two months ago, they had found *Speeder One* and *Two*. To save time when they did their test flights, they didn't move the speeder in use all the way back to the shuttle bay but kept it by the exit tunnel that led to the meadows.

The hauler was operated by a joystick and held enough seats to accommodate thirty-some people. Where a windscreen should have been placed, a screen with transparent data helped the driver maneuver it securely, as it was also able to tow their speeder.

After maneuvering Camilla's wheelchair onto the back of the hauler, they drove to the first opening in the tunnel wall, which led to a staircase that took them to Camilla's house. Built in the late 1700s, it was one of the few original settlers' houses still standing. Walker and Philber also lived in similar houses and had their own access points to their respective homes.

Brandon easily carried Camilla up the stairs, past the basement, and entered the newly renovated dining room. He placed her gently on her chair at the end of the table. Darian walked up to her grandmother and took her hands.

"You feel a bit cold," she said quietly as Samantha joined them.

"Aw, don't fuss, Darian," Camilla said, smiling broadly. "I'll be warm and toasty in no time. But perhaps bring me my mohair shawl?"

"I'll get it," Samantha said. "Living room?"

"Yes, thank you, dear," Camilla said.

Returning quickly with the shawl, Samantha found Darian had left the room. "Where did she go?" Samantha placed the shawl around Camilla's narrow shoulders.

"I asked her to bring down the journal. I think we're due for some more information. In fact, it might settle you a bit. I know you're our fearless leader, but you take on too much of the responsibility." Camilla, her gentle voice holding no criticism, was merely stating the facts as she saw them. "Once we find the one the NIECs choose to be the captain, your burden will ease."

Samantha had given this subject a lot of thought over the last two months. As much as the others had their respective roles, she was alone at the helm. Sharing the responsibility would be a welcome change when that day came. She just hoped whoever possessed the required qualities would end up being someone they could relate to and work with.

As they gathered around Brandon's casserole, Samantha finally began to relax, looking at the people who were now as close to her as family. Next to her was Darian, the woman she could never stop looking at. Her wavy, chocolate-brown hair, almost always kept in a low ponytail, was rich and shiny. Brown eyes, which could be flat and penetrating or warm like honey, regarded the world with equal parts curiosity and suspicion. With a fondness for running and working out, Darian moved with grace, her physical strength impressive. So far, they had only kissed. Secretly, on particularly lonely nights, Samantha wished they had moved their attraction further along, but they had so much to do and even more to plan. Between her job as the head librarian and working on the alien technology, she barely found enough hours to sleep.

Samantha let her gaze travel around the table. Walker, infatuated with Camilla, his big teenage crush, had stealthily cut her meat for her. Camilla's hands were always weaker in the evenings, but Walker understood not to be obvious about helping her. Carl, the youngest among them, was shoveling food into his mouth as if he were afraid to go without. He had turned out to be a great scholar when it came to interpreting the finer nuances of the alien lettering and syntax. He would be the one reading from the journal later.

Raoul, their physician, was talking to Darian about growing up in West Hollywood in Camilla's care. Orphaned at age eight, Darian had lived with her "Gran" until she graduated from the police academy. She had made detective at a very young age and gave it all up to help Camilla move back to Dennamore. Darian had thought it was a temporary thing and that she'd return to LA when Camilla was settled. That was before she fully experienced the *yearning* and then, with Samantha, found the alien artifacts.

The *yearning* happened to the people of Dennamore who moved away from their hometown for any purpose. Whether it was instant or took them almost fifty years, like with Camilla, sooner or later they felt the urge, the yearning, to return home. For Darian, who had never set foot in her grandmother's hometown, it had been a complete surprise to feel it creep up on her.

As they moved into the parlor, where newly renovated antique furniture easily provided seating for everyone, Carl accepted the journal and opened it to where they had left off. Before he could start reading, Philber returned and was provided a plate of food by Brandon before joining them.

"I have a suggestion," Carl said carefully. "Because Samantha talked about how we never meant to keep this to ourselves this long, perhaps we need to skip ahead to where Bech'taia writes about the *Velocity*? If we want to move things along faster, I mean. I've seen it referenced in the midsection of the journal."

Everyone looked over at Samantha, who in turn exchanged a glance with Darian. "Why not? We have to find out how to get in there before we can even contemplate moving forward."

"I have another suggestion for you all to mull over," Philber said, "but let's hear what Carl has found."

Carl turned a few pages farther into the middle of the large book and cleared his throat. "This is all written in the alien letters." He flashed them a broad grin. "I'm so glad you finally dared to let me use my NIEC, or I'd be totally out of the loop. Okay. Here goes. 1877. July."

It has finally dawned on me. I've even come to accept it. We are not going home. The Elder Council has finalized their decision to bury the ship. Any chance of leaving will be buried right with it. Gai'usto has, however, not accepted anything of the sort. Instead, he holds secret meetings with some other loyal crewmembers who stay in the dormitories where the uncoupled people live. I have heard some of what they discuss, and one idea sounds more insane than the next.

When I try to voice my opinion, he dismisses me, and it makes me so angry. We are coupled since only one year ago, and I love him. Part of me understands it is his frustration and stress that makes him show these less attractive traits, but I have now demanded they keep quiet long enough during their next meeting to hear me out. Gai'usto understands this is not a suggestion. In fact, it is an ultimatum. Either we will be equals, as a coupled pair should be, or he will move out of our humble cabin and live in the dormitory.

Carl looked up. "I like her."

Samantha nudged Darian gently. "Some traits are strong within your family."

"Oh, please. She sounds more like you than me." Darian snorted. Carl continued.

The meeting was postponed twice, but eventually we met by the lake in the woods. It was time for me to make my case, and I started by breaking the law, as I took an illegal computer with me. I am an excellent mathematician, but for some calculations you do need the assistance of a computer.

I showed them my estimates and how my plan could allow us to keep settling down on this world, in so many ways a paradise compared to home, and still have the option to leave if we had to. It was obvious that they had not expected that approach. Their ideas had included violence, mutiny, insurrection, and there I stood, clinging to my computer and suggesting that we persuade the Elder Council to build an underground facility, store the NIECs and our communicators safely there, and then sink the Velocity *in the very lake where we were meeting.*

I had well-constructed counterarguments for any they could think of. Before the night was over, the twelve men and women before me had accepted my plan and were prepared to put it to the Council.

Carl quickly browsed a few pages before he began reading again.

The decision has been made. In the end, it did not take much convincing to persuade the Council, especially since the uncoupled young crewmembers weighed in, and the Council realized they might have an uproar on their hands if they insisted on an irrevocable solution. We are going to excavate enough bedrock for the tunnel system required. After building a rudimentary pump system, we will temporarily drain the lake and build a chamber for the Velocity. *Only the Council members will know the access point, which will be marked on maps that only they will have access to. As Gai'usto and I will be among the crew working on this project, we will be sworn to secrecy, along with the others. For the first time in my life, I will commit treason against the Elders and go against this vow. I do not agree with their view of not spreading the knowledge among the rest of the crew. One day the Elders will be gone and replaced by a younger generation. I fear that the knowledge about the ship— its location, even where we come from and how we ended up here—will fall into oblivion. Gai'usto thinks I am exaggerating when I talk about this probability, telling me that our culture is too great, and too strong, to ever be forgotten. I do not think so. Several children have already been born here, Earthborn, and the risk is great for them to grow up knowing little to nothing about Dwynna Major and the people we left behind, the people we were sent out to help. So, while I swear the oath of silence, I will make my own markings on all the maps I come across, to guide the way to the ship for those who need to find it.*

At least by placing the ship underneath the lake and keeping a guarded archive of our technology, we may be able to try for home one day. If not us, then perhaps the upcoming generation. Just knowing this is possible has lifted the spirit of me and everyone else. I get through the days much easier, and some days I feel truly happy. We work hard from sunup to sunset, Gai'usto and I, to hide the ship before the indigenous people of this nation, or anyone else headed deep into the wood, come across it by accident.

"Dwynna Major?" Camilla turned to Samantha. "That is the name of their origins. We've come across it several times, and I'm always fascinated how it became Dennamore after a while here on Earth."

"I would agree." Darian stood and began pacing, which wasn't uncommon for her when she was thinking out loud. "We have to gather what maps we can find. Bech'taia marked them, and if we locate the same mysterious marking on several different ones, then that's a good place to start." She twirled her ponytail around her hand and then stopped in the center of the room. "If you ask me, it sounded like it's a prerequisite of Council members to have sticks up their asses."

Carl snorted. "Yup. That about sums it up."

Samantha groaned. "You have no idea. I feel like Desmond Miller is trying to fuse with me. He's a shrewd man and can probably sense I'm up to something. Perhaps Philber too. I stumble over him every time I turn around."

"Our esteemed Council chairman has a nose for conspiracies. Another reason for us to find the *Velocity* and push our plans forward," Walker said. "I have an idea. Everyone here knows people in Dennamore that we trust, both on a personal level and when it comes to their credentials. Why don't we start recruiting? With only eight of us, we need more people. To be blunt, we don't know when we'll actually find the way to *Velocity*. Miller might have enough time to cause us real problems before then. What do you think?"

Samantha was relieved. Perhaps it was her lack of self-confidence of late, but it felt good that she didn't have to make the suggestion. "I think it's time too," she said now, hearing her own voice sound stronger than it had all day. Maybe several days.

"Agreed." Philber raised his hand. The others nodded affirmatively as well.

"How do we do this? Should we think of names and run them by each other, get the go-ahead, and then proceed to bring them in?" Raoul asked.

"Sounds reassuring. That way, we're all responsible for the choice for what will essentially be our crew." Samantha pulled a notepad and pen from the side table to her. She jotted down the suggestion, and when everyone voted yes, she went on to the next question. "We will have to start moving NIECs and speakers." She indicated the communication device attached to her shirt. "Maps too. And we'll be taking a great risk doing so. We won't be able to hide the fact that we've disturbed centuries of dust in the oldest part of the archive."

"At least we have a back door in since you found the small elevator that leads into Town Hall." Camilla sighed. "I regret that Darian, Brandon, and I won't be able to come up with very many suggestions for potential crewmembers. Having lived here for three months doesn't cut it, I'm afraid. Besides, we've mostly spent time with you lot." She winked at Walker, who had the misfortune to blush a little.

"Then you'll be in charge of setting up and keeping track of the NIECs, etcetera." Samantha smiled. "You will be the taskmaster, Camilla, and the other two can do the heavy lifting."

Darian deliberately raised her eyebrows at Samantha. "She'll work us to a pulp, and we just finished the reno of this house." She indicated the log house around them.

They remained in Camilla's living room for another hour, hashing out more details, even tossing around some names that already came to mind with some of them. Samantha found herself content to listen after a while and again study this family of friends she'd come to love. And then there was Darian, who was butting heads with Raoul, all tongue-in-cheek, over name suggestions. Only after Camilla had fallen asleep against Walker's shoulder did they end their meeting. It was after two a.m., and several of them had to catch some sleep before going to work in the morning.

On these late nights, the ones who had access points to the tunnel in their basements used them to go home. Carl and Raoul usually accompanied Philber and then walked the short distance from his home to their more modern houses.

Samantha usually spent those nights at Camilla and Darian's. They now had a beautiful guest room, and even if Samantha had shared Darian's bed before the guest room existed, they hadn't returned to that arrangement. Samantha told herself it was better this way. They were too entangled in the matter of the alien technology and damn spaceships to take another step forward romantically. But Samantha also knew that if Darian had invited her into her bed, or come to the guest room in the night, she would have gladly received her.

Samantha knew she would never give up hope that this could happen later. Judging from how Darian looked at her and occasionally caressed her in passing, or even kissed her like today, albeit quite chastely, Samantha's interest was reciprocated. One time, when Camilla had had a bit too much red wine and then some of her strong painkillers, she had waved her hand at Samantha and Darian and called them "sizzling."

When Samantha was finally tucked into the soft guest bed, she had to agree, remembering their earliest kisses. Sizzling was putting it mildly.

CHAPTER TWO

Holly logged out from her stationary computer and rubbed her eyes. Only then remembering she was wearing eye makeup, she cursed and reached for the small mirror she kept in a desk drawer. Examining the expertly applied eyeliner, she saw it was still intact. She ran her fingertips along her lower lash line and brushed away a few specs of eye shadow that she'd rubbed out of place.

Normally, she didn't bother with more than a minimum of makeup, but when she was teaching via link like today, the ring light she used washed her out. She didn't think she was very vain, but she was particular. Looking her best boosted her confidence and gave her that extra edge. Frances sometimes teased her about it, calling her Ms. Perfect. The name had annoyed Holly on occasion, but for the most part she had laughed it away and understood that Frances meant no harm. The thought of her wife whom she lost to cancer seven years ago made Holly pause. Losing Frances after an excruciating year of battling the relentless disease had made her return to Dennamore. She was already famous in her fields by then, and the dean of the university where she taught was ready to bend over backward to keep her on the faculty. Holly went to Albany several times every semester but did give her lectures online, like today.

Holly chastised herself for getting lost in thought when she needed to change and get going. Energized at finally having the opportunity, and the right weather, to hike to the meadows, she jumped up and went to change. She only had to remove her blouse, as she was already geared up from the waist down. After choosing a blue turtleneck and an off-white knitted sweater, boots, and lined windbreaker, she grabbed her camera bag that sat ready in the hallway. Her pulse was elevated at what she might find as she headed out the door.

The last couple of days when the weather had prevented her from going to the site where she had spotted, and filmed, the strange vessel and the hole in the ground, had been torturous. She had watched, and re-watched, the video and stills she had taken, and each time she could barely believe her eyes. Using her video software and photo editor to zoom in, she had found strange markings on the side of the vessel that was lit indirectly from below. They looked like code, which was mysterious in itself.

She met a few people walking toward the meadows, but as it was an ordinary weekday and still early afternoon, most of the Dennamore inhabitants were either at work or school.

The air was crisp, and Holly had to be careful not to slip on any of the icy patches as she made her way toward the trail that tourists used to reach the lake and meadows, and also to hike up the mountain. Holly loved being in nature around her hometown, but she preferred to stay close to civilization. Doing this, especially without telling anyone else, was both in character for her, and not. She had friends in Dennamore, but nobody that she had ever let in fully. Perhaps that was because she always felt like an outsider. Being adopted and not related to the founding ancestors, like most of her peers were, had created a barrier. Never bullied, or disliked, Holly still had felt excluded. Frances used to say that half the barriers around Holly were self-constructed, and perhaps she'd been right.

Samantha Pike, the head librarian, was one of the people Holly had become reacquainted with when she returned to Dennamore six years ago. Needing Samantha's expertise and the resources of the library for her research, they had become friends, however not especially close. Months could pass between the times they grabbed a coffee together. Holly didn't mind her own company; her work took most of her time, and her interest in photography and space consumed the rest.

The meadows doused in sunlight was a completely different vision than the other night, and at first, Holly was disoriented. She turned and looked over at the lake. Then, turning back, she spotted the rock formation where she'd set up her telescope. After walking over to it, she looked out over the meadows and tried to estimate the distance to what she'd seen.

She pulled up her tablet and found the video of the phenomenon, stopping it where it clearly showed the ground, the rectangular hole, and the outline of trees and mountains in the far background. Holding the tablet before her, she walked toward the site, intermittently scanning the ground.

As it turned out, the ground on the meadows clearly revealed the outline of a perfect rectangle. Holly thought it might be obvious to her because she knew where and what to look for. Anyone oblivious to its existence would probably just walk past without noticing it. She bent down, careful to remain on the outside of the faint perimeter, running her fingers along some withered grass that seemed trapped. Dirt lay in a string next to it, which made sense if somehow this part was able to sink and perhaps slide sideways. The possibility sounded ridiculous, and Holly didn't doubt that if she confided in anyone, they'd consider her certifiable.

She took several pictures, following the entire rectangle, and then made closeups of the trapped grass and dirt. Opening her camera bag, she pulled out her grandfather's old surveyor measuring tape and pulled it along the lines, typing the numbers into her cell phone. Eight by fifteen yards. Afterward, she stood there, cautiously looking around. Nobody was within sight, so as absurd as she felt, she knelt just inside the line and pressed her ear to the ground. She couldn't hear a thing, naturally. Snorting at herself, she stood and walked to the center of the rectangle. There she stopped when she saw something glimmer. It wasn't shiny, but it reflected light. Crouching, she saw a metal object, like a three-inch pipe, sticking up just enough for her to spot it. When she looked around for more, she saw an even more faint outline in the wild, dry grass, stretching the entire length of the center of the outlined area.

Remaining by the metal pipe, Holly tried to figure out what this meant. Did this, well, hatch, open in two parts? That would make sense. She snorted again. As if any of this made sense.

After another quick glance in all directions, she pressed her ear to the ground again. Nothing.

"Huh." She rolled back onto her feet, hugging her knees to her while she studied the protruding metal part. How long had it been there? People could have walked along the meadows and never stumbled upon this for ages. She'd found it only because she knew where she'd seen the light and the vessel.

She took more photos of the pipe from all directions, and when she zoomed in on the camera screen, she frowned. "What's that?" she murmured. Something glimmered at the bottom of the pipe, but it also seemed a lot deeper than she thought. Carefully, she leaned over it and looked. She was straight above it but couldn't see anything. She placed the lens of the camera against the opening at the top of the pipe and took several shots. This meant taking the photos in complete darkness.

Yet when she looked, she saw a light. This time it was distinct. Octagonal.

"Damn." Using her phone now, she shone the flashlight into the pipe, but it was impossible to judge how deep it went. Not even hesitating now, she pressed her ear to the pipe—and this time it wasn't quiet. A distinct hum reverberated and made her fall back. And it wasn't just the hum. The air inside the pipe, against her sensitive ear, was warmer than the air around it.

Darian was perusing the first list of ten people that the others had come up with. She was glad they knew who to approach since she didn't, but a small part of her felt she might not be the right person to be the chief of security, since she wasn't as well versed in Dennamore lore as the others. However, these doubts lessened each time she attached her NIEC and everything she needed to know about her duties seemed crystal clear. She looked down at the names of complete strangers and decided she'd done enough for one day. After getting up, she poked her head into Gran's bedroom, where she was watching TV and resting. "Hey. I'm going to work out, all right? I'll be in the tunnel."

"In the tunnel?" Camilla put down the remote she'd just used. "Need some space?"

Gran knew her well. Darian had always had a need for privacy, which hadn't always been easy to find in Gran's condo in West Hollywood. She knew this was why Gran had feigned an interest in camping and rented cabins every now and then when Darian was a teenager, to give her some breathing room.

"Yeah." Darian nodded. "I'm on my speaker and wearing my NIEC."

"Good. Have fun." Gran returned to her channel hopping.

Darian continued downstairs and then down into the basement. There she rounded the now-exposed wall that was made of one large piece of bedrock. The surface was as smooth as glass, and intricate lines and dots blinked and flickered in it. As she approached, the wall where the lights were parted and revealed the long, narrow staircase leading down into the tunnel. She jogged down the stairs, and as she entered the tunnel, the muted light increased and showed how long and wide it was.

Darian walked past the hauler that was parked next to their access point, one of Camilla's electric wheelchairs strapped to it. Gran had one down here and one she used when leaving the house. Indoors, she still managed to walk, albeit with a cane and preferably with a person on her other side.

"Okay," Darian murmured and began running. She usually ran five miles, and today was no different. As she fell into the soothing feeling an even tempo always brought her, her thoughts went to Samantha. The other day, she had seemed so stressed it had worried Darian. They needed to find a captain, fast, and more crew. Only yesterday, after yet another day of not determining a common denominator between the maps of Dennamore that could show them the entrance to the Velocity's location, Samantha had seemed so closed off and tense. Darian knew, they all did, that it had had to be below the lake, but how to unravel the secret about how to access it was eating away at them, yet mostly at Samantha, who shouldered the weight of moving them forward in the research. Perhaps they'd been too cocky. Their first discoveries had all happened one after another, but then they'd hit a plateau.

After returning to her access point, Darian began the slow movements of tai chi. It didn't take her long to find the flow, and she let her mind go blank. This was one of the ways she had kept her sanity as a detective at the LAPD—clearing her mind, keeping her body lithe and strong.

After a while, Darian noticed how her movements changed. She flowed from a meditative state to being alert, and the way she sliced her hands through the air had nothing to do with tai chi. She barely had time to register that her precise, deadly kicks, twirls, and jumps had to be because of the NIEC. She let instinct take over. Taking aim, she ran toward the smooth wall of the tunnel, kept running up along it for three steps, pushed off on the fourth, performed a somersault backward, and landed in a crouch, her hands raised, ready to fight.

A sound behind her made her rise and pivot in one fluent motion.

"Stand down, fighter," Samantha said coolly, but Darian saw her take two steps back. "That was some move, Dar."

"Samantha. I'm so sorry. I didn't hear you come down." Darian lowered her hands. "I didn't mean to startle you." *Or launch at her, but she almost had.*

"I'm fine. You looked amazing. Don't think I've seen you do that last trick before." Samantha came closer.

"Neither have I." Darian tapped her temple. "New trick, I think. I was doing tai chi, but my NIEC kicked in. Literally."

"Did you feel out of control?" Samantha frowned, touching Darian's upper arm briefly.

The small caress made Darian relax. "No, though perhaps to a degree. I wasn't aware of when exactly the tai chi turned into some alien ninja sport."

Samantha smiled and came closer. "It was actually quite beautiful," she said, cupping Darian's cheek. "I watched for a few moments." Her eyes had darkened to a forest green.

"You watched me?" Darian returned the smile.

"Can you blame me? I can't recall when I've actually had you to myself for more than five minutes in weeks. Or months?" She let go and held up her hands. "I know, I know, I'm exaggerating, but time flies and...I suppose I miss the early days when we were so innocently trying to figure our mystery out."

"It's still such a mystery, but I know what you mean. A few months ago, you and I were on our own a lot. I mean, I love the others. They feel like family. But…"

"But." Running a gentle index finger down Darian's neck, Samantha tilted her head. "I do miss that."

"I do too. And I'm sorry I'm so sweaty now that we do have a moment." Cringing at her words, Darian took Samantha's wandering hand and kissed her palm.

"I don't mind. Honestly." Samantha pulled Darian closer and kissed her, soft and searching, as if reacquainting herself with Darian's mouth.

So grateful to find that the spark was still mutual, Darian turned them around and nudged Samantha up against the tunnel wall where she just performed the somersault. She returned the kiss, inhaling the scent that was Samantha's signature. Fresh, a little dark, classy. Pushing her fingers through Samantha's strawberry-blond hair, she managed to dislodge some hairpins that pinged like little bells as they landed on the floor.

"So good," Darian murmured into Samantha's mouth. "So damn good."

"Mm." Samantha tugged at Darian's shirt, pulling her closer yet. "Agreed."

These kisses had to be the best of all. Darian could barely believe how the long-pent-up tension between them went from nearly zero to a hundred in seconds. She was on fire, and the way Samantha pulled at her shirt showed the feeling was mutual. When images of tearing Samantha's suit off and pressing her naked body against the hauler flickered through Darian's mind, she clenched up, and she knew that for her, the day when she finally was able to get that close to Samantha couldn't come fast enough. "Wait…" Darian smoothed the now-wild hair around Samantha's face. "Got to slow down. It's that or having my way with you right here." She gasped for air as Samantha pulled back half an inch, her upper lips pulled back in what had to be a feral smile.

"So what?" Samantha hissed. "It's been too long."

"What has?" Darian hugged Samantha close. "Sex in general, or us getting more intimate?"

"Both." Muttering, Samantha buried her face against Darian's shoulder. "Of course, you're right. And I'm supposed to be the level-headed one. Not much of that lately either." She sighed and clung to Darian. "Just don't let go quite yet."

"Are you kidding? I could hold you like this forever." Closing her eyes, Darian allowed a gentle hum of total contentment to spread through her. Sure, parts of her wanted more, but emotionally, this was bliss. "And about you stressing? You know we understand, don't you? We truly do."

"I know you want to understand, but there's so much to do, so much to consider."

"And it's not all on you." Darian wanted to rock Samantha to try to soothe her but had a strong feeling that being rocked wasn't this woman's thing.

"I suppose. Am I arrogant for being so agitated?" Samantha pulled back enough for their eyes to meet. Hers were back to their usual lighter-green tone with golden flecks. The image of them was forever burned into Darian's mind.

"Arrogant? If you'd been Philber, I would have said 'hell, yeah,' but you? No. I think your agitation stems from being dutiful and incredibly responsible." Stepping back farther, Darian took Samantha's hands. "We have names of candidates that you guys have vetted now—ten names—and the future captain may be among them. Either way, once they're up to speed, we'll have more people to help us with everything."

Slowly, Samantha began to relax, only to tense as a pulsating sound began around them.

"What the hell's that?" Darian turned in a circle, trying to figure out where the noise came from. "Damn, that's loud."

Samantha closed her eyes for a moment. "It's the proximity alarm."

Darian's NIEC took one second longer, but then the information flooded through her brain. "It has to be at either one of the access points or the meadows." She ran over to the access point that led to Camilla's and her house. "Come on. We need to get to the computer console."

They ran up the stairs, and soon they stood at the large console in the basement. The first thing she did was to mute the alarm klaxons.

"God, that was loud." Tapping in commands, so used to the alien interface by now that it was second nature, Darian only vaguely registered that Samantha had her computer that they'd found aboard *Speeder One*. It was connected to the other computers like it and all the consoles in the tunnel were.

"It's the meadows," Samantha said. "Someone's found the sensor."

"What are the odds someone would stumble upon that? That little metal part is tiny." Darian logged into the surveillance system put in place almost two hundred and forty years ago. They couldn't see outside, but at least the chute that launched the speeders from the tunnel was intact. "Nobody has breached the hatch. Yet."

"Wait. I'm performing a thermal scan. There's a faint outline, but that's all I can hope for, as the hatch is made from alien alloy. Here. Look. One person's out there."

Darian moved over to Samantha and watched her adjust the scan. The outline of a person, yes. Were they crouching? Perhaps trying to dig around the sensor. What if they harmed it? Was that even possible?

"I'm going to run a diagnostic on the sensor," Darian said and returned to the larger console on the basement wall. "If this person has damaged it…" She tapped in commands and slid her fingers along colorful long lines in an intricate pattern that still was logical only to her.

"And?" It was Samantha's turn to look over Darian's shoulder.

"No. It's all right, so far. Whoever's up there, at least they haven't poked and prodded yet." She exhaled sharply. "Again, how the hell did they find it?"

"Pure chance…or…" Samantha stopped in midmotion as she was about to return to her computer. "Or they've seen *Speeder One* come in."

Darian thought her heart would stop. "What? But we're cloaked."

"Not always just as we enter the chute. I used to have to turn the cloak off, as it made it easier for me to maneuver, and now it's as if there might be a glitch. I don't know if that's the case, but I've noticed the cloaking system can flicker. I didn't think we were actually visible—but what if we were?"

"The odds of someone spotting us on the meadows in the middle of the night, if we were uncloaked for a second or two, are still astronomical!" Rubbing her forehead, Darian was beginning to feel cold and vaguely registered that she was still wearing her sweaty workout clothes.

"I know. That said, we still have to find out who's up there. Can we get there in time? Or send someone?" Samantha had only just uttered the last words when Philber and Walker showed up on her computer.

"What the hell's going on?" Philber growled. "That damn alarm nearly gave me a heart attack."

Darian relayed the information to them. "We need to figure out who this person is. Oh, damn. What if it's Desmond Miller?" She loathed the Elder Council chairman, who had his nose in everyone's business and wanted to micromanage everything that went on in Dennamore. He was not to be trusted.

"That's even more unlikely. I can't see him muddying his precious Jimmy Choo shoes. I swear that's all I've ever seen him wear." Samantha crinkled her nose. "So no, not him—this time."

"A random person? Walking a dog in the middle of the night perhaps?" Darian sighed. "Know anyone with nocturnal habits? And no, I don't mean prostitutes."

Samantha sounded as if she were about to choke. "God, woman. No. I can't think of—wait.'"

"You do have someone in mind." Darian wrapped her arm around Samantha's waist, curious now.

"No, not really, but…I have a friend that sometimes comes into the library for books other than her usual social- or political-science material. She's an avid amateur astronomer. It's always been her thing, from what she's told me over the years. I'm not saying it's her, on the contrary, but someone like her. A stargazer."

"That's an idea. Or, if we're really unlucky, your garden variety of a peeping Tom. Ew." Darian bumped her hip against Samantha's. "Actually, your idea is more appealing. The question is, should we try to get to the meadows? I mean now. Catch them in the act, so to speak. They haven't caused any damage yet, but they might."

Samantha closed her eyes briefly. When she opened them again, she squinted against her computer. "It'd take too long. I suggest we send a probe."

"A what, now?" Darian tried to access the same knowledge Samantha had. It took a few precious seconds, but then her NIEC provided the answer. "Of course. Damn. When the knowledge is there, it's obvious. Like peeling a freaking onion."

"The question is, can we launch it from here?" Samantha groaned. "Doing it planet side isn't the same as sending a probe in space. Not that I've ever done that, either."

"Hey. We'll figure it out." Darian placed a hand at the small of Samantha's back. "Good thing we're up in the middle of the night."

Both their speakers gave a muted ping. "How about sending a probe?" Walker asked.

"A great idea." Darian smiled. "Now we just have to figure out which one and how." She placed a kiss on Samantha's cheek. "Let's do this."

CHAPTER THREE

Samantha jumped into the hauler next to Darian. Used to manning the helm, Samantha punched in the commands and set the hauler in motion. On their way to the shuttle bay where *Speeder Two* still sat, she knew they needed the larger computer console there. It had taken them an additional four weeks after finding the speeders to locate the enormous console, well-hidden until it was accidentally triggered, like so many of their other finds. That time, it had been Walker working on his alien computer, with Camilla, when suddenly a vast portion of the wall lit up.

Samantha let the hauler come to a stop at Philber's access point, where the stocky man waited for them, his trademark bag slung over his shoulder. Being in his sixties and initially not in the best of health, he had experienced an improvement during the last few months. He thought it was because of the NIEC's influence, but Raoul, their chief medical officer, insisted it was because Philber was not housebound with his nose in his "musty old books" all the time. Now Philber jumped onto one of the other seats of the hauler, not bothering with more than a "let's go" in lieu of a hello.

A few minutes later, a carved-out elevator took them up a level to the shuttle bay. After parking the hauler, all three hurried over to the wall, which sensed them, or their NIECs, rather, and opened three large screens.

"We should start with the smallest probe." Darian tapped in commands, and her screen filled with an image showing the array of the probes. "The less of an intrusion the better."

"This person has already spotted something they know is out of the ordinary. Let's not waste an opportunity to use a more substantial probe." Philber shook his head. "So, what if they see it?"

"I'm not only talking about that person. We don't know if anyone else is around, and also, why scare the living daylights out of them?" Darian placed her hands on her hips. "And as chief of security, this is my call." With Philber, there was always some struggle when it came to enforcing the chain of command. He was a stubborn guy who was used to getting his way and could be called a know-it-all, which was not unfounded, but this was a security matter.

"We might get the chance to do both," Samantha said calmly. "Keep going, Darian."

Darian pulled up the new knowledge relayed to her by the NIEC. Pushing at fluorescent lines and tapping the colorful dots glowing in the dark, glossy bedrock wall, she engaged a probe that held a sensor with the ability to record, about the size of Samantha's little finger.

"I need you to help me use the navigation, Samantha," she murmured as her fingertips flowed across the computer. "We need to direct it to move just about body height and not hit anyone. I can manage that part, but as to steering it right, you're the star there."

"I'm on it." Samantha's screen filled with a map-like set of lines. She slid her index finger in a jagged line and then let go. "I added the coordinates. Now, if the person at the hatch is gone, we can have it circle until we set coordinates to send it toward town. What we can't do is have it go still. It can't hover."

"Are you saying *Speeder One* can hover, but that little thing can't?" Philber huffed. "Ridiculous."

Samantha had to smile. He was rather entertaining in his grumpiness, unless he took it too far and became obnoxious. "Here we go. All set. Deploying." She pressed her finger to a large blue dot. After a few seconds, the screen went black long enough for Samantha to worry it wouldn't work. Then she was nearly blinded by the strong sunlight and the blue, cloudless sky.

"Let's see, then." Darian rubbed her hands as she zoomed out the view from the tiny probe. "This is launching from our position about five hundred yards from the hatch sensor."

"And it's fast." Samantha stood behind Darian now, following the hurtling sensor as it sped along its set trajectory. "And I see the area. And…one person."

"Is that a boy? Looks very slender. Young, from this distance." Philber joined Samantha and squinted at the screen.

"No…I think it's a woman." Samantha moved back to her console and tapped in more commands. "Slowing down to a circling pattern. We'll see her from another angle soon."

"What's the altitude of your little doohickey?" Philber asked.

"Twenty feet, for now. I don't want to alert her by having it arrive at eye level." Samantha pulled a magenta-colored dot back along a lime-green line. "There we go. Less dizzying, better image."

"Well, what do you know," Philber said, huffing. "Whoever she is, she brought a backpack and tools. She's been there before."

"Could be," Darian murmured. "Do any of you recognize her?"

"Not yet. She's wearing a cap. I have to risk getting pretty low to spot her features. But even if we don't make out who she is, we can use the sensor to see where she lives." Samantha cringed at her own words.

"A bit creepy, but I'm here for it." Darian smiled. "What's she doing now?"

The woman, seen at a forty-five-degree angle from above, pulled out a camera from her bag and began snapping pictures. She even knelt and took closeup shots of the sensor. Samantha sighed. They were going to have to identify and reach out to her before she took this to the press or, worse, Miller, or merely showed the photos to friends and family, who in turn might want to try to solve the puzzle.

Samantha felt a headache begin to pound again, wondering what this stress did to her blood pressure.

"She's fiddling with the zipper of her bag. Now's your chance, Samantha." Darian spoke quickly.

Samantha reacted automatically, pushing at sensor levers and directing the sensor to six feet. As it made a new lap around the woman, Samantha saw her features clearly. "I can't believe it!" She stared at the screen as the sensor moved along in the narrower circle now. "Holly Crowe."

"Holly Crowe? The professor?" Philber snapped his head up and stared at Samantha. "It's her? That darn thing swooped by her so fast, I could barely make her out."

"It'll round her again now. Look for yourself." Samantha pointed at the screen.

The sensor made another turn, and Samantha was just about to punch in the command for a still image of the esteemed professor when the sensor suddenly halted. It seemed to wobble in place, despite not being able to hover.

"It's...stuck?" Darian worked her console. "I don't understand. It should plummet."

The screen showed Holly Crowe's face grow bigger on the screen. A frown marred her ethereal features, and her green, almond-shaped eyes were narrow slits as she stared right at them. Straight, brown eyebrows pulled together in a scowl. Then the image of the screen went crazy, as if the sensor was tumbling out of control.

"What the hell's going on?" Philber covered his eyes. "Damn."

"Is the probe malfunctioning?" Darian began running diagnostics.

"No," Samantha said after a few beats. "The probe's working, but she's caught it."

"What?" Darian stopped moving and looked from Samantha to the screen. "Oh, God. She did."

Holly Crowe was back on the screen, and it was eerie how she seemed to glower at them.

"At least we know who to approach. And it must happen quickly. Today." Samantha stood. "Philber, I'll ask those of the others that are available to join you here. Darian and I will go talk to Holly. At least I know her enough to not frighten her."

"Somehow, I don't think it's possible to scare that woman," Philber said, muttering. "Last time I had a run-in with her, she took my head off. She's made from stern stuff, that's for sure."

"Well, that might serve her well." Samantha leaned over her console. "I'm launching a larger probe. Now that Holly has the first one tucked away somewhere, in her pocket or in her backpack, judging from the darkness, it's easy to set the other probe to follow its signal. I need you to monitor and let us know via the speakers where she's going, Philber."

"Yeah. Got it. I think I'll enjoy this James Bond kind of shit." Philber grinned and looked like he was having far too much fun by now.

Darian motioned at her clothes. "I'm not exactly fresh. If you start moving in her direction, I'll catch up with you, after I clean up, if you need me to. Just let me know."

"All right." They took the elevator down with the hauler and sped off to Camilla's house. Darian drove, and Samantha made a joint call with the others via her speaker. As they ran up the stairs at their access point, Darian disappeared toward her room.

Camilla stood ready next to Brandon, her chin raised and with an obvious glitter in her eyes. "I'll join the boys and keep them in check," she said lightly, but tension showed around her lips. "Be careful, dear."

"Thank you, Camilla." Samantha nodded at Brandon and then put on her coat. As she hurried out into the cold weather, she cursed as she fumbled for her scarf and gloves in her pockets. Glad she wasn't in her boots with four-inch heels, she ran to her car and got in. Throwing the car in gear, she tore down the residential street, knowing this would be frowned upon, but not caring. Turning north, she drove toward the meadows and the beginning of the trail that led to them and the lake. It wasn't that she didn't respect and quite admire Holly Crowe. What worried Samantha as she sped through the quiet streets of her Dennamore was that she knew Holly wasn't one of them. She was adopted and not of alien descent.

CHAPTER FOUR

Holly walked toward the lake, her strides long and purposeful. She should be heading back home, and part of her was dying to examine her photos and video clips on her computer. A greater part of her just needed to calm down. Ever since she caught the object that had circled her repeatedly, her heart had pounded. The lake area, despite the water acting weird and not "on schedule" the other night, was one of her favorite places to cleanse her mind. The rustic wooden benches around the perimeter all provided a nice space to sit and enjoy the view of the dark water. Once she felt calmer, she was going home to investigate her findings further.

Choosing a bench closest between the meadows and the woods, she pulled out her foldable seat pad and placed it there to sit on. She let the camera bag slide to the ground and pushed her hand into her left breast pocket. Taking out the small, cylindrical object, she unwrapped the tissue she'd used to cover it. She turned it slowly between her fingers. It was made of charcoal-gray metal, though she couldn't distinguish what kind, and had thin grooves along its entire length. One end was not metallic, rather glass-like, obsidian in color, and the other end, which she judged was the backend, tapered off slightly. At first, she thought the grooves glittered in the sunlight, but then she realized she held the narrow object close to her face, in the shade.

"What the…"

"Hello, Holly," a female voice said from behind her, making her jump. She hid the object in her hand as she turned around. Relieved to see it was just Samantha Pike, the head librarian, she managed a smile.

"Hi, Samantha. You startled me." Holly frowned. Samantha was out of breath, but she wasn't dressed to go running. And if she were out for a walk, why would she be gasping for air?

"I didn't mean to." Walking closer, Samantha pointed next to Holly. "May I join you? I need to catch my breath, it seems." She didn't wait for an answer but sat down.

"Why do I get the feeling that us running into each other here isn't a coincidence?" Holly asked, shifting to face Samantha. She wasn't afraid. This was someone she knew. But an onset of nerves made her feel jittery.

"It's not. I came to talk to you." Samantha adjusted her cashmere scarf, pulling it up around her ears. "Cold here, sitting half in the shade."

"What can I do for you?" Holly asked coolly. She wasn't sure she liked where this was going.

"I saw you in the meadows. You found something you didn't expect." Samantha spoke in a way that showed it wasn't a question. "And you captured something else too, didn't you?"

"How can you possibly know any of that?" Holly gripped the small cylinder harder in her hand. "Cornering me this way isn't like you."

"I know you're curious, perhaps even apprehensive, but I promise you, that's nothing compared to what I've felt like, on and off, the last few months. You're not the only one making discoveries. You're in good company." Samantha broke eye contact and looked up at the sky. "What made you examine that particular part of the meadows? Did you see something? A light phenomenon? Or an aircraft?"

Holly's mind raced, and she credited her ability to catalogue pros and cons, then examine the potential fallout from her options to her education and profession. She quickly concluded that trying to lie to Samantha was futile. That didn't mean she was going to give everything away instantly. "I saw a square-shaped light reflect in what looked like some experimental vessel."

"I knew I didn't set the landing properly. It took too long." Samantha sighed and ran her gloved hand over her face. Her eyes, green like Holly's own, but a completely different hue, looked tired, the skin around them tense.

"Excuse me? Did you say that *you* landed that thing? Where is it now—underground?" Holly leaned forward, intrigued rather than cautious now.

"Yes. I did." Samantha held up her hand. "And the only reason I'm telling you like this, here by the lake, is because we have to inform everyone soon. We didn't even consider anyone finding out by accident, which was shortsighted, of course." Samantha placed a gentle hand on Holly's arm. "And before you ask any questions, I have to ask you if you brought the small item you caught back with you. We can't have any of the technology lying around for more people to stumble upon. Not yet."

"What is that thing?" Holly gripped it harder but didn't answer Samantha's question.

"It's a sensor." Samantha squeezed Holly's arm. "Please. Do you have it?"

"Yes."

"Oh, good." Samantha relaxed against the backrest but didn't ask for it back. "Now, listen. You and I know each other. Even if we haven't been close, we have seen each other almost every week at the library or in town. I would suggest you know me as a level-headed, sane person, right?"

"Absolutely."

"And the same goes for me. If I ask you to come meet some of my friends, most of them people you know, would you do that?" Samantha let go of Holly, perhaps to not come off as less than sane. "It's important."

"Where?"

"Brynden 4." Samantha tilted her head as if waiting for something.

"Bry—*that* house? One of the original houses? I thought it was vacant. Someone bought it?" Confused now, Holly shook her head. As far as she knew, the original owners had moved away decades ago.

"Camilla Tennen and her granddaughter Darian returned a few months ago. They live there, and so does Camilla's assistant, Brandon. I realize you don't know them, but I thought the grapevine would have filled you in." Looking surprised, Samantha shrugged.

"I was never really part of the grapevine phone chain, not even back when we were teens. I'm not of old Dennamore stock, remember?" Smiling tightly, Holly mimicked the shrug with one of her own. It was ridiculous, as she loathed gossip, to feel left out for not even being considered for it.

"Okay. Anyway, they'll be there, of course, and also Chief Walker and Philber. You know them."

She did. Everyone in this town revered Chief Walker for how he had carried out his duties over more than forty years. Philber was a fellow scholar, albeit in a different field.

"You want me to join you now? Just show up at these strangers' house and insert myself into whatever you have going on there?" Her back rigid now, Holly shot Samantha a glare she knew was icy enough to make the most full-of-themselves students back down. But clearly Samantha was no undergrad student, and she didn't even blink.

"I know this is strange. It's beyond strange, but I think I know you well enough to say that you'll find it fascinating as well. And— just to be clear. We're not doing anything illegal."

"With Walker there? Didn't even cross my mind." Sighing, Holly stood. "Well, since my curiosity is bound to keep me sleepless for the rest of the week, I'll go with you. I walked here."

"I drove. You can ride with me."

Holly nodded, and as they began to walk, she slipped her little, what did Samantha call it, sensor, back into her pocket. She was going to hang on to that small object until she'd heard what this group of people had to say.

Darian opened the door when she saw the two women walk up the flagstone path toward the house. Guarded, but reserving her judgment, she studied the tall, lanky woman next to Samantha. With long, sure strides, she seemed efficient even in the way she moved. Jaw-length, jet-black hair cut with precision, including the bangs. Almond-shaped transparent green eyes, a soft, wider nose, and full, curvy lips made for a stunning face that suggested an Asian-American heritage.

"Welcome to Brynden 4. I'm Darian." Darian extended her hand as Samantha and the woman stepped inside.

"Thank you. Nice to meet you. Please, call me Holly." Holly's grip was firm but not hard. "This is an unusual situation, so why stand on ceremony?"

Equal parts impressed and a tad affronted at Holly's way of taking the initiative, Darian nodded. "Agreed. And you're right. This is unusual. I don't know how much, if anything, Samantha has told you on your way here, but I hope you don't have anywhere to be. It's going to be a lot." She shrugged.

Holly studied her in silence while she took off her jacket and hung it on the hooks Brandon had mounted for their winter gear. "I have no commitment today. You must realize I have a lot of questions."

"Trust me. We do get that." Smiling now, Darian motioned toward the parlor. "Gran and I set up what we need to show you in here. Normally we do our research and have our discussions in the library, but Gran's a bit under the weather with her arthritis today."

They walked into the parlor, and Darian could tell that Holly was taken aback for a moment at the sight of the four people in there. Samantha took over and made the introductions.

"Holly, this is Camilla Tennen, who owns Brynden 4. Camilla, this is Professor Holly Crowe, a friend of mine. We've known each other for years."

"Holly, this is a pleasure." Camilla extended her hand, and it reassured Darian to see how gently Holly shook it, clearly mindful of the frail, swollen joints.

"The pleasure's all mine, Camilla. As unexpected as this is, I'm a fan of your house and always dreamed of a chance to see it from the inside."

"You're welcome anytime." Camilla nodded regally, but the warmth in her smile was unmistakable.

Samantha continued to introduce Brandon, Raoul, and Carl, but when she came to Walker, who was already on his feet along with the other three men, he surprised Darian by pulling Holly in for a hug.

"Dear Holly. It's been too long." He patted her shoulder. "It's good to see you."

"I feel the same way," Holly said, her smile genuine and less guarded now, showing off even, white teeth.

"Holly's father and I were part of the same photography club in high school when he was a senior and I a mere freshman." Walker smiled and his eyes shone. "He was always a great friend after that since. I miss him."

Holly merely nodded and turned to Philber, who stood next to Walker. He certainly didn't appear to want to hug her. "Philber."

"Prof—Holly. Unexpected, to say the least." In Philber's mouth, the words sounded bordering on accusatory.

"I'd say so." Holly raised her chin, and Darian broke in before the ambiance became even more awkward.

"Please have a seat, Holly. Sit down, everybody. Can I get anyone something to drink?" Darian motioned for them to use the table with padded chairs, knowing that anything else would hurt Camilla's sore body.

"Let me get some beverages," Brandon said lightly. "You're needed here."

Darian sent him a grateful smile, for the umpteenth time wondering what she and Camilla would do without this man. He knew them so well, and he adored her grandmother, which was the most important part.

When they were all seated, Darian nodded to Samantha to take the lead in how they addressed this subject with Holly. Only the way Samantha gripped the scroll she took from a side table and placed on the table between them showed she was uneasy.

"It's hard to figure out in what order we should share our finds with you, Holly, but this is one of the first things we came upon. It was stored in the library archives, in a part where nobody has set foot apart from me and my predecessor. It was covered in dust and kept among old Dennamore artifacts, most of them centuries old."

"In our library?" Holly's eyebrows went up. "If it's that old, it belongs in a museum, even a local one."

"That's the ultimate goal, of sorts." Samantha pressed the two protruding parts at the end of the scroll, and it clicked open, exposing the first part of the semi-transparent sheet that was covered in alien signs.

Leaning forward, Holly looked at the scroll, frowning. "You're claiming this is an old object? That doesn't make sense, considering the plastic roll with the strange signs."

"That's what we said," Camilla stated, giving a short laugh. "This is just one thing. Once we've showed you the rest, you'll understand—or at least begin to."

"To a degree." Samantha sounded somber. "Holly is like Brandon, not related to the first Dennamore inhabitants."

"Oh." Darian was disappointed but not deterred. "It doesn't matter. She still deserves to know what she's stumbled upon, and it'll give us a hint of how we can explain it to the rest of the people— many of them are not related to the first ones, after all, as Dennamore has grown a lot over the years."

Holly, now rigid and with her mesmerizing eyes turning into narrow slits, looked from the scroll to each of them, one by one. "Are you saying this 'secret' of yours is better understood by the ones who originate from here by blood?" She sounded infinitely cooler than just a moment ago.

"Not better understood—easier experienced," Samantha said. "And as you're adopted, it won't work fully for you."

Holly shook her head. "This sounds...insane. I don't know whether to laugh or be offended."

Darian could tell how torn their guest was and was relieved when Brandon entered with an assortment of beverages and cookies. "Brandon, tell me, have you ever felt left out or less likely to grasp what we're up to, just because you're from out of town?"

Brandon blinked. "Eh. No? Well, perhaps for a moment, I was disappointed to not be able to use a NIEC, but other than that, I'm as read-in as the rest of you, even if my skills aren't, hm, induced."

Apparently, Holly had decided on which emotion would take precedence, because now she threw her head back and laughed.

CHAPTER FIVE

What were the odds that these people, all inhabitants of the small town tucked away in the remote corner of the Adirondacks, would develop severe delusions at the same time? Holly covered her mouth as her unexpected bout of mirth mellowed into giggles. She *never* giggled. In fact, she believed that most giggles stemmed from an onset of nerves or general silliness. Something to be avoided. And to be honest, if these people were delusional, she was heading toward the same condition. She had seen things she couldn't explain and even had some hard proof in her jacket pocket.

"An astute, if surprising, reaction," Camilla said. "It beats storming out of the house."

"Nah. Holly's made of sturdier stuff." Philber nodded. "Any initial questions, Professor?"

"You're joking, right?" Holly had herself under control now and willed herself to relax against the backrest of her chair. "I have nothing *but* questions. So many, I don't know where to start."

"Then I suggest we tell you the story of our finds first. You can interrupt and ask questions to your heart's content," Camilla said. She looked over at her granddaughter, Darian. The dark-haired woman oozed authority and strength in an unmistakable way. Wiry and moving in a lithe, pantherlike way, Darian could obviously hold her own.

"All right." Darian began telling the story from her and Camilla's point of view—the yearning to return to Camilla's hometown that surpassed any other loyalty or emotion, the decision to restore

Brynden 4 and thus needing the original blueprints. Darian's voice softened when she spoke of running into Samantha, which suggested that Dennamore's accomplished, assertive librarian had made quite the impact on the LA detective.

"And then it all started with our find in the basement." Darian pulled up a leg, hugging her knee. "We'll show you later, but just so you understand how remarkable it was, it turned out to be a large computer console leading to a tunnel that runs under a big part of Dennamore."

"A tunnel?" Holly's brain was firing up her synapses as she tried to puzzle Darian's words together. "Does that opening in the meadows lead to that tunnel?"

"It does. Anyway, we found a journal by a woman named Bech'taia, which stems from the late 1700s. She was Camilla's and my ancestor. It was also full of strange signs and symbols we couldn't decipher." Darian continued to describe each new find, and Holly was torn between a healthy dose of disbelief and filing away all the information so she could revisit it later.

"And when Samantha went back to the oldest archive in the basement of Town Hall, she found the NIECs." She patted the ornate box sitting on the table next to the scroll they'd claimed was an antique.

"What exactly is a NIEC?" Holly asked. She ached to put her fingers on the box and open it, but she was also wary of it, concerned about what was inside.

"This is a Neural Information Expertise Connector." Samantha took over and flipped open the lid after pressing along some thinly chiseled lines on the lid. Holly leaned forward and examined the object sitting in what looked like velvet-clad indentations. The inside of the box looked like red velvet and cradled a metallic oval with some thin nylon-looking threads that ended in small metallic dots.

"It attaches to your skull and provides the knowledge you need." Samantha turned around and raised her loose hair with both hands. At the nape of her neck sat another oval, and the threads extended from it and disappeared into her hair.

"Don't be freaked out," Darian said. "They don't hurt. They don't alter anyone's personality. They haven't tried to harm us in any way, and we've used them for months." She placed a gentle hand on Holly's shoulder. "They allow us to maneuver the shuttle you saw."

"This is not of this world. Not if it's as old as you say. That much is obvious." Holly spoke coolly. It was the only way she could stay in control of her rampaging thoughts. "Are those pins you're all wearing part of this technology too?" She pointed at the small domes on their lapels or necklines.

"These are called speakers, for lack of a better word. They're simply a communication system. We also found what you could call alien laptops, which we've used for communication and research." Darian smiled encouragingly. "I know this is a lot to take in, but please consider who's in the room. I realize that Gran, Brandon, and I are strangers, but the rest are people you've known, or known of, for a long time. We're not messing with you."

"If I thought for a second you were, I wouldn't be here. The question is, all this that you've told me, what's the plan, what are you doing with it, apart from joyriding in some spaceship in your free time?" Holly raised her chin as she saw the others exchange glances.

"We intend to bring more people into this situation. You just beat us to it by a few days." Samantha spoke calmly. "Yes, we discovered all this, but it's not ours. It belongs to all the people of Dennamore, including the ones who aren't descendants of the original settlers. You see, apart from the vessel you spotted, there is another ship, the mothership, if you will, that we haven't been able to reach yet. Can we persuade you to join us in the search for the entrance to where it's been hidden for centuries?"

Whatever Holly might have guessed would be Samantha's next words, this request wasn't it. "An even bigger ship? But where?" She rubbed her temple that had started to ache in the same way that it did when she had sat at the computer for too long.

"Underneath the lake," Geoff said. Nobody added anything else. Instead, it was as if they were waiting for her to speak.

Holly let her gaze meet theirs, one by one. Stopping when she reached Carl's, the young man sitting next to Philber, she saw his eyes glitter with excitement. She tried to envision what repercussions this mind-boggling find would have for a young mind. For a kid his age, it had to be like striking gold. Alien technology, if that was what it was, and what else could it be? Spaceships. Items that connected with your damn brain. Her own brain circled back to the incredible information about a mothership under the lake. How did they know that? Was it written in one of the scrolls or in the journal they mentioned? Or... Holly's analytical mind raced. Images of how the unexpected lake lights had shocked her when she was out to photograph the night sky flickered across her retina. "The lights. All this time? That's the ship, well, doing something?"

"That's what we think. We have corroboration in the material we've gone through, and we are presently studying old maps where the entrance is supposedly marked. We don't know if it's submersed or sitting in a cave. But we have to get to it." Standing up now, Darian rocked back and forth on her feet. "Are you up for having a look at some of what we've found?"

Holly nodded. "If you don't show me, I won't fully believe you."

"No wonder." Samantha got up. "Darian and I will do just that you while the others keep working on the maps."

Holly noticed that the others seemed fine with that decision, even expecting Samantha to take charge. It wasn't surprising, as this woman radiated authority. Holly followed her and Darian down into Camilla's basement, which was lit by spotlights throughout.

"Feel the wall to begin with," Darian said and placed her own hand on the smooth surface next to the furnace. "This was one of the first anomalies I stumbled upon on my end."

Confused, Holly did as Darian suggested and felt her eyes widen at how warm the wall was. With its glasslike surface, she had expected it to be cool. After a moment, she felt a small vibration against her palm. "There's a tremor." Now this was strange.

"Yup." Darian motioned for Holly to follow her as she rounded the wall. "And then there's this."

The back of the smooth wall was equally smooth but lit in all kinds of colorful ways. Holly had to reach out for support and luckily found the backrest of an armchair. "Damn."

"That about covers it," Samantha said. She slid her fingers along the glowing lines and dots in an intricate pattern. The wall barely made any noise as it slid open and a light went on, showing a narrow staircase. "Are you ready to continue?"

Holly merely nodded, not sure she truly was ready, but nothing on this planet could have stopped her from going down the stairs with Samantha and Darian.

Afterward, it was something of a blur—the vast tunnel, the hauler that did indeed look like a golf cart, and, most shocking of all, the space shuttle sitting just below the chute that led to the place she'd explored only a couple of hours ago. Darian and Samantha talked about the elevators at both ends of the tunnel, leading to the shuttle bay and Town Hall respectively. Stepping aboard the shuttle, called *Speeder One*, apparently, took what was left of the cohesion in Holly's knees. Slowly she sank onto one of the seats meant for passengers or crew. Around her, the ship came to life by itself, but Darian explained that it sensed her and Samantha's NIECs.

After a tour of the speeder, Holly climbed down the steps to the tunnel floor, and as she stood there, taking in what these women had discovered, she knew that her world, her *life*, would never be the same again.

"You asked me if I want to be part of this," Holly said, then cleared her throat as her emotions nearly got the better of her. "I'm glad you asked. I don't know how I know this, but I have to be part of this, a descendent or not."

"Oh, thank God." Darian grinned broadly. "I was afraid we'd end up scaring you off."

"Not this one," Samantha said, smiling as well. "We've known each other for years, Holly, and I'm glad to have you be part of the group."

"Thank you. How often do you meet? Is there a roster, or do we pitch in in a more organic way?" Holly couldn't help stroking her hand over the piece of the hull she could reach from underneath. The metallic alloy was not as smooth as the walls of the tunnel, and when she looked closer, she saw it shifted in an intricate pattern. It reminded her of the way the metal in a Japanese katana looked after being forged by a master.

"Both," Samantha said. "Carl has school, he's a senior in high school. I work, and so do Raoul and Brandon. Geoff and Camilla are retired, and Darian is on leave of absence. Philber works, of course, but is his own master when it comes to his hours. This means that we have to schedule some things."

"I teach online three mornings every week, but other than that, I'm flexible." Holly reluctantly followed Samantha and Darian, who began to walk back to what they called Camilla's access point.

"That sounds great." Darian turned to Samantha. "See—we're getting help, and it won't all be on your shoulders." Her voice was tender, and Holly didn't think she read things into the glance the two women exchanged. She sensed something almost tangible between them, something Holly hadn't experienced for herself after Frances died. She had immersed herself in work and not even considered actively pursuing a new relationship. Now she told herself that it was at least nice to see that romance happened to other people, even if it wasn't what she was after. Knowing her own affinity for singlemindedness, she imagined her entire focus, apart from her work, would be on these amazing discoveries and nothing else. Nothing, absolutely nothing, could ever be this exciting.

Holly stubbornly ignored the snickering inner voice that said, "Famous last words."

CHAPTER SIX

Two days later, Holly found herself poring over maps and translated documents in Camilla's library. The previous day had seemed longer than a year, as she had been tied up with lessons and a faculty online meeting that dragged out far too long. After getting up at six a.m., she had impatiently waited for the time to pass, reading through student assignments on autopilot, wishing time would pass quicker. At nine a.m., she texted Darian and asked if it was too early to come over. To her relief, Darian seemed just as eager for her to join them as she was, and now she had been working on the documents for three hours.

Brandon had come up with coffee and tea in thermoses, and Holly turned to the table where she kept her mug, afraid of accidentally spilling her drink on the documents. Most of the maps were copies, but the newest one Samantha had located in the archive at Town Hall was the original. Holly turned back, looking over at Darian and Walker, who were translating scroll texts. They seemed entirely focused, which told Holly that even if some months had passed since their initial discoveries, their dedication and, yes, obsession, hadn't lessened. This didn't bode well. Holly was aware of her single-minded personality, how she could immerse herself in her current interest until she forgot to eat and could even forego sleep.

Taking one of the magnifying glasses from the table, she scanned the part of the map that described the outline of the lake. She identified the symbols that she had decided suggested the location of some buildings at the far end that she knew didn't exist anymore.

Guessing they might have been hunters' cabins, or dwellings for the ones not "paired off," as the aliens—oh, God, would she ever get used to calling the first inhabitants of Dennamore that?—referred to committed relationships. Holly let the magnifying glass follow the lake's perimeter and found more markings on the west side of the lake as well. Toward the east, where the town was now located, she couldn't find any such symbols. Instead, the lines that described the tunnel, including the hatch on the meadows, were clearly indicated.

"Huh." She rubbed her neck, which smarted some after being bent in an unfamiliar angle for hours.

"What?" Darian looked up, blinking. "Everything okay?"

"Sure. It's just...Can you remember any ruins or markings around the lake from old cabins?" Leaning back, Holly tucked her hair behind her ears.

"Cabins?" It was Walker's turn to look up. "Some people have asked to buy land from the town over there, wanting to build cabins, or even year-round homes, but the municipal laws state that it's not allowed. I've photographed the area a lot and have never seen any traces of older structures. What have you found?" He got up and, with Darian, joined her at her table.

"This symbol, according to the translation, means habitat, or dwelling. It can also mean protection, according to another document." Holly pointed to the sign on the map.

Darian squinted, as if searching her memory or, most likely, her NIEC. "You're right. But it's more. I mean different. Not just protection." Darian turned to Walker. "What do you think?"

"Damn. That's a tiny symbol." Using one of the other magnifying glasses, Geoff bent over the table. "No wonder we haven't spotted it. I probably thought it was a speck of dirt. And the symbol. My NIEC tells me it's a 'gills block.'"

"A what?" Holly wrote the words down. "Are you sure? Gills as in what fish breathe through?"

"Yes."

"And block." Tilting her head, Holly snorted. "Here I thought if I could just figure it out, it would make sense."

"Welcome to the world of the folks from Dwynna Major." Darian grinned. "Nothing makes sense until it does."

"Dwynna Major?" Holly frowned.

"Dennamore. Dwynna Major. It's the original name of this place we call home. And, from what we've found, the name of where the aliens originated." Walker nodded. "If I didn't know your capacity for learning, I'd worry we might give you a brain meltdown."

Dwynna Major. Somehow, this name of an alien location made things even more real. "I think I'm running on being numb right now," Holly said, shaking her head. "Only way to deal with all this is to keep going." At least that was her usual method of operations. Born a genius? Skip classes in school and become a double major in college at age thirteen. Hard to decide which subject to later pursue. Make sure you get tenure for both as a professor. Your wife dying of breast cancer. Negotiate for teaching online and flee to the place where you grew up.

"I need to see these sites in person." Holly reached for a modern map of Dennamore. She measured the different scales and marked the location of the "gills blocks." "No time like the present. I need some air and to clear my head a bit anyway."

"I'll come with you," Darian said. "You're having lunch with Camilla soon, right?" She looked over at Walker, who nodded with a broad smile.

"The highlight of my day," he said.

A twitch in Holly's chest made her swallow hard. The look in Walker's eyes when the topic of Camilla came up reminded her of Frances, and she had no time for falling into that particular rabbit hole. Fortunately, she was distracted as they gathered up the modern map and photographed the area around the lake on the old map with Holly's cell phone right away. While walking downstairs, Holly had reclaimed her bearings.

"I have my hiking boots in my car," she said to Darian as they reached the hallway. "Do you need to change?"

"Nah. Since we'll be around the lake, I think hiking boots and jeans will do fine. I'll just bring my backpack with my alien computer. I already have everything else." She indicated her NIEC and the speaker on her lapel.

"Excellent. We can take my car. See you outside?" Holly put on her all-weather jacket.

"Sure thing. I'll just be a minute."

As Holly fastened her boots, Darian showed up in almost identical clothes, which made them smile. "Great minds think alike. Guess we both shop at the local outdoor store." Holly slipped into the driver's seat and started her Jeep. Darian jumped in next to her, tapping her speaker. "Darian to Samantha." She turned to Holly. "Good thing it only vibrates when Samantha's at work."

"I'll say." Holly wondered what toll all the secrecy had taken on this dedicated group of people during the last few months. Yes, it was exciting and the biggest, most world-altering discovery in the history of humanity, but it also meant the responsibility was overwhelming. If Holly, who was the new kid on the block in the group, could detect the tension emanating from Samantha, Darian must be worried.

"Samantha here. What's up?" The cropped-short words spoke volumes. There was definite stress in her voice.

Darian frowned and sat straighter in the seat as Holly pulled away from the sidewalk.

"We're fine. Holly and I are going to the lake to check out a few places marked on the latest map you discovered. What's going on at your end?" Darian spoke lightly, but Holly saw how she moved her hands restlessly.

"Just been to a meeting with the council members and some of the other town hall employees. Apart from Miller going on and on about cutbacks, etcetera, he also asked me to stay behind." Samantha gave a sigh, sounding more tired than annoyed now. "He asked pointed questions about my work schedule and so on. He's picked up on my friendship with what he calls 'the individuals at Brynden 4'... as if you're suspicious people. He infuriates me to no end, that man."

"I know. He's horrible," Darian said.

"He's beyond despicable." Holly wasn't sure her voice registered on the speaker and gave Darian a questioning look. When Darian moved her hand in a circle, indicating for Holly to continue, she kept talking. "Desmond Miller managed to get himself elected because he knew what people wanted to hear, and now he's trying to implement a stealthy kind of dictatorship. This is my area of expertise after all. Social and political science. His method is nothing new, but it can be effective—to a point. Eventually these people go too far."

"Thank you. Both of you." Samantha sounded somewhat calmer. "Wish I could go with you to the lake. I'll page you when I'm out of here to check if you're still there."

"And we'll do the same if we find anything. We'll do a joint page then." Darian lowered her voice. "Stay out of that man's way, okay?"

This made Samantha chuckle. "I will. Trust me."

Ending the conversation, Darian tightened her ponytail and then adjusted her baseball cap. "I could throttle that dude."

"Samantha carries a lot on her shoulders." Not wanting to overstep, Holly felt it important to be honest.

"She's the hub—at least so far. Soon enough we'll have more people interested in taking part in this…um, project. And when the NIEC chooses a captain, Samantha can take a step back and let that person take the lead. No doubt she'll still be in the inner circle, in a manner of speaking. I don't see this working out without her."

"Or you." Holly turned a corner and drove onto the country road that would lead them to the lake's parking lot. "All of you."

"I'm the chief of security, according to my NIEC, so you have point."

Feeling a pang of disappointment over the fact that she would never receive a rank by a NIEC, Holly merely nodded. Flashbacks from her childhood flickered through her mind, despite her best attempt to will them away. She was never bullied or ostracized, but most of the Dennamore inhabitants made clear distinctions about who was part of the direct lineage of the first settlers. Holly huffed inwardly at the thought of what those snobs would say about the fact that the first settlers were a whole different kind of immigrants.

"You grew quiet." Darian shifted in the seat to look at Holly. "I'm sorry the NIECs work with only a certain type of DNA. We've tried several with Brandon, but they just don't switch on. It truly is a bummer since a person with your expertise is golden for what lies ahead."

"And what lies ahead?" Darian's words both saddened and warmed Holly.

"The way I see it, and I know the others agree, is that we have to find *Velocity* and then prepare to go to space. We have to find the origin of our ancestors." Darian spoke with conviction.

"How can you know this? I mean, how can you be so sure?"

"You know the emotion the people here call the yearning?"

Holly nodded. "Yes. A myth about why so many people return to their hometown. The returnees are supposed to heed an irresistible yearning to come back home."

"You did. Philber told me. He said you used to live in Albany," Darian said.

Holly wanted to throttle Philber, even if it was no secret. "I did. And yes, I came home. Not because of any yearning, obviously."

"How can you be sure?" Darian asked kindly.

"I came home after my wife died. I needed to help my ailing mother, who later passed away. I didn't respond to any yearning, merely practicalities." Holly realized she was speaking too sternly. "It was seven years ago," she said, softening her tone.

"And why did you stay?"

Holly had answered that question before, and her usual response was that she had gotten used to teaching online and being her own boss. The truth was much more complicated. She didn't want to dismiss Darian, or give her the standard answer, but Holly wasn't sure if she was ready to examine her own reasons to stay, let alone share them with someone who'd been a stranger a few days ago. To her relief, they reached the parking lot just as the silence threatened to become awkward.

Holly parked as close to the lake as possible and then stepped outside, grabbing her ever-present camera bag. Darian carried the map as they made their way to the pathway the town had constructed around the lake. During the Lake Lights Festival in August every year, locals and tourists gathered to be enthralled by the lights in the dark water. Holly always thought they resembled the aurora borealis because of the way they moved under the surface. To think they were emanating from a large spaceship was mind-blowing.

As they walked in silence around the black, still lake, the ambiance was close to eerie. Holly was grateful that Darian seemed to be as lost in thought as she was. When they reached the northern part of the lake, they compared the modern map with the photo of the old one on Holly's phone.

"This is it, right?" Darian pointed at a spot farther north. "This protrusion. Wait. Let me pull up a compass on my phone." She tapped her screen a few times. "This shows the altitude as well." She peered in between the trees. "Doesn't seem impossible to just keep due north. It's just a few hundred yards. A quarter of a mile at the most."

Holly nodded. "I agree. Let's go." She didn't wait but started making her way past low shrubbery that followed the path around the lake. Among the trees, it was darker, but she had no problem seeing where to put her feet.

Behind Holly, Darian unfolded the map. "We just need the compass to find it. If this is as precise down to the umpteenth of an inch as everything else those people created, we'll walk right smack into it."

As it turned out, when they reached the spot on the map, they walked right smack into a small camp where a woman sat by a fire, apparently cooking something.

"Hello," the woman said, flashing a bright smile. "This is unexpected. Welcome." Probably of African-American descent, she had long, naturally curly black hair kept in a braid that reached her shoulder blades. Dressed in purple winter gear and wrapped in a lilac-colored blanket, she sat in a rustic-looking, classic Adirondack chair, a book in her hand.

"We didn't mean to disturb you," Darian said and stepped around Holly. "I'm Darian Tennen, and this is—"

"Holly Crowe. I recognize you from the library. I'm Claire Gordon. This is my camp. Well, sort of. I come here a lot to read and hang out." She stood and put another couple of chopped branches on the fire.

"Alone?" Holly finally found her voice. "And yes, I recognize you also. From the library."

"I might be Samantha's best customer when it comes to the science-fiction shelf." Claire pointed at a few stumps. "Have a seat. Rest your feet. I'm just about to make myself some coffee. Interested?"

"Well, we reached our goal, and I'm always down when it comes to coffee." Darian took off her gloves and placed them on a stump she sat on. "Thank you."

Holly mimicked what Darian did and took the opportunity to glance around the clearing. Behind Claire stood, unfathomably enough, a small tent. Who in their right mind camped at this time of year? The temperature went down to far below freezing during the nights. Behind the tent a rock formation rose more than twelve feet in the air, Holly surmised. Unless she had misread the map, it was located right next to the mark of the gills block.

Claire handed each of them a mug of coffee. "Careful. Hot. And just black, I'm afraid. I don't carry milk out here."

"Understandable." Darian looked up at the majestic trees around them. "Why are you out here, if I may ask?"

"This is what I do when I'm not working. I hike, camp, and read sci-fi." Claire sipped her coffee after blowing on it. "This is my very favorite spot."

"Do you have many people pass here?" Holly asked.

"Not really. The rocks behind me hide this clearing pretty well during the months when the shrubs aren't green. I think most would walk right by me unless they saw the fire." Tilting her head, Claire studied them closely. "And speaking of that. You said this is your goal. That has me curious."

Darian sent Holly a quick glance, and it was obvious she wanted to know Holly's opinion of this woman. But all Holly knew, and it was practically nothing when it came to Claire Gordon, was that she was a regular at the library. Holly gave a small shrug, leaving the decision up to Darian.

"We heard there might be old ruins around this clearing," Darian said lightly after turning her attention back to Claire. "Have you spotted anything like that?"

"Ruins? Here?" Claire stopped her hand holding the mug of coffee halfway to her mouth. "In the woods? That sounds unlikely. I mean…who told you that?"

"We came across it on an old map," Holly said, carefully choosing her words. "It's not supposed to be big. Somewhere behind you and the tent, from what I can tell."

Claire turned and looked at her dome-shaped tent. "There? Huh. We can go have a look, but I've been coming here for years, and I've never seen any ruins."

"Considering they may have initially been built from wood, the chance of finding anything isn't great." Darian stood, placing the mug on the stump after drinking some more. "Great coffee, by the way."

Claire moved lithely around her tent and stared at the ground. "Honestly, I have no idea what to look for." Holly could tell she was still intrigued.

"We might have to come back with shovels and rakes," Holly said. "After centuries, the sediment layers can be deep."

Darian stood in front of the rock formation, studying the ground as well. Then she stepped closer to the rock, craning her neck back. "Wait." She closed her eyes in a way that Holly had already begun to recognize as "listening" to the NIEC. Opening her eyes again, Darian reached up and began brushing away moss.

"Help me." Darian stood up on her toes to reach farther. "Damn, my five-eight isn't enough."

"Show me what to do." Holly was a good three inches taller than Darian.

"Look for indentations." Darian stepped back. "There should be four of them."

"What the hell?" Claire, who was almost as tall as Holly, came closer. "What indentations?"

Holly nearly snorted out loud. She had begun to realize that Claire might be next on their list of people they needed to inform, as she sort of claimed a stake of the site they needed to explore. Holly brushed at the moss, and now Claire helped her. As it turned out, Claire found the first indentation, or hole, rather.

"Wow. Look at that." Pushing moss and debris away with both hands, Claire pointed at it. "Damn. It looks drilled. It's a perfect shape."

Of course it was. Holly gaped, even if she had seen even more fantastic things.

"Now that we know which level that's on, the other three have to be to the left of it." Darian took a branch, obviously not able to wait. She pushed at the rock, and together the three of them uncovered three more perfect holes. As far as Holly could tell, they were spaced with the same precision.

Claire shook her head. "If we hadn't just brushed away eons of moss and crap, I would have thought you'd drilled those just the other day to play a trick on me or someone else. But that moss was nearly stuck, damn it. How the hell can this be?" She turned around, her hands on her hips, glaring at them. Her braid whipped through the air fast enough for Holly to hear it move.

"You deserve to know, Claire. Can you be patient while we call our friends to come have a look? Don't worry." Darian held up a hand when alarm flashed over Claire's face. "You know some of them. Or of them, at least. Holly here is new to our group of friends."

"Very new," Holly said dryly. "Are you of Dennamore descent, by the way?"

"Of Dennamore descent?" Claire looked at Holly as if she were crazy. "What does that even mean?"

"Holly." Darian shook her head. "What she means is, do you have ancestors going back to the time when Dennamore was founded?"

"Sure do." Claire shrugged. "My dad is very proud of that fact. He says we were the first black family to settle here. Not sure I believe that, but he's adamant about it."

"You experience the yearning?" Darian tilted her head.

"Nope." Claire shook her head. "For a very simple reason really. I never left."

"Oh. Right." Darian blinked. "May I ask one more question?"

Claire retrieved her mug and threw out the cold coffee. Pouring herself a new mug full, she indicated the pot. "Help yourselves. And why not? Ask away."

"What do you do for a living?"

Claire raised her chin. "I'm a car mechanic like my dad. We've worked together at our garage since I graduated from high school."

Smiling now, Darian unzipped her jacket and reached in for her shirt lapels. "Perfect. Now, I'm going to use my communication device to tell our friends where we are. Please stay and meet them?"

"Okay." Claire seemed at ease, but Holly detected tension at the corners of her mouth and around her eyes. No wonder.

"All hands, this is Darian. Please converge on my coordinates ASAP. We have found part of what we were looking for. We have also made a new friend."

There was a pause, and Holly took the time to study Claire's expressions, because so many of them passed over her face like a movie reel.

"Samantha to Darian. Are you safe?"

"Affirmative. Bring extra gear, all right? And a few small ladders."

"Affirmative. Samantha out."

"Samantha Pike?" Claire gaped.

Holly nodded to not drown out the other voices that confirmed they were on their way. When the last one, Philber, had checked in and let them know that he, Walker, and Camilla, would remain at Brynden 4, Claire sat down in her chair again, wrapping the blanket around her.

The fire looked like it might be about to die. Holly put on more branches and made sure she didn't suffocate the flames.

"All right," Claire said and pulled her knees up. "Since we're going to be here for a while and we're also having company, you might as well put on more coffee."

CHAPTER SEVEN

Samantha walked through the woods toward Darian's location. Next to her, Carl and Raoul were talking with each other, speculating what this new find might bring. Samantha's mind was too full of thoughts that refused to be categorized. As a librarian, she loved organization, and perhaps that's why she felt the safest when she could compartmentalize her thoughts. Even her feelings, at times, she confessed to herself. No wonder she was so stressed as all the pieces of the puzzle that was her life right now seemed airborne and erratic. Adding her feelings for Darian to that…God.

"It's right around that area of dense forest. It's really dark in here." Carl turned to include Samantha in his and Raoul's conversation. "Gives a feeling of how it was for the settlers. Have we come across any notes of how alien our scenery was to them? I mean, they could have been used to pink trees or something where they came from. Dwynna Major."

"No notes of pink trees," Samantha said and had to smile. The eighteen-year-old Carl, soon to be nineteen, possessed an unyielding optimism and stamina when it came to their discoveries. He was smart and insightful, but in many ways a big kid. When they decided that it was up to him, being of age after all, whether to use a NIEC, tears had run down his face as he attached the device to the base of his skull. When it attached, Samantha had observed his reaction, her heart thundering in her throat. As it turned out, Carl responded faster and more accurately to the NIEC than any of the older ones in the group. Raoul theorized that it might be because of Carl's age. His brain was still developing and thus more susceptible to manipulation. Samantha had shuddered at this theory, but since Carl was fine, and thriving, she tried to let her trepidations go.

They rounded the trees and found themselves in a clearing framed by a large rock formation. In front of it, Darian and Holly sat with a woman Samantha knew well from the library. Claire Gordon, wrapped in a blanket, was calmly sipping from a mug.

"There's coffee," Claire said. "Welcome to my now-so-very-popular, but humble, abode." She made a comical face. "Hello, Samantha."

"Hello, Claire. This is unexpected." Samantha walked closer and introduced the men. "Coffee sounds great. I left work early, and that means, no afternoon coffee break."

Darian poured coffee into three small cups from Claire's stash of items in the tent. "This is Claire's spot where she hangs out to read. Until we barged in and started tearing up the place, she hadn't noticed anything out of the ordinary here."

"Unless you count wildlife and the beauty of the woods," Claire said, her tone tinged with irony. "Who knows when the wildlife will return after all this commotion. I'll have to find a new spot."

"I'm sorry." Darian sighed. "I really am. I'm the last one who wants to invade someone's privacy, but what we're looking for is important. It's beyond important."

"I've gathered that. And I forgive you because now I'm seriously curious what brings such an eclectic group of people to my clearing as if you'd found gold." She finished drinking from her mug and stood. "Should we show them the holes?"

Samantha hadn't seen this assertive side of Claire at the library, perhaps because patrons were supposed to be quiet and mindful of other people's focus there. Here, the woman moved as if she were showing them around her living room in her home. And in a way that was true.

"Over here." Holly pointed behind the tent where the rock formation was vertical and towered above them. She indicated four holes, each almost two inches in diameter and five feet off the ground.

Carl pulled a flashlight from his backpack, where Samantha knew he kept a small toolbox, "just in case," as he put it. He directed the beam into the hole. "Damn. I can't see a thing. Dirt and debris. I need a branch or something to scrape it out."

Darian picked up four thin branches from the ground and handed them to the men and Samantha. They spread out, the shorter among them using the narrow, extendable ladders, and began working on a hole each. Samantha's was filled with what looked like composted soil. "Careful when you do this, so you don't pack it in and risk clogging the hole completely."

"Gotcha." Carl used a twisting motion with his branch, which seemed effective as the debris inside came out at a steady pace. After working like this for a few minutes, Samantha couldn't extract any more. She estimated the branch could reach approximately ten inches into the rock. "Carl, may I borrow your flashlight?"

"Sure." He pulled it from his back pocket and then kept working on his hole.

Samantha motioned for Holly and Claire to join her, as she wanted them to be part of this discovery. If Claire also became invested, it would mean they were expanding their group organically, which was a good start. "Let's see if we can make out what these holes are for." She shot them a smile.

Claire nodded, returning the smile. Holly stood on Samantha's other side, fully focused.

Letting the beam of the slender flashlight shine into the hole, Samantha pressed her face in next to it and squinted. The hole was drilled somehow; there was no question about it. Had their ancestors done it, or was this some weird forestry technique she had never heard of? The inside of it looked as smooth as the rock in Camilla's basement, which sent chills through Samantha. Shifting to get the light to shine in from another angle, Samantha thought she saw something reflecting the beam farther into the hole. Excited, she tried to angle the flashlight further but dropped it onto the moss at her feet. Going rigid, she realized she hadn't seen a reflection at all.

Slowly withdrawing, she took the flashlight Holly had retrieved for her. "Listen...listen up everyone. Be gentle with the branches. There's a light at the end."

"Wh-what?" Claire's eyes grew wide. "A light?"

"But of course. Then they made these holes." Darian smiled brightly. "Holly, you're a godsend. You found this!"

"Please," Claire said. "I'm about to lose my mind. What light?. Who are 'they'? And why do you all look like you won the lottery?" Claire's hand rested on her hips now.

"Come see," Samantha said softly, motioning for her to move closer. "And don't think that what you're feeling now isn't something we've all experienced during the last few months. You'll be fine."

Claire studied her with a serious expression. After a full ten seconds, she abruptly turned and pressed her eye to the opening. "I feel kind of stupid right now," she muttered before she grew rigid and curled her fingers against the rock as if trying to hold on to it. "Damn."

"Damn, indeed," Samantha said.

Claire stumbled backward. "The light's tinted pink."

"This one's yellow. Bright yellow." Carl smacked his palm against the rock next to his hole.

"Baby-blue," Darian said after pressing her eye against hers.

"I can't see yet," Raoul said. "At least not enough to judge the color."

Holly walked from hole to hole, looking into them with an unreadable expression. At Raoul's, she reached for a thinner branch, little more than a twig, and used it in circular motions for a few seconds. She looked into the opening again. "Purple, hinting toward lilac."

"Holy crap." Claire rubbed her forehead. "What is this stuff?"

"That's what Holly asked us a few days ago," Samantha said. "And we could answer a lot of her questions then, but these holes are new to us."

"They have to have something to do with the lake," Holly said. "About the entrance to the *Velocity*."

"Wait...what? What is the *Velocity*?"

Darian held up a hand. "I don't know about you, but I'm getting cold. Why don't we add some fuel to the campfire and warm up while we give Claire the crash course in Dennamore's true history? And then, in the future, when we recruit people, we have to bring in more at a time, or we'll go nuts at repeating everything over and over."

Raoul and Carl found a large log at the opposite end of the clearing and rolled it up to the fire. It provided three seats. Together with Claire's chair, and the two stubs, they could all benefit from the now-roaring fire. Samantha made sure she sat on the log next to Darian. Their closeness, together with the fire, made her stop shivering so badly.

While they heated more water, for tea this time, Darian explained to Claire the short version of their amazing finds since last August. Claire, in turn listened impassively until Darian was done. She then turned her focus to the flames, and after grabbing an oven mitten, she pulled the pot to her and added water to the mugs. Six teabags found their homes in the mugs before she handed them out.

"If you guys weren't who you are, I would say you're certifiable, the lot of you—colorful lights in holes or not. And I'd also call you cruel." Claire spoke with such aplomb; Samantha wasn't sure what to think of her reaction.

"How do you mean...cruel?" Darian asked.

"I'm a sci-fi lover. No, beyond that. When I'm not living my best life as a mechanic, I live and breathe science-fiction novels. I've dreamed of stumbling across something, anything, that could have an unexplained tinge to it, for as long as I can remember. I always felt I was born far too soon. I should have been born far into the future, where humans travel through space as easily as when they now take the car to go grocery shopping. Now you tell me you have a space shuttle and that you're looking for the mothership." She stopped talking and looked from one person to the next around the campfire.

Raoul cleared his voice. "When you put it into context like that, I can see where this might come off as cruel, but I assure you, we're not pulling your leg. Everything Darian said is true, and she's just scratched the surface."

"I guessed that much." Claire locked her gaze on Samantha, and her nearly black eyes clearly demanded nothing but the truth. "Why are you telling me this? I mean, why tell me anything at all? How do you know I can be trusted?"

Samantha weighed her answer carefully. "Because it's necessary. We need help. We need more people to be involved. Until a few days ago, we've been the same group of eight people that were present from the start. It's not enough. We need at least seventy-six, preferably more. Holly stumbled upon some artifacts, and we brought her in. Same goes for you. You were here, and to be honest, I have doubts about it being a coincidence, even if I can't figure out why— yet. As for trusting you? Why not? And besides, this will come out eventually, no matter what or how we go about things. It's just…it's important that we do it in the best way possible." Samantha gripped Darian's hand as she tried to judge Claire's reaction.

Claire looked over at the rock. "You think I'm drawn here because of those things?" She spoke slowly. "I've come here since I was a kid…"

Samantha knew she didn't have to state the obvious. This place, this exact spot in the vast forests that clad the mountains surrounding Dennamore, was the spot that had pulled Claire Gordon to it for years. Samantha thought Claire was about her age, perhaps slightly younger. A lot of years to sit under the same rock, for sure.

"So," Claire said, drawing the word out. "Am I to wear one of those NIECs Darian talked about?"

"Only if you're comfortable with it." Samantha knew they were moving fast. Too fast, she feared. "There's a lot about them you need to know before you can make an informed decision. As a science-fiction afficionado, you've surely read about scenarios when expectations and deductions have sent people down the wrong path. This is true for our situation as well. It's up to each individual to determine how far they're prepared to go, what they're prepared to do."

A prolonged silence, though not uncomfortable, gave Samantha the chance to enjoy the sounds of the forest around them. Despite the noise the humans created, the animals and birds still moved around them. Samantha sipped her tea, inwardly grimacing at the absence of half-and-half, but she needed the heat. Darian felt warm against her right side, and if they had been alone, Samantha would have rested her head against Darian's shoulder. At times Samantha would have given anything to have Darian's arms around her. She had been used to working at a certain pace at the library, and stress wasn't even on the menu back then. Perhaps she wasn't cut out for this sort of thing after all? Enduring stress was not for everyone.

"All I have to do is think about how it would feel if I walked away from this, from you guys, and never knew what those holes are for, or what else you'll find, and what my place could have been in all this." Claire put her mug down and regarded them sternly, one by one. "So, NIEC and what else you throw at me—I'm in."

Holly walked back with the others, listening to the conversations behind her and in front of her as they maneuvered along the narrow path. Just in front of her, Claire walked in silence as well. Her thick braid moved with every step, swinging back and forth on top of Claire's daypack. What was this woman really thinking? Was she filled with the same feelings as Holly, a mix of excitement, trepidation, adventure...and all of it under a cloud of disbelief? Or had reading so much science fiction preconditioned her to think this was all bound to happen one day? Perhaps Claire had dreamed of watching an extraterrestrial ship land in her backyard and its crew asking her to join them and travel through space.

Holly wasn't a stranger to self-criticism. It had followed her throughout her life, and unlike what some might think, it had only served to strengthen her self-confidence. Now the same soul-searching thoughts made her wonder if she simply projected her own reactions onto Claire. Or, worse, if it was an echoing envy of when she grew up, knowing she was adopted and not part of the proud heritage of this town.

"How did you take it?" Claire's voice broke Holly out of her reverie. She had slowed down and now walked next to her on the path.

"Excuse me?" Holly quickly sorted her thoughts into their respective compartments in her brain.

"When they told you all this? Space shuttles, alien artifacts, the enigmatic NIECs?" Claire pushed a branch with naked twigs out of the way.

"As I stumbled upon them landing their shuttle, found a strange object glowing in the ground on the meadows, and actually caught a strange little flying metal cylinder, I was primed for an explanation—any explanation—because I felt I was going a little mad." Shooting a glance behind her, she then stealthily plucked the sensor from her inner pocket. "They don't know I still have it. Or if they do, they haven't asked for it back."

"Whoa." Claire looked at the cylinder, her mouth forming a perfect O. "That's fantastic."

"Here." Holly could tell Claire was dying to hold it but too cautious to ask. "It's heavier than you think."

Claire took the cylinder and turned it over in her hands. "That a lens?" She slid a fingertip over the glass-like end.

"I think so. They could see me, anyway, so it makes sense."

"What did you think of this business with the NIEC?" Claire handed the sensor back.

"I don't qualify for one, unfortunately. I don't have the right genes." It literally hurt Holly to say the words. "However, they still want me on the team, as they insist I can be useful in so many other ways." She shrugged, doing her best to sound casual.

"Damn. That's not fair." Claire shook her head.

It wasn't, but she would make the best of it. Holly gave Claire a smile, not wanting this woman to pity her.

Darian paged Camilla and the others at Brynden 4, updating them, as they walked toward the parking lot by the lake. After discussing their different schedules, they all decided to meet in two days, in the evening. As apparently Brynden 4 had become the hub of all the meetings lately, Walker and Brandon would make dinner for everyone.

"We'll have to figure out another way to meet once we add more people," Carl said. "Camilla's house is amazing, but if we're going to be seventy-six plus, we might have to rent a place."

"We won't need that after we open the entrance to the mothership and to *Velocity*." Holly surprised herself that she suddenly felt comfortable taking part in the planning. She was, after all, the second newest in this group.

Samantha smiled and nodded at her. "You're right. That's exactly what we need to focus on the most. Once we have access to it, we can truly start recruiting and having a place to store all the old artifacts. I have a feeling some of the stuff we've found on the shelves in the archive over the last few months will only come into its own once it's in direct contact with the ship."

Holly was grateful that she hadn't overstepped. These people were not about ego, in a very liberating way—except perhaps Philber. But, on the other hand, that was his usual attitude.

As it turned out, Claire lived only four blocks from Holly and offered her a ride home. The four cars drove off one by one, and as Claire maneuvered the quiet streets of Dennamore, neither of them spoke much. After pulling over to let Holly off at her house, Claire reached out and stopped her just as Holly unbuckled the seat belt, then squeezed her arm gently.

"Yes?" Holly let the belt slide off her and turned to face Claire.

"On Thursday. At Brynden 4…you will be there, right? I mean, we all said we would, but it's kind of…I just would feel better if someone new to this is also going to be there. I mean, for sure?" Claire ran her fingers along the steering wheel, following the ridges in the faux leather.

"I'll be there. I wouldn't miss it for the world." Holly watched the tension around Claire's perfectly shaped full lips dissipate.

"Good. It's just that after we said good-bye at the parking lot, I started feeling as if it was all a dream. Impossible and outrageous, you know?"

Holly nodded. "That's how I felt after I came home two days ago. I was stunned, overwhelmed, awestruck…but also—it felt unreal. So, yes, I hear you. Should we meet up and walk there, or perhaps taking the car is better?"

"I'd like to walk, if that's okay. Five thirty is fine. I'll have time to hit the shower. Perfect." A broad smile transformed Claire's face. "Thanks."

"No problem. Thank you for dropping me off." Holly raised her hand in a wave after she got out of the car and closed the door behind her. She watched Claire wave back and then drive off.

After she walked to her mailbox, she gathered the contents in one hand and pulled out her keys with the other. The mundane routine seemed odd after the amazing discovery today, as if her life up to now had been based on false assumptions. Wondering if anyone else among the others felt that way, she unlocked her front door and stepped inside. After she locked the door behind her, she found herself unable to move for several moments. Thoughts of the holes with the glowing lights they'd found in the forest, how Claire Gordon had been sitting there, almost like an unknowing sentry, were almost too hard to grasp.

Forcing herself to remove her jacket and then continue to the kitchen, she pulled out a frozen dinner and popped it into the microwave. She was suddenly exhausted, probably more from sensory overload rather than the short hike. Sitting at the kitchen table and not even caring what she was eating, she wondered how she would be able to focus on prepping for her lecture the next day, when all she wanted was to keep researching everything to do with the location of the *Velocity*. She wasn't surprised at her single-mindedness. It was a well-known trait that used to drive Frances crazy, but it was part of her personality. It was the passion behind her desire to drop everything else and dedicate herself to Dennamore's alien history that stunned her. If she hadn't known better, she would have thought her life depended on what they discovered in the days to come.

CHAPTER EIGHT

Holly tried to shake the feeling of slight ridiculousness when her inner voice compared the gathering at Camilla's with some odd secret society from a Victorian novel. They sat in a circle in the library upstairs, and Samantha headed the meeting.

"Now that we're all gathered, and everyone's been introduced, I, for one, am delighted that our group is growing. And, to be clear, just because I'm the unofficial leader here, I refuse to be the one who can veto anything. This responsibility is too important for someone who isn't the chosen captain to take on. That is why we need to find a captain as soon as possible, but you all know that."

"What do you mean, exactly, 'find a captain'?" Claire, who sat opposite Holly, asked.

"The NIECs have the ability to determine existing or potential expertise in a person. So far, it hasn't chosen someone to be our indisputable leader—our captain—but it will, soon enough." Darian motioned to the scroll boxes on the table. "We can never ask anyone to try one on. Everyone must make that decision for themselves. The only one here who we have doubts about trying one on is Camilla, and that's for health reasons. Everyone else carrying the alien genes here has used them without any adverse effects."

"I want to try it. It's a weird feeling. It's like I have to." Claire rested her elbows on her knees. "I mean, we have a doctor present in case something happens, right?" She glanced at Raoul, who nodded calmly.

"All right." Samantha opened one of the boxes. "We'll mark this one with your name afterward. We used to color-code them, but now that we're slowly growing in numbers, we're running out of colors."

Claire sat up straight. "What should I do?"

"In the beginning we bothered with parting the hair and so on, but it's not necessary. Just leave your hair how you normally wear it and hold the oval just below the base of your skull. The NIEC will take it from here."

"You have any idea how creepy that sounds?" Laughing nervously, Claire kept her eyes locked on the object in the scroll box. "Wow. It's smaller than I thought. Good. And those, what do you call them, tentacles, are tiny."

"Filaments. Here you go." Samantha handed Claire the NIEC. She studied it for a moment and held it angled toward the ceiling light. "All these patterns and symbols. Looks very *Stargate*ish to me." Claire didn't hesitate after that but pushed it in under her curly hair. When her eyes widened, Holly knew the oval had attached. She had seen it done only once, by Darian, two days ago, and now she waited to see Claire's reaction. It took perhaps two seconds, and then Claire gripped the armrests of her chair. "Um. Dizzy. Just a little."

Raoul placed his fingers against Claire's wrist. "Steady pulse. You're fine. The first time can be a bit overwhelming."

"Uh-huh." Claire opened her eyes. "Wow. What a rush." She regarded them through narrow slits. "Yet I feel totally normal. I mean, like me, not some alien, suddenly. Not sure why I was expecting that." She chuckled and slowly let go of the armrest.

"Here's the scroll that came with your box. Can you make out anything of the alien language?"

Claire took the scroll and automatically began reading from the right lower corner and moving up and then to the left. "Of course. It's as easy as reading English. Suddenly." She kept reading, and then she began laughing. "But of course. It shouldn't surprise anyone."

"What do you mean?" Camilla asked, leaning over Raoul to look at Claire.

"I can't be a hundred percent sure, but I have a strong feeling that if you hand me some blueprints of the shuttles or the *Velocity*, I'll be able to read all of them." Claire lowered the scroll. "I just know."

"You're our engineer." Walker grinned. "Makes sense."

After watching Claire's emotional acceptance of the NIEC, Holly tried to identify her own conflicting emotions. Part of her felt remnants of the crippling sense of not belonging that she used to struggle with, while the rest of her was so sure this was a false emotion—that she belonged just as much as the others around the table did. She wanted to tell them, but watching Claire's bubbly personality as she spoke about her new impulses and thoughts made it impossible. This was Claire's moment. Getting a NIEC was extraordinary, and Claire deserved to see that through without interruption. And she should certainly not be disturbed by Holly, who couldn't be in on this particular experience.

Soon, the maps were out again, as were the photos they'd taken in the woods two days ago.

"Do we need to go to the other areas marked in the forest, or should we focus on the one next to Claire's camp?" Holly asked.

"Good question. I find it compelling that Claire's been drawn to this exact spot, and not the other two, over the years. Does that mean this is the best choice?" Samantha tapped her lower lip. Leaning over the map, she placed her well-manicured finger with a perfectly blunt nail on the spot she was talking about.

Holly stood and stretched her back, taking a few steps to the left and ending up looking at the map from the north. She regarded the newly marked areas and the lake. From there, she followed an imaginary line to where she had seen the hatch on the meadows open. She blinked twice. "Wait." Perhaps something in her voice startled the others, because they all quieted at the same time and snapped their eyes up to meet hers. "I've looked at these maps a lot over the last days, and by that, I mean obsessively. Yet for some reason, I haven't turned them around until now. Do you see it?" She looked down at Philber, who sat just in front of her.

"No? What? What am I supposed to see?" He leaned over the map.

"No. Pull back. Stand up." Holly patted his shoulder. "You're too close. I've been too close too. Perhaps we all have."

"No wonder. We've been looking for entrances and so on. The map's damn detailed." Walker frowned but also stood and joined Philber.

"I still don't—hey, wait a goddamn minute…" Philber took off his reading glasses and rubbed his eyes before putting them back on.

"What are you seeing?" Walker nudged Philber. "You're never one to hold back. Come on."

"Holly?" Philber turned to her. "It should be you."

"All right. Okay if I draw on this one, as it's a copy?" Holly pulled one of the maps closer. "I'll need a long ruler."

Darian moved quickly to a desk that sat in the corner and returned with the items. "Here. And here's a pencil."

Holly placed the ruler on the map and began to draw—one line from their latest discovery over to its eastern counterpart, then down to the southern one. From there, she measured the exact same length to the west end of the lake that ended in a sharp dip toward the meadows. From that point, she drew a shorter line to the hatch leading down to the shuttle chute. "This is one part of it. The distances are perfectly measured. Then there are your houses." She made small dots where Camilla's, Walker's, and Philber's houses were located and drew lines from them to the hatch. Adding another line to the Town Hall, she frowned as she regarded the map. "I know several of the other old houses aren't there anymore, but they're clearly marked on the map." She kept drawing lines. "There."

"Holy crap," Darian whispered. "I can't believe it. I mean, I can, but…damn."

"That's nothing short of amazing." Raoul had come to stand behind Holly. "It forms a word."

"What word? I don't recognize it." Camilla sounded impatient now. "Snap out of it, everyone, and fill me in."

"It says *Velocity*," Darian said, smiling. "Look, Gran." She followed the lines with a blunt nail.

"Oh, my God." Camilla gaped. Then she turned to Holly, who just stood there, holding the pencil with cold fingertips. "But, Holly, how could you possibly see this? I mean, did you recognize it as an alien symbol?"

"Not at first. I just noticed how symmetrical those important points seemed, and it seemed logical to try to connect the dots. And the more I looked, the clearer it appeared." Holly shrugged, knowing her explanation sounded too casual, too out of the blue. "I'm sorry, but I can't explain it any better than that."

"Welcome to the club," Carl said, grinning broadly. "That's typically how we end our sentences in this gang."

Holly was sure Carl had no idea how reassuring his words were, how included they made her feel. "Good to know."

"A part's missing, though," Samantha said and circled the table after everyone sat down again. She pulled a notepad closer and drew something with a marker, using quick, sure strokes. "Here's the symbol for *Velocity*. See? One line is missing. If we add that to Holly's brilliant lines, it will end up around…eh…here?" Samantha placed her right index finger on a structure Holly knew didn't exist anymore, whatever it was.

"What is that?" Darian asked, resting her elbows against the table. "It's right on the north side of the lake."

"It used to be the old water tower. They must have chosen that place because it's the most elevated part of town. It's not there anymore." Philber scratched his feathery hair. "Fortunately, nothing else has been built there."

"I remember," Samantha said and made a mark on the copied map. "There's a little plaque, right? Nobody in Dennamore pays any attention to it." She smirked. "Except us nerds."

"What can possibly be the significance of that spot? I suppose it has to be added to our to-do list," Raoul said. "And speaking of that, what is actually next?"

"We need to revisit Claire's camp as soon as possible," Holly said, not sure why she was the one who took the initiative. "Now that she's wearing a NIEC and has become the designated engineer, she might understand what to do with those holes more than anyone else."

"That's an excellent point," Samantha said, looking grateful. "The same team as last time?" She looked around the group.

Claire beamed. "Absolutely. I can't wait to back and see it all with new eyes. When?"

After some discussion, they agreed to meet by the lake on Saturday, to fit everyone's schedule. Holly felt it was too long of a wait but realized that Raoul, Claire, Carl, and Samantha had a schedule to keep.

"Anyone interested in coming along to the other place by the lake, the one marked with a plaque, before then?" Holly asked, looking hopefully at Darian. To her relief, Darian nodded. "Absolutely. You game, Brandon?"

"I'd like that," Brandon said after checking with Camilla, who merely flicked her hand and pointed to the journal.

"Walker and I are going to keep going through this. It's our favorite pastime," Camilla said.

"Well, almost." Walker winked at Camilla, who gave him a mock scowl.

"Indiscreet already, Young Geoff?" she asked silkily.

"Crap. She called him Young Geoff. Not a good sign." Darian grinned.

It didn't take a genius to see how Walker adored Camilla, who apparently had been his teenage crush back in the day. It was equally obvious that the feeling was now mutual.

After some coffee and tea in the parlor to round out the evening, where other topics than the alien artifacts were welcome, Holly found herself more and more at ease in the group. It was vital, as she, along with Brandon, needed the full acceptance among the ones of alien descent to fit in.

"Glad I didn't bring the car after all," Claire said when they put on their jackets in the foyer later, "as it's such a beautiful evening." She peered out the narrow window next to the heavy oak front door. "Look at those stars."

"Same here. Want some company?" Holly pulled on her gloves as the cloudless night sky made the air colder.

"I'd love that." Claire held the door open and waved to Samantha and Darian, who stood in the doorway to the parlor. "Thank you for today."

Holly waved also and stepped outside. They were the only ones walking home above ground, as Carl and Raoul could use the tunnel and get home easier via Philber's house. Walker apparently often spent his nights at Brynden 4 and had made no effort to leave at all.

The residential streets were empty for the most part, only a few people out walking dogs or going home from friends or family. Holly found it restful to stroll at a normal pace next to Claire. The woman was a seasoned hiker, after all, and it had dawned on Holly that Claire might be used to, and prefer, a faster pace. As it turned out, one of the reasons Holly didn't have to speed up was that Claire kept looking up at the stars. After a few blocks, when they were about to turn right, she stopped in the middle of the intersection and tipped her head back. The moon cast silver-blue highlights along Claire's curls when she turned a full circle.

"What are you doing?" Holly looked up at the sky, but then the image of Claire's expression of awe drew her attention more than the beautiful night sky, and she gazed at her as if it was the first time. Her dark-brown eyes glittered as they reflected the stars. The muted streetlights warmed her dark skin and emphasized Claire's high cheekbones and high forehead. She was average height, about five-six to Holly's five-eleven.

"I can't help but wonder…which one is it? Which one of these stars is the sun shining down on Dwynna Major? Any of them at all?" Her dreamy way of speaking added to her beauty, and Holly had to tell herself to breathe. "It'd be so cool if we were actually looking at the home of our ancestors."

The pang of the all-too-familiar feeling of not quite belonging threatened to make an appearance. "The way things are moving along, you all will find out about that sooner than you think." Holly could hear how forced her words sounded.

Claire apparently noticed the same. "What do you mean 'you all'? You're part of this too—you were before I was."

"By two days." Starting to walk again, Holly pushed her gloved hands into her coat pockets. "And I'm glad I'm part of the group, but I'm not from Dennamore."

"A lot of people aren't from Dennamore. Who knows how many of them will be able to add to this project anyway?" Claire lengthened her stride. "It can't have been easy for you to watch me get my NIEC." Her voice showed understanding but was, thank God, without pity. Holly confessed to being a proud, private woman when it came to certain things. Pity was one of them.

"Thank you for saying that. And even so, I wouldn't have wanted to miss it for anything. The look on your face when it connected to your mind…I'll never forget that." Relieved that she sounded her collected self again, Holly shot Claire a smile.

"It was like nothing I've ever felt before. It wasn't there. And then it was—feeling entirely natural. So odd." Claire raised her hand to the back of her head even though the NIEC wasn't attached. "I know Samantha and Raoul were adamant about my wearing it only a few hours at a time in the beginning and with a few hours in between as well, but I miss it."

"I can understand that, but they know so much more about all this than we do, and I'm glad they're being careful. If you got carried away and accidentally injured yourself…That'd be horrible." The idea of the NIEC harming Claire made Holly's stomach clench. Surprised at her pointed reaction, Holly avoided looking at her companion for a few moments.

"How long have you been back in Dennamore?" Claire asked, perhaps sensing that changing the topic was a good idea.

"Seven years. My wife passed away, and I moved back to tend to my mother. I teach online, social and political science, which makes me able to continue my research."

"And your mom? She still with us?"

For some reason, it didn't sound presumptuous that Claire said "us." "No. She passed a year after my return. My father died right after I got tenure at the university, four years before Frances, my wife." Why was it so easy to tell Claire this? Normally, Holly never brought personal things like this up—and certainly not with someone she'd just met.

"You've seen a lot of loss." Claire didn't elaborate, but her words showed two things. She had understood, and she wasn't going to dig for details. Holly appreciated both.

"I'm equally interested in hearing what it's like to work with your father full-time?" Holly smiled when Claire chuckled at her question.

"My dad is pretty easygoing, unless I screw up with any of the cars. He has high standards, which is as it should be. Luckily, I'm a brilliant mechanic. Certainly better than the two other men I work with. They see more of 'Mr. Gordon' than I ever have. 'Mr. Gordon' is what we call Dad when he's all up in our faces telling us what we've done wrong." Claire laughed again. "Fortunately, Dad is a real gentle giant. He just wants things done right. He has an engineering degree and designs motorcycles, which means that fixing people's cars is up to me and the guys."

"Impressive." Holly thought of her own soft-spoken father, working at the bank in Dennamore all his adult life and so proud of his adopted daughter for her academic prowess. Her mother had worked as an elementary schoolteacher until she retired. Growing up in the Crowe household had been easy. No raised voices, just acceptance, love, and encouragement. When Holly came out to her parents, they had already guessed, and they had loved Frances.

During the rest of the walk, they talked about ordinary things, and the sound of Claire's voice, how it rose and fell, its timbre, made Holly relax fully for the first time in days. When they parted to walk toward their respective houses, Claire surprised Holly by quickly stroking up and down her left arm.

"I look forward to Saturday. Good luck with the plaque. Oh, wait." Claire pulled out her cell phone. "I just realized I don't have your number. I want to hear what you find there." She looked expectantly at Holly, who didn't hesitate for a second about giving out her private number. Claire tapped against the screen, and soon Holly's pocket gave a muted ping.

"There. We're connected." Claire began walking backward. "Bye!"

"Good night." Wincing when Claire barely missed a lamppost, Holly then stood motionless for a moment, somehow transfixed, until she was out of sight. Pulling out her house key, she walked up the short garden path to her front door and entered the house that looked exactly like it had when she grew up. In here nothing had changed. Within Holly, nothing was ever going to be the same.

CHAPTER NINE

Darian walked next to Brandon as they crossed the parking lot over to Holly's small hybrid car.

"Weather's on our side," Darian called out as she adjusted the backpack containing tools, her alien computer, and some instruments.

"A relief since I can sure do without that icy rain that fell last night." Holly greeted them with a small wave. "Hi, Brandon. I appreciate all the hours you put in yesterday."

"You're welcome." Brandon pulled out the copy of the old map. "You set some coordinates this morning with Samantha, via link, right?" He glanced over at Darian.

"Yes. She's the navigator, after all, and I figured, why reinvent the wheel?" Darian took the map and put it on the hood of Holly's car. "I figured we'd take some rudimentary measurements when we reach the plaque. Is it big, this plaque? I mean, are we going to have to dig around for it?" She looked up at Holly, who shook her head.

"Not at all. It's in another clearing, quite close to the lake, but I think you need to know where it is to spot it. Most tourists are here for the lights in the summer and skiing in the winter. Nobody cares about an old water tower."

"Unless you're a population that wants running water in their faucets." Darian rolled the map up and looked expectantly at Holly. "Lead the way."

Holly shoved her camera bag farther back and pulled on a pair of leather gloves. She began walking along the same side of the lake where Darian had stood when she saw the lake lights for the first time.

After about a hundred and fifty yards, Holly motioned toward a narrow, discreet sign that simply said *Dennamore Water Tower*. Constructed like the wooden pathway that circled the lake, a narrower path led ten yards or so into the forest. There, an unassuming brass plate simply stated when it was built in 1820 and taken out of commission, in 1962.

"They sure could build things to last," Darian said, leaning closer to the plaque to read the smaller print. The little monument was apparently constructed on top of a deep, subterranean stream that also provided the lake with its water. To this day, this was where the inhabitants of Dennamore got their water. "Let's see if we can determine the angles from here." Darian unfolded the map again and handed it to Brandon. Taking out her computer, she pulled up the information she needed, but then she had to reach for the closest tree as a, by now familiar, whoosh went through her system. "Damn."

"Are you all right?" Holly quickly stepped closer and cupped Darian's elbow. "You went pale."

"Just my trusty NIEC finding this a good time for another upgrade." Darian drew a deep breath but managed to smile. She could still get nauseous for a moment.

"Upgrade?" Holly frowned.

"Of me, in a manner of speaking. I'm not sure if the NIECs reads us to make sure how much of an upgrade we can tolerate at a time, but they portion them out. Often when we find ourselves at a point where we need it—oh." Darian saw the map so much more clearly now. She waved her fingers reassuringly at Brandon, who seemed ready to leap and carry her back to the car, much like he had after more than one party in her teens. "I'm good."

Darian circled the plaque, which sat on a four-foot-high stone column. "This is it, but I need to scan it."

"Scan it? With what?" Holly studied Darian closely, clearly not about to miss a thing.

"I don't—wait. With this." Darian took her computer and turned it on its side. She felt for the sensor she suddenly knew was there and slid her finger along the nearly invisible slit.

"What's that? Another feature we had no idea was there?" Brandon stood next to Darian, clearly not entirely sure she was a hundred percent yet.

Darian looked down at the now oddly familiar object in her hand. Five inches times four, a quarter of an inch thick, and with one big, still-black screen, it was not heavy, but it had some weight to it. "It's more than a scanner," Darian said, her hand trembling, but she knew it was just adrenaline from the rush. "It's like their version of our smartphones, but infinitely more advanced, of course."

"Of course," Holly muttered.

"How do you turn it on?" Brandon asked.

"Like this." Darian slid her right index finger along the right side and, at the same time, let her thumb on the same hand trace the bottom edge. It reminded her of the pinching motion she used when zooming out from text or pictures on her cell phone. She jumped when her speaker pinged, and at first, she expected to hear the voice of someone paging her, but then she realized it had connected to her...her... Darian closed her eyes briefly, and then the name came to her. "This is a *trackpad*." The screen lit up, and the alien text ran from the right corner and upward, fast, as if it had rebooted and was getting used to its new owner.

"And what does it do, apart from scan?" Holly asked, sounding mesmerized.

"As you heard, it made my speaker ping. The screen can provide an image of who I'm talking to, among other things. Kind of like a video call. It's a small but powerful version of the computer, I suppose like a tablet, and it can of course calculate, record, and analyze." Darian straightened. "And now that I'm not feeling like I'm about to throw up all over your shoes, let's scan the area around the plaque." She handed the computer to Holly. "Keep it open, please. I know what to do, but I'd rather just get a backup copy of what we found on the computer as well."

"Got it." Holly followed Darian as she circled the plaque, tapping in commands on the bright screen that obediently scanned and recorded everything.

"There's something I don't get," Darian murmured. "It has registered the plaque or, I should say, the base of it. Then look here. You don't have to understand the language to see the specs." She motioned for Brandon and Holly to flank her. "See these thin, glowing lines radiating from the center of this well, or water source? They're in a perfect ninety-degree angle from each other. And they are exactly, let's see, 3.145 yards from the center of the well. That's a very precise measurement, isn't it?"

"Pi," Holly said.

"Excuse me?" Darian blinked.

"That's right, Holly." Brandon slapped his hand on the plaque. "Pi, Darian. Any of your old school math still in there?" He grinned as he pointed to her head.

Darian finally understood that Holly wasn't talking about some baked goods, but Pi as the mathematical constant that showed the connection between a circle's circumference and diameter. "This is why I'm the chief of security and not the engineer or navigator," she said with a crooked smile. "Thanks guys. I'd like to think I may have figured it out, but—"

"You would," Brandon said.

"Does this mean that we should make the circle using the tips of those lines or make four smaller circles?" Holly turned slowly to look at the moss and needles on the ground. "Or do we dig?"

"I think we need to identify the four tips, as you call them, first of all." Darian tucked the trackpad into her back pocket and dug into her backpack. Pulling out a small spray can of paint, she handed it to Brandon after a quick glance at Holly's leather gloves. She took out the trackpad again and placed it on the pillar. "Let's see. Yay. Like this." Suddenly small, yellow dots glimmered on the ground in all four directions. Something was wrong, though, as they were not still, but trembling. Wasn't the trackpad calibrated correctly? Standing closer to the pillar, Darian moved the trackpad around on the plaque, thinking she might not have found the dead center. Or the right angle. She slowly turned the device clockwise. Then it was as if she felt, rather than heard, a click from it. Darian looked out on the moss. There they were. The yellow dots. Not moving at all.

Brandon had pulled out his cell phone and tapped his screen. "I'll put it away in case it interferes with the other technology. I just wanted to run my compass app. And I was right. It's exactly aligned with the cardinal directions."

"And look at this." Holly stepped in between Darian and Brandon. "North, west, south. There." She drew lines with her finger from their location in the three directions. "And then east." She showed the angle with her other hand. "It creates a pattern. This part is as vital as the others."

"I might be jinxing things, but I feel we're going to find out a lot tomorrow," Darian said, reaching for the trackpad. As she closed her hand over it, something shifted under their feet. Holly supported herself against the pillar but then took a few steps back.

"Let go of it." Brandon took Darian by the arm and pulled her back. "Let's get out of the area the trackpad marked."

Darian stumbled backward, and now she saw the pillar start to shake. "But I could lose it."

"Hold on to my hand and grab it then." Brandon gripped Darian's hand hard as she leaned in and snatched up the trackpad and shoved it into her breast pocket. As she was pulling back, the dirt under her feet began to separate. Her feet slipped as roots broke and flipped up as if they were elastic bands.

"Darian!" Brandon braced himself and tugged at her, Holly holding onto him from behind. Brandon seemed to have a good grip of her arm, thanks to the material of her jacket, but Darian feared she might topple him if the ground didn't stop shaking.

"What's going on?" she called out. "If it was the trackpad, it should have stopped when I removed it."

"We don't know that," Holly said, also raising her voice as the rumbling continued.

With a snap, a thoroughly mechanical sound, the ground opened under Darian. She fell, and the pain in her shoulder made her cry out, but it also meant Brandon hadn't let go. Clawing at his arm, she looked down but saw nothing but a black hole. What she heard, though, scared her. A dark, roaring, almost gurgling sound rose from the hole in the ground. The pillar was gone. It had fallen into the hole that seemed to go on forever.

"Darian, hold on." Brandon groaned out the words as he was now on his side, having fallen flat on his stomach right at the edge.

"We have to call for help," Holly said from somewhere behind Brandon. Darian was now in agony from the tearing at her shoulder. She dared to let go of Brandon's arm with her free hand and felt against the side of the hole. A thick root sprang from the dirt, and she wrapped her cold fingers around it, clinging to it and to Brandon.

"Call 911. I can't hold her much longer."

"No!" Darian whimpered. "That'll blow the whistle on everything before we're ready. Please. Let me try first."

"But you're hurt. I heard the shoulder go. I *felt* it." Brandon grimaced as he looked down at her.

"Just give me a sec." Darian pressed her face to the dirt and inhaled the scent of nature. "I've got a good grip on this root. If Holly can reach me from your right, Brandon, she can help pull me up by my jacket."

"You get one attempt. One." Brandon gritted his teeth.

Holly's head appeared at the edge of the hole. "Okay. Let me get a good hold." She reached down with both hands and took fistfuls of the fabric of Darian's jacket from below her left arm. "On the count of three. All right?"

Darian dreaded Brandon pulling on her right arm but knew this was the only way. "Yes."

Brandon nodded grimly.

"One—two—three!" Holly pulled hard and fast just as Darian pushed her way up along the root. She cried out in agony as Brandon tugged her over the edge by her injured shoulder, whimpering again as the world around her turned gray and fuzzy at the edges. When it slowly cleared again, she found herself lying in a fetal position, cradling her shoulder. Brandon was talking to someone on the phone, and Darian tried to sit up, ready to argue.

"It's just Raoul. He's going to come help us get you back to the car. You need the emergency room." Holly had taken off her jacket and wrapped it around Darian. "Want to hear something strange?"

"What?" Darian whispered through the searing pain.

"The hole closed itself once we had you out. As soon as your legs were free, it zapped shut. The pillar and the plaque are gone. So are the dirt and moss."

"What covered it?"

"It just looks like naked bedrock. It seemed to flip up from below." Holly pushed the hair from Darian's face. "Hey, you're not going to pass out on me, are you?"

"Nah. I've had worse." Darian tried for a smile, but the effort made her wince. "Not a lot worse, but marginally."

"Raoul's on his way. Should I call Samantha, or do you want to do it?"

Darian groaned. "It can wait—"

"No, it can't. If Samantha was injured and didn't tell you asap, what would you think about that?" Brandon cupped her chin.

"All right. See your point." Darian leaned against Holly. "Darian to Samantha." If Samantha didn't answer, and part of Darian hoped she wouldn't, it meant she was in a meeting or with a visitor.

"Darian. What's wrong?" Samantha sounded tense. Clearly, she had kept her speaker on voice alert, and not just the very discreet buzzer mode that they normally used when they were among other people.

"I fell and hurt my shoulder. Raoul's coming to help me get to the clinic. I don't know how long it'll be." Darian could hear how raspy her voice sounded.

"I'll meet you there. You're not alone, are you? I mean, right now?"

"No. Of course not. Brandon and Holly are with me as planned."

"I should be there with you." Samantha's voice didn't give away her emotions, but Darian could guess how much effort it took for her to sound this calm.

"No. Don't do that. I'll be out of here by the time you get here. I'd love it if you'd come to the ER though." Darian moaned as the pain went from an eight to a ten.

"Damn it, Darian. How bad's your injury?" Samantha was starting to lose her collected tone.

"Not sure. It's my shoulder. We'll see what Raoul says. He'll be here in a few minutes, I think."

"All right. I won't let you strain yourself by talking to me any longer, darling. Just keep it together until he gets there, all right? I'll see you soon."

There it was. Another "darling" spoken by this woman whom Darian could never get enough of and without whom this entire adventure would lose its magic. "Okay. Drive safely." Darian ended the call by tapping the speaker, but even that small gesture made her cry out.

"I have you. Try to relax against me." Holly held her gently while Brandon crouched next to them.

"I'm sorry I hurt you, kiddo," he said, the term of endearment he'd given her when she was little slipping over his lips.

"You saved me from falling all the way down, however far that was," Darian whispered. "I'm just going to need some painkillers and a sling. Probably just a sprain."

"God." Brandon ran a hand over his face. "Camilla's going to kill me."

"Gran is going to thank you." Darian reached out a trembling hand, and he took it between his. "I'll be fine."

"Yes, you will," a new voice said from behind as Raoul joined them. "I got a call from Samantha, who said she was going to the ER, but I told her to go to Brynden 4. I just realized I can treat you much better and safer aboard *Speeder One*."

Samantha didn't bother to knock but barreled through the doors of Brynden 4. In the foyer, Camilla was getting ready to be assisted down the stairs to the basement. A dirty and disheveled Brandon stood in the doorway leading to the stairs, looking pale.

"Where is she?" Samantha had to push the words over her lips.

"Getting into *Speeder One*. Holly and Raoul are there, and Carl was just out of school and came to help." Brandon spoke curtly.

"She's so bad off she can't walk on her own? What the hell?" Samantha moved toward the stairs, but Brandon held up a hand.

"She's hurt her shoulder badly. It makes it hard for her to move." He cleared his throat and grabbed hold of the doorframe. "It's my fault."

"What?" Samantha did her best to reel herself in, and when doing so, she noticed how Brandon had problems keeping his balance. "Hey. You have to sit down." She grabbed a stool that stood in the corner. "Here."

"Please, Brandon, do as Samantha says." Camilla's tone was stark, but the underlying tremor showed how worried she was. And she was right. Brandon loved Camilla and Darian. They were his family, and now one of them was injured.

"I'm sorry, Brandon. I didn't mean to snap at you." Samantha wanted to tear down the stairs to the basement and get to the tunnel, but the man before her had saved Darian, and still he was agonizing, thinking he'd hurt her. From what Samantha had gathered over the speaker while they were en route back to Brynden 4, Darian could have been killed if Brandon hadn't caught her. "Now you listen to me. Don't you think a busted shoulder beats a broken neck?" She knew she was being harsh, but Brandon looked like he was close to having a coronary.

"When you put it like that," Brandon murmured and ran a hand over his bald head. "But she's in so much pain."

"I'll go to be with her, and Walker is helping Camilla. Come back down when you feel ready. I know Darian will want you there." Samantha kissed Brandon's forehead and then hurried through the door and down the stairs. As she reached the tunnel, the echo of a shrill scream made her stop and support herself against the wall. When it was followed by a growl ending in "Son of a bitch!" Samantha ran over to the shuttle and up the ramp.

Inside, Raoul and Carl had converted some of the crew seats into an LSC-bed, which stood for Life Support Care. On it, a writhing Darian glared at the two men and Holly, who had all taken a step back.

"Darling." Samantha hurried over to Darian and placed a gentle hand on the uninjured shoulder. "What's going on?"

"He's trying to inject me with something from the ship that hasn't even been tested. I hate needles. I hate injections. I hate foreign substances in my freakin' body!" Darian was pale and sweaty, with dirt smeared all over her clothes and face. "And when I flinched, my damn shoulder hurt like crazy."

"Listen. I understand, but Raoul must look at your shoulder. Can he do that if you get to pinch me if it hurts?" Samantha smiled, even if her heart ached at the sight of Darian's obvious pain.

"I don't want to pinch you." Darian groaned. "But all right. Just no needles."

"I promise no needles," Raoul said as he carefully approached. "That's what I tried to tell you. These are dermal infusers. I've scanned the agents, and my NIEC tells me they're fully compatible with regular human physiology. I could give it to Holly or Brandon without a problem."

"Huh." Darian closed her eyes briefly. "I still don't like it."

"You'll like my examination even less if I don't give you something." Raoul took a gentle grip of Darian's chin. "Just close your eyes…or, better yet, look at Samantha."

Samantha placed herself at a good angle for Darian to glare at her but merely squeezed the hand of her good arm. "It'll act really fast, I'm sure. There you go."

Raoul placed the gunmetal-colored pen-like instrument against Darian's jugular vein. A faint hiss and then it was done. Samantha watched Darian's face go from contorted in pain to relaxed in seconds.

"Whoa." Darian tilted her head. "Now, that wasn't so bad." She snorted. "I can sure be such a baby about some things."

"I can testify to that," Camilla said from behind Samantha. Walker had helped her into a seat from where she could see everything that was going on. "How are you, sweetheart?"

"Pretty good. There's this kind of nice, loopy feeling, but the pain is um…manageable." Darian peered at her grandmother. "Don't worry, Gran. It takes more than this to do me in. Where's Brandon?"

"The poor man is in shock, whether he acknowledges it or not." Camilla sighed. "He'll be joining us after he's changed clothes and gathered himself some."

"I can understand how he feels," Holly said from where she stood at the head of the LSC-bed. "It was a few horrifying moments there, before Darian was back on solid ground."

The sound of quick steps came closer and up the ramp. Claire barreled through the hatch, her eyes huge. "How is…oh, thank God." She stopped next to Holly and fought to catch her breath. "I got the alert but couldn't get away in time to help."

"You're here now." Samantha nodded gratefully to Claire. "It's been dramatic, but now I think we need to let Raoul work."

"I'm not budging." Camilla waved her hand to the others. "The rest of you can debrief each other, but I'm staying with Darian." She set her jaw in a way that left no margin for argument.

"Me too. I'm not going anywhere either." Samantha met Darian's gaze. "Not a chance."

Darian's expression softened. "Thank you."

"Then I suggest the rest of us move to the aft of the shuttle." Walker motioned in the direction with his chin. "I, for one, want to know what's going on."

"So do I," Philber stated from the hatch. "Ah, a full house." He stopped by the LSC-bed, awkwardly patting Darian's left foot. "You all right?"

"Super." Darian made a swaying thumbs-up.

Samantha watched the others as they entered the part of the shuttle where she knew more seats could be unfolded, but then she returned her focus to Darian. "All right. Better get started before that medication wears off."

"Way ahead of you." Using an unfamiliar instrument, Raoul cut off Darian's jacket, sweatshirt and T-shirt. He left her sports bra on, and when he stepped away to get something else from the tray he'd pulled from the wall, Samantha saw for the first time the extent of Darian's injury.

"Oh, my sweet Lord," Brandon said, having entered without any of them noticing. He too stared at the mottled skin on Darian's shoulder, where the angle of the shoulder joint looked distorted.

"Take a seat here with me, Brandon," Camilla said sternly, but her frail hands were gentle when they guided the burly man down next to her.

"Hey, Bran. I'll be fine. I'm getting super-duper-freaky alien meds. And Raoul here will do magic." Darian giggled and crinkled her nose.

"If you sit still, I'll do my best to live up to such a glowing review." Raoul returned with a set of instruments, none of them making any sense to Samantha or her NIEC. He picked the smallest of them and began running it over Darian's skin, which was changing colors before their eyes, and to Samantha's amazement, after a few passes back and forth, it began leaving healthy pink skin in its wake. For the larger swellings where the skin was already bruising a deep blue-black hue, Raoul shifted to a larger, transparent, cylindrical object. When he gripped it, a bright lilac-colored light lit up a slit that ran along its full length. Raoul moved the object around Darian's shoulder, keeping it an inch from her skin. The lilac light was even more effective than the smaller device. It was as if it painted on healthy, unbruised skin with each stroke.

"That's the broken capillaries," Raoul muttered to himself. "Darian, I'm not sure how much your pain meds will help with the last part. Tell me if you need more, okay?"

"Mm-hm. Sure thing." Darian smiled blissfully.

"Samantha, I need to scan her shoulder from both sides, just to be sure. I'll do the front first, but then I will need help rolling her toward you." Raoul raised his eyebrows.

"Understood." Samantha stepped closer.

Raoul placed what looked like a nylon fabric on top of Darian's shoulder and clavicle area, smoothing it down. Then he ran what looked like a tablet over it. Like magic, a perfect scan of Darian's bones, tissues, and blood vessels appeared in a highly defined picture.

"Now toward you." Raoul pushed his hands flat under Darian.

Samantha bent and pushed her hands in as well, much like an embrace. She pulled Darian toward her. A muted whimper from Darian made Samantha press her lips against her temple. "Shh. I have you. Just relax, and we'll be done faster."

"Okay." Darian's voice was small. "It hurts."

"You can get more medication once we finish the scan. And there. It's done." Samantha lowered Darian back against the LSC-bed.

"It's not fully dislocated, Darian," Raoul said. "It's on the edge and will only need a nudge to slip back into the socket. What's worse is that your clavicle is broken, but I have what we need to fix that."

"Wait...what?" Samantha blinked. "Are you saying you can mend fractures?"

"Not all, but when they're not misaligned, it's easily done with a bone-stitcher."

"It's unfathomable," Camilla whispered. "Do you have something for an aching grandmother's heart, perhaps?"

Raoul sent Camilla a gentle smile. "Your heart should stop aching when you see Darian back on her feet, and that'll happen before you know it."

"Pfft. Cocky, aren't we?" Darian rolled her eyes, whether from the effect of the medication or due to Raoul's words.

Raoul merely shook his head and gripped Darian's upper arm. Before anyone had a chance to react, he had popped it back into its socket with a practiced movement. Darian yelped but then smiled broadly. "Oh, wow. You can be cocky all you want. If I weren't gay and my heart not already taken, I'd kiss you."

Raoul glanced at Samantha, who didn't know what to say. Darian was speaking under the influence of alien drugs, after all, but even so, her words had made her heart skip a beat, or several.

"You will feel even better in a little bit," Raoul told Darian. He chose another instrument that reminded Samantha of a flashlight from her childhood with its broad, flat end covered by a glass-like surface. He placed it against the skin above Darian's clavicle and tapped the end twice. Another colorful light spread along the skin underneath it.

"Whoa. That's hot. Yikes. Almost too hot." Darian's eyes popped open, searching for Samantha. "Is that right?"

"It's as it should be. I promise, I'm not burning you. The heat comes from the broken collarbone fusing. Just hang in there." Raoul patted Darian's hand. "You're being a trooper. This is new territory for you."

"And for you," Camilla said quietly.

"Not really, Camilla." Raoul checked a small window on the handle of the bone-stitcher. "Another couple of minutes and you'll be feeling much better, though I recommend that you rest over the weekend.

"No." Darian glared at Raoul. "We're going to the woods to figure out the holes in the rocks. Too much going on."

"If you insist on coming along, it'll be on the back of my four-wheel bike. You're not walking or putting any strain on my handiwork." It was obvious Raoul meant business.

"Okay. Thank you. That sounds very cool, actually." Darian closed her eyes again. "Amazing how comfortable these beds are. I've never been in an ER that had a comfortable chair or gurney—ever."

Samantha could tell Darian was fading fast and realized all that had transpired had worn her out. When Raoul removed the bone-stitcher and Darian didn't even wake up, Samantha gently bent and kissed her lips, not caring who saw.

"Why don't we let her rest for a little while we update ourselves on what happened in greater detail?" Samantha turned to the others. "I'll spend the night with her to make sure she's all right—if that's okay, Camilla?"

"More than okay." Camilla took Brandon's hand. "Now, can you please start to take full breaths, my dear. She's fine. Fully repaired. And you, my best friend in the world, saved her. And me." Camilla placed a kiss on Brandon's cheek.

"I'll do my best." Brandon looked marginally better, but Samantha knew it would take him, Camilla, and her a while to stop thinking about what could have happened. From now on, they needed to approach the artifacts and landmarks with a lot more care.

CHAPTER TEN

The following day, Holly watched Darian climb on the back of Raoul's terrain four-wheel bike after the group had added the heaviest equipment to its rack. Holly was carrying her daypack, mainly consisting of her camera equipment, water, and energy bars, as per her usual routine. She chuckled inwardly, as there was nothing routine about what she and the rest of the group were doing.

"All right," Samantha said where she stood to Holly's right. "Let's just make sure we're all on the same page. Brandon and Carl will head over to where the plaque used to be. And while doing so, you two will be very cautious. Brandon, you're in charge. Carl, you're the one with the NIEC, so you keep your wits about you."

"Got it. Caution and wits." Carl saluted with his right index finger, making Samantha frown and smile at the same time.

"Raoul and Darian will go with the rest of us to Claire's camp, where we'll unload the equipment. Then they'll continue around the lake with their trackpads and try to locate the other two places where we think there might be similar holes in the bedrock. And again, Darian, it was an amazing find, the trackpads."

"Hey, it was my NIEC that decided it was time. Pretty sure it had nothing to do with me. I was the only one there with a NIEC."

Holly had started getting used to being one of two in this group who could never utilize any of the alien technology. She knew it was mainly because the others made her feel important to the group, regardless of her status, and it seemed as if they appreciated her affinity for taking charge when things drew out too long, which she was about to do now.

"I thought of something. If Raoul and Darian find the other two sites, *and* if we reach some form of progress at Claire's camp, we might need to divide ourselves among all four sites." She let her gaze travel around the others.

Samantha brightened. "I like how you think one step ahead. You're definitely more macro in how you see things, Holly. I tend to micro-manage my life." She shrugged lightly. "All right. We have a contingency plan. Let's go."

It felt natural for Holly to fall into step next to Claire again, as they began to walk to the camp. Perhaps the feeling stemmed from a bonding experience of being new to the group, but that wasn't the only reason. Something about Claire, perhaps her glowing intensity and how she showed her enthusiasm for these fantastic discoveries without holding back fully matched what Holly felt on the inside but always had difficulty sharing. Frances used to say that Holly was like some level-ten puzzle box. Not until you knew all the right things to do and say around her did she open up to others. Holly had claimed that was an exaggeration, but after the death of Frances, who clearly had possessed all the keys to Holly's secret traps and hidden doors, she realized it wasn't by much.

"Good thing there's no snow," Claire said as they moved from the walkway around the lake and onto the path into the forest.

"Yes. The fewer tracks we leave behind, the better." Holly looked at the ground. "We don't make many marks on the moss and pine needles. Not even the bike is stirring up too much."

"Unless another humongous hole opens up and shoves it all aside. Good thing no locals are interested in the damn plaque for the water tower. Tourists aren't keen on the area here at all. Even if there were snow, they'd be on the slopes rather than around the lake."

Claire was right. Holly rounded a group of trees she recognized from the other day. "Do you feel different walking to your camp wearing the NIEC?" Holly shot Claire a quick look, hoping she wouldn't mind the question.

"Not yet. I'm aware of my speaker and the trackpad in a very different way, of course, but that doesn't seem to correlate to the forest. I have a confession though. Since I got my alien computer yesterday, I stayed up half the night going through it, trying things out. There were calculations and information about technology that should have been like a foreign language to me, but my brain treated it all as if it were something I've always known. It's the freakiest thing."

"I wish I possessed the gene. I truly do." Holly managed a smile. "But hearing you talk about it actually makes me feel a bit connected after all."

"I didn't mean to gush." Claire winced. "I keep forgetting that you're not wearing one. It sort of feels like you do. I can't explain it."

"Hear, hear," Samantha said from behind them, where she headed up the rear. "You put words to my thoughts, Claire."

Surprised, Holly turned her head back and saw that Samantha looked entirely genuine. "That's nice to know."

Samantha made a gesture, palms up. "From my point of view, having been the impromptu leader, it's a godsend. Like I said before, I think we complement each other, which goes for a lot of the personalities in the group."

"Once we have seventy-six crewmembers, it's going to feel a lot less personal, and a lot harder to manage," Holly said. "I'm glad to be able to be a part of this, even if I'm not genetically a match."

"You were meant to be with us," Samantha said gently. "I'm not prone to fatalism, but that's how we all feel. Same goes for you, Claire."

Claire beamed and then pointed ahead where the four-wheel bike turned a corner. "That's it. We're almost there."

Holly heard Raoul turn off the ignition, and the woods became very quiet until birds started making some noise again. They caught up with Darian and Raoul, the latter putting up foldable chairs while Darian was busy starting a fire.

"You okay doing that?" Samantha asked lightly.

"Yup." Grinning, Darian soon had the fire going. "I know we brought hot beverages, but I thought, why not make good use of Claire's fire pit?"

"Good point," Holly said and helped get the equipment off the bike. She unfolded a small camping table. Soon Claire's and Samantha's computers sat there, ready to be used. Holly pulled up a chair next to them after waving Darian and Raoul off as they returned toward the lake to go look for the other sites marked on the old map.

"Let me go scan the holes," Claire said and grabbed the small ladder. She took her trackpad and tapped in a few commands. To Holly's surprise, two thin, rigid filaments extended about four inches in each direction, on either side of the top.

"Now there's a feature we have yet to learn about." Samantha looked down at her own trackpad. "Hm. Guess I'll have to ask Claire how she did that later."

Claire walked closer to the rock formation and ran the trackpad from one hole to the other. Even if Holly sat four yards away from her, she could hear the pinging sound from the trackpad.

"Something's registering." Holly stood. She was eager to find out what, exactly, but didn't want to disturb Claire's focus.

More scanning, furious tapping, and then another scan. Claire eventually, after what felt like an eternity, turned to Holly and Samantha, her eyes huge and glowing. "Damn."

Whatever Holly had thought Claire would say, that wasn't it, yet it said it all. Whatever she had found out, it was huge.

"Tell us," Samantha said. "I'm recording, just so we don't forget anything."

"Everything is downloaded into my computer already, but that's still a good idea. I might just lose my marbles, and then who knows if I'll even remember my name." Claire kept looking at her trackpad. "This rock formation is, as we sort of know already, one of three. It is also part of the opening mechanism when it's time to launch the *Velocity*."

Samantha was almost on her feet but slumped back down on her foldable chair. "Really?"

"Not just that. The scanner showed me everything, and now I know why the ground opened by the water tower plaque yesterday." Claire sat down on her chair. She closed her trackpad and pushed it back into the slot on the side of her computer. "Here. See?" She pointed at what looked like an aqua-tinted map of Dennamore two hundred and twenty years ago. "See that square there?" She tapped the location of the plaque. A new window opened, showing a square opening. Alien text appeared to its right.

"What does that say?" Holly asked, slowly sitting as well.

"It describes the measurements, and the depth, of what it calls the entrance." Samantha looked up, blinking hard. Tears filled her eyes and ran down her cheeks. "It does say entrance. Excuse me." She wiped at her cheeks. "All hands. This is Samantha. Claire's unlocked a huge part of our mystery." Her breath caught, and she had to clear her throat.

"You all right?" Of course, Darian didn't miss a thing.

"I'm fine. Just emotional. The hole you almost fell into yesterday? Claire's scans say it's the entrance."

"You're kidding." Darian sounded perplexed. "That dark pit?"

"Yes." Samantha wiped her cheeks again.

"Well, that's fantastic news. And speaking of news, we were just going to page you guys. Since we now have the trackpads, it's much easier to locate the other sites. No need to get up close and personal with every rock we see in the woods."

"Ah. Yes, of course." Samantha smiled through the tears. "Good luck finding them, all the same."

The others checked back in, one by one, and last were Carl and Brandon. "If this is the entrance, how the hell do we get down into the pitch-black monstrosity of a hole—and isn't there water down there? Scuba diving?" Brandon was obviously not a fan of the hole where he'd nearly lost Darian.

Holly motioned for Samantha to connect her speaker on her behalf. "Brandon. Carl. Let me talk to Claire about something. Hold on." She turned to Claire, who was focusing on her computer again. "Is there a way for you to receive Carl's scans in real time on your computer?"

"But of course. And that's a brilliant idea." Claire touched her speaker. "Carl. I'm going to send you a code for your trackpad. It'll make it possible for your scans to enter my computer as you perform them." She slid her fingertips along the glass-like surface that sat where a laptop would normally have a keyboard. After creating intricate, colorful patterns of lines and dots, Claire stopped. "You still there, Carl?"

"Sure. Wait. Whoa. That's a new thing. Some antennas, or whatever, poked out of the trackpad." He sounded startled.

"We know. It's happened here too. Apparently, something to do with my being an engineer, according to my NIEC." Claire opened another window on her computer. "We're all set. Scan as much as you need to."

"Got it. Scanning."

As Holly looked at the screen in fascination, it filled with signs and lines, from the bottom right corner and to the left. She couldn't spot any of the few signs she had learned by heart, perhaps because the text floated onto the screen so fast.

"I'm saving it, but I think I understand the gist of it," Claire murmured. "Samantha?"

"I understand some. The NIECs sure homes in on our specialties. For you to suddenly understand not only the text, but also the engineering elements to it, the technology…and it has been just two days! What you will find out in time is that you retain more and more knowledge every time you use the device."

"Cool." Claire hastily looked up at Samantha and Holly. "I think our next step will be to figure out how to get to the *Velocity* through the opening Darian found."

"Found. Yes. That's one word for it." Holly walked over to the rock with the holes. "So, what do these things actually do? Any information about that?"

Claire nodded. "They will work together with the other two sites. When we enter the opening by the old water tower, eventually these holes will send laser-like rays. Where they meet, a fourth ray will be sent down into the lake and over to sensors on the meadows."

"Lasers?" Holly stepped away from the holes. "What type of lasers? Signaling or flesh-scorching?"

Claire merely shrugged. "I doubt they're flesh-scorching. If anything, they're going to be powerful enough to go through water and not be distorted. But you're right. Just to be on the safe side, let's not jump in front of any of them." She returned her focus to the computer. "And that's the rest of the scan." After reading some more, Claire blinked. "Seems we better not put off going down in that hole."

"What do you mean?" Samantha walked closer and read over Claire's shoulder.

"Darian's involuntary opening of the entrance yesterday evidently started a countdown. We have to get down there and make our way to the mothership. If we don't do it now that the water is being pumped out, it will flood back up again, and according to the diagnostic automatically performed by the trackpad, there's an elevated risk that it can bring back impurities from the surrounding underground caves that might have an adverse effect on the instruments and mechanical parts that keep the water out of the cave where the *Velocity* is kept."

"It's in a cave?" Samantha breathed the words and gripped Holly's arm. "Natural? Manmade? Or, should I say, alien-made?"

"This text suggests it's alien-made." Claire tapped some of the symbols. "It's huge, with measurements I've never heard about before, but the NIEC shows me the measurements in yards with no calculations required."

"And how big is it?" Holly wasn't the bouncy type, but she found it hard to stand still.

"Approximately 75,000 square feet, like a soccer field. Height is, wow, can this be right? Two hundred feet."

"It's massive," Samantha whispered.

"All hands, this is Darian." Darian's bright voice interrupted Claire's recount of amazing facts.

"Yes, go ahead," Samantha said.

"We've located the first of the two sites. If we hadn't had the trackpads, I doubt we would have found them...or it would have taken us months and months. The third should be even easier, as we can triangulate by using the coordinates of the first two."

"That's great news." Samantha placed a hand on Claire's shoulder. "While we have a party-line going, Claire has some information as well. Go ahead." She nodded to Claire.

Holly listened intently as Claire rattled off the new finds. Knowing she had to retain everything they found the old-fashioned way, she also pulled out a writing pad and pen, jotting down the measurements Claire had found for the cave.

"Things are happening fast, Samantha," Darian said, her voice softer. "Like a ketchup bottle."

"Excuse me?" Samantha frowned. "What do you mean?"

"You know, the old type of ketchup bottle, made of glass? You shook it, slapped the bottom, and just as you started to give up, the whole damn content spilled onto your fries."

A boisterous laugh broke in, which Holly quickly identified as coming from Philber.

"Our police detective is correct," Philber said. "We've received your data and will see what we can perhaps add to the interpretation. We've also managed to decipher more of Bech'taia's journal. For not wearing a NIEC, Camilla's dangerously good at this."

Holly could hear the admiration in Philber's voice, which was miraculous in itself. Normally, the only one Philber admired was himself. Perhaps *his* NIEC was having a good influence on him. She snorted to herself. Nah. If anything, Holly gave Camilla's considerable charm and charisma credit for Philber's unusual behavior.

"Can't wait to hear about that as well." Samantha exchanged a few more words with Philber and had begun to sign out when Darian gave what could only be described as a squeal.

"Are you getting this? We did it. I mean, we found it!"

"What? The third site already?" Samantha moved closer to Holly and pulled out her own trackpad. "I'm seeing only a massive data download.

"Me too," Claire said, rubbing her palms against her pants. "And it's a lot of coordinates and settings. Settings for what?" She began sliding her fingers in intricate patterns again. "Damn. No. Not that. More like...something like that. Yes. Yes!" Claire now slapped her knees hard and then grimaced as she gently rubbed her palms together. "We now have the exact coordinates for the hatch leading into *Velocity's* cave."

"Damn." Samantha sat down. "Ketchup bottle, indeed."

❖

Darian stepped off Raoul's bike when they reached the sign pointing to where the old water-tower site was. "I've got to take another look at it. I mean, now that we know its true significance, I just have to see what it looks like after it closed again. To be honest, I can't remember much else than panicking at the thought of dropping toward the center of the earth, or something." She shrugged.

"Let me pull the bike in among the trees, and we can walk. It's not far. And you'll tell me if you're feeling unwell, all right?"

"I promise. I actually feel better and better." Darian wasn't exaggerating. She did feel well, and certainly better than anyone with a dislocated shoulder and broken clavicle had the right to feel on day two of the injuries. "I'm pretty grateful that you figured out the medical equipment aboard *Speeder One*."

"Nothing to do with me, really." Raoul pushed the bike along the path and then into a small clearing, where he whipped out a camouflage net and threw it over it.

"Whoa. You come prepared." Darian surmised it was her bias that hadn't thought the rather handsome and stylish young doctor could be so hands-on practical. Well, he'd showed her.

"Boy Scouts." Raoul grinned. "I hated parts of it, but I can't deny learning quite a bit."

"I never did make a good career of my six-month stint in the Girl Scouts, which wasn't because I disliked it. But a bully situation was going on, and I was too fragile at the time to deal with it." Darian sighed. "I really enjoyed everything about it except Ronda and her clique of mean friends."

"Fragile?" Raoul asked kindly.

"It was a couple of years after I lost my parents in a car crash. I just couldn't deal."

Darian helped Raoul secure the net, and then they began walking to the site. The air was cold, but she could still hear birds. Around yet another bend, Darian almost stepped on Brandon, who was waiting on the path for them.

"Carl's busy with his piece of technology," Brandon said, studying her carefully. "And you're not even pale anymore." His tone was something between relieved and suspicious.

"Sorry about that." Darian gently fist-bumped Brandon's arm. "I feel totally fine."

"Hm."

"Hey, guys!" Carl waved them over. He was kneeling just outside the perimeter of the large square that had opened yesterday. "I've managed to perform more readings, and I think Claire's on her way over as we speak. Wasn't it lucky for us to come across an engineer?"

"It was." Darian knelt next to him. "Can I see?"

"Sure thing." Carl handed over his trackpad. "If you hold it like this," he said, nudging Darian's hand until it was horizontal, "and then you push in that command." He tapped the upper left corner. "See?"

Darian blinked at the alien text running like some upside-down waterfall along the screen. "I do. I do see." But that didn't mean she was believing her eyes. "If it's this easy for me to understand, then I would imagine Claire will find it even more so." Darian pointed to two intersecting lines. "No wonder we almost short-circuited the damn thing yesterday when I placed my trackpad on the plaque and then turned it. We should be happy we're alive." She took Brandon's proffered hand as she stood.

They waited until faint voices were approaching, and even then, Carl made sure it was the others in the group, rather than some off-the-beaten-track tourists, before they called out.

Holly, Samantha, and Claire joined them. "I think everything is controlled from here," Claire said, reaching for Carl's trackpad. After studying it, she nodded slowly. "Yeah. That's what I figured. Did you see this already, Darian?"

"I did. An accidental hatch breach, right?" Darian moved closer to Samantha. "You guys detected something really cool too."

"We did or, I should say, Claire did, yes." The way Samantha's broad smile rejuvenated her face made Darian realize how relieved she was to have someone else be able to take charge.

As if on cue, Holly spoke. "I've been tracking the new finds as you all made them. As far as I can tell, things seem to happen quicker now. It can either be because we're physically getting closer to the areas in question, *or* it's because you're adding to your expertise, as with Claire, and with Raoul's extended knowledge of the medical equipment, etc."

"That's an important observation, but there has to be more to it. I get the feeling that those among us with the non-alien DNA are playing a part." Darian motioned around the group. "There's no true science behind that claim, but it still feels that way. Just the fact that Samantha was starting to feel the brunt of leadership too acutely for her health makes me wonder if you two," she pointed at Holly and Claire, "truly are the sign that it's time to start recruiting on a larger scale than we initially thought."

"You might be right," Raoul said, and Samantha nodded. "I don't understand, at least not yet, how the NIECs can sense the presence of anyone without the DNA marker. Camilla, Brandon, and, now, Holly."

"Either way, that's my working theory for now," Darian said. "Let's keep a lookout for signs that corroborate it."

"Samantha to Walker. You and Camilla there?" Samantha adjusted something on her speaker.

"Present and accounted for." Walker's calm baritone voice was heard throughout the clearing.

"We're all standing at the water-tower site. Let's not waste time. We need to try to open it and find a way to go inside. We can't do it now because the risk of someone stumbling upon us is too great. We need to meet up for a more well-planned attempt after dark. What do you all say to that?"

"Yes, you're right," Camilla said over Walker's speaker.

The others in the group nodded. "The sooner the better," Philber said. "Anyone have second thoughts about it?"

Nobody said a word.

"How's the list of potential recruits going, Walker?" Darian asked.

"We have twenty to begin with. Those of us who have lived here longer can divide them up among us, which means two to three people to reel in per person, or thereabout."

"Sounds doable." Holly wrote something on her notepad. "That needs to commence tomorrow."

"Then why don't you all come back to Brynden 4 and get warm and fed?" Camilla asked. "And now, Brandon, you're not cooking. I'll order in."

"But—"

It was no surprise to Darian that Brandon sounded a bit offended.

"It won't be as good, but we'll suffer through it," Camilla said, and Darian could hear the smile in her voice. "And I'm far too eager to hear about everything to have you ostracized in the kitchen."

"Very well," Brandon muttered but then gave Darian a smirk. "You're the boss, Ms. Camilla."

"Well then. You're all welcome to take a load off here and recharge your batteries." Camilla sounded pleased.

"Well played, Gran," Darian said to Samantha as they walked around the hatch in the ground, keeping well away from the edge. "She wants to make sure we're all right."

"I realize that. Especially you." Samantha put her hand against the small of Darian's back. "And I know you look like nothing happened to you yesterday, I mean, you look fine, but I think a rest isn't wrong."

"Physically I do feel fine, yes." Darian pulled away from the rest of the group, glad Samantha didn't remove her hand. "Emotionally, I'm not a hundred percent. When I fell...I did think I'd just keep plummeting. It was..." She swallowed hard.

"It was frightening," Samantha said, her voice trembling. "For me too, after the fact. And Brandon isn't over it either. Good thing Raoul's laser focus kicked in once we got you back to the speeder. He has a knack for not letting his emotions run away with him."

"He sure does. And if it weren't for him and his NIEC, I'd be a lot worse off. Perhaps in the hospital, even."

"Which would mean I'd be out of commission too, as nothing would have kept me from being at your side, Dar." Samantha moved her hand in small circles against Darian's back. "I mean it."

"I know. Same goes here." Darian leaned into Samantha, not worried about anyone else paying attention. "It's funny. When Raoul and I walked from the bike to here, I remembered being bullied at age eight. In the Girl Scouts, of all places. I could see the girls in a circle around me, as clear as if it happened yesterday. I hadn't even thought about that for years. But he mentioned the Boy Scouts, and there I was, in the middle of a circle of scornful little California girls, and one thing they kept repeating was that they knew I didn't even have any parents. I never did tell Gran about that last part, but I think she knew something must have happened since I was a member for only six months."

"Only? That's a lifetime for a kid." Samantha pressed her lips to Darian's temple. "So, a vivid memory, huh?"

"Very vivid. Shockingly so." Darian had to smile at the concern in Samantha's eyes. "Now, don't get all worried about it. I was a kid and I'm over it. It just took me aback that it popped into my head like lightning. That's all."

"It's well worth noting. Perhaps the NIECs are having that effect on our minds as they're teaching us the intricacies of the alien technology and language."

"I'll enter it in our log," Darian said.

"You ready to go?" Holly called out from the other side of the hatch.

"We are." Darian raised her hand. "See you all back at Brynden 4."

As they walked back to the parking lot, Raoul last, as he had to get his bike, Darian felt something settle within her. It had nothing to do with her childhood memory, but instead with being part of this group of dedicated, loyal people, knowing with more certainty than she'd ever felt in her life that they had her back—and she theirs. And then, of course, there was Samantha—elegant, brilliant, and able to take Darian's breath away with one glance. Deep inside, Darian knew, if it weren't for Samantha, yearning or no yearning, she would have been planning to return to Los Angeles. Now, all she had to do was look at Samantha, and she knew nobody was more important to her.

CHAPTER ELEVEN

"Y ou can't be serious!"

Samantha looked from Darian's stern expression over to Raoul's calm demeanor.

"I am. Very much so." Raoul, who was the type who only got calmer the more stressed or angry others became, spread butter on a bread roll.

"You're suggesting we stick a NIEC on Gran and then subject her to alien medical practices, despite having already decided to be reckless with her by performing alien medical procedures on her while not knowing what it does to a NIEC-less person."

"Exactly. The same alien medical practices that healed you in less than a day," Raoul said.

Samantha glanced over at Camilla, who hadn't spoken up yet. Camilla merely raised her perfect eyebrows but kept eating.

"I have to say I agree with Darian," Walker said slowly. "It's amazing that it can heal mechanical damage like a clavicle or torn muscle tissues, but Camilla has preexisting conditions."

Holly shook her head. "Being new to this group, I find it fascinating that Camilla is so calm about waiting her turn to talk about her own medical concerns, should she even want to. Especially among all of us. Raoul, I believe you're close to violating HIPAA."

Everyone grew quiet, and to Samantha's surprise, the reprimand, because that was what it was, made Raoul's cheeks color faintly.

"Darian," Camilla said gently, but even Samantha could detect the steely undertone in her voice. "I know you always have my best interest at heart. I really do. But don't forget that I'm the one who decides what is best for me. We've had this discussion before."

"But—"

Camilla held up her right hand, which was apparently enough to ward off any more arguments from Darian. It was still obvious from how Darian set her jaw and kept her shoulders stiffly squared that she wasn't done.

"And Walker, don't fall into the trap of being too protective. It's not sexy." Camilla smiled at the clearly flustered man.

"Well, perish the thought," Philber said merrily, reaching for more chicken.

"Raoul, HIPPA or not, I know you're eager to help me, but Holly's not wrong. Now, that said, I have a question, and as it might be of interest as I'm not the only old person around the table, I will give you permission to talk about this here."

"Thank you, Camilla. I got carried away. I apologize." Raoul looked a decade younger as he placed his utensils on his empty plate.

"Is it possible to try treating, let's say, my right hand only, and without adding a NIEC to the mix just yet?" Camilla tilted her head, and Samantha couldn't take her eyes off the stunning woman. She could imagine how Camilla had taken Hollywood by storm, and how she'd had to fight to be taken seriously as a writer and fended off attempts to turn her into yet another starlet. No doubt, Camilla had eventually won most over and steamrolled the rest.

"That's actually a great idea." Raoul looked carefully at Darian, and Samantha had to hide a smile by wiping her mouth with a linen napkin.

"It sounds a lot less reckless, at least," Darian said through gritted teeth.

"It does, doesn't it? Something we may attempt tomorrow afternoon?" Camilla stuck her fork into a green bean. "Anyone who wants can watch. I think I'll charge admission."

Claire snorted and then began laughing in earnest. "I just adore you guys. This is such a family." She smiled as she too added another piece of chicken to her plate.

"You don't know the half of it," Philber muttered. "Just as you think things are moving along at a decent pace, someone finds something, does something, hurt themselves, or falls in love." He shot Samantha a knowing glance.

"Oh, God," Samantha muttered, her cheeks warming. It had been too much to hope for, to be kept out of the line of fire.

"Who's in love?" Carl asked, finally looking up from his plate, now empty for the second time.

"Philber, mind your own business." Camilla snapped at him. "And Carl, when people want you to know about that, they'll tell you. All right?"

"Yes, ma'am," Carl said, virtually hiccupping at being in her crosshairs.

Philber merely started eating again.

After leaving the dinner table, Samantha and Darian moved to their favorite seat, the settee in the parlor, and Camilla joined them in her wheelchair. She maneuvered it until she was facing Darian head-on.

"Sweetheart, listen now. I know you fear losing me. That's where all this anger and resentment comes from. I have a couple of questions for you though. You know the pain I live with. My joints have deteriorated this winter here in the north, but going back to LA isn't an option. Wouldn't you want me to find a lasting relief, the chance to actually heal?"

"Of course, Gran. That goes without saying, but—"

Again, Camilla raised her hand, the swollen, red joints clearly visible. "And if I start with one hand, and that works, and there are no horrible side-effects, can you imagine supporting me by allowing Raoul to treat my other hand, then my hips and knees?"

Darian drew a trembling breath. "I don't want you to have another single moment of pain. Ever."

"Philber has a heart condition, and his NIEC hasn't hurt him. The opposite, in fact. I just wish it would do something about his ornery nature, but alas." Camilla smiled and wiped an errant tear from Darian's face. "Don't bite Raoul's head off. He's a good doctor and wouldn't take more risks now with his patients than he did earlier. I want you there with me when he treats me. And you, Samantha, if you would care to be. Walker will have to sit it out, and that's mainly for his sake. The man can be pretty mushy, and as I said, that's not sexy."

"Gran. Please." Darian laughed but hid her face in her hands. When she lowered them, Samantha saw she had truly calmed down. Camilla must have noticed the same as she bent forward and kissed Darian's cheek, patted Samantha's hand, and then wheeled over to the couch where Walker and Philber sat.

"How are you doing?" Samantha asked.

"I'm okay. I think. For the most part."

"I suppose we'll be distracted soon enough." Samantha arched her back and rolled her shoulders. "We should leave in about an hour or so."

"Agreed." Holly pulled up a chair, and Claire did the same. The four women regarded each other seriously. "I have my climbing gear in the car," Claire said. "Never know when it'll come in handy, and see, I was right."

"I'm going down into *Speeder One* and get a few things I spotted last time I worked on the inventory list." Samantha tried to hide her unease. "I have to confess that I'm not the sporty type. I may end up slowing the ones of you who are."

"No, you won't." Darian spoke as if that was obvious. "We'll each have our task. We're all needed."

Samantha guessed it was partly Darian's loyalty to her speaking. "Thank you. Yes, of course."

Holly nodded. "We all have different qualifications, and I think, with each day, we'll see more and more how we all will fit together."

Samantha had to smile. Those words coming from the woman who really must feel like an outsider at times were reassuring. "I'll put my qualifications to the best use, while the rest of you perform the outdoorsy tasks."

"I'll be right there with you, using my brain rather than my muscles," Philber called out from the couch.

"Sounds good," Samantha said, and she meant it. Whenever she worked alone with Philber, he dropped some of his gruff ways and let his professionalism show. His methodology when it came to researching the artifacts and the journal was second to none.

Darian changed the topic, and they spent the next hour relaxing and talking about anything but their upcoming assignments. When it was time to get ready, Samantha and Darian went down to *Speeder One* and fetched the equipment and instruments Samantha had set aside earlier. It all fit in Samantha's large backpack, which Darian helped her put on, as some of the instruments were fragile.

After some deliberation, they decided to take Samantha's and Claire's cars. Camilla and Walker were going to stay at Brynden 4 and be with them via speaker link. Claire had shown them all how to connect the speaker via the trackpad to add video to their communication. As they took their seats in the vehicles, Samantha gripped the steering wheel as she pulled out into the empty residential street. This was going to be one of the pivotal days in their exploration. She could feel it.

Holly walked with the other seven to the old water-tower site. Claire was just behind her, studying the readings on her trackpad as they got closer. Philber and Carl spoke in low murmurs at the far back, but otherwise, everyone seemed lost in thought. To accommodate Holly not having a NIEC or a speaker, she was carrying a regular walkie-talkie for emergencies only, and so were Samantha and Raoul. They were also the only three who had their cell phones.

Around them, the forest was quiet, and only the swaying lights from their flashlights made it possible to see anything in the opaque darkness among the trees. It wasn't as cold as it had been a few nights ago, but Holly still shivered, probably from elevated levels of adrenaline.

The clearing came into view, and Samantha slipped out of her backpack. "Just keep the flashlights going for a bit. I have something that'll make it a bit easier to work." She opened her pack and pulled out what looked like small, square pieces of glass. She pressed them against a few boulders and trees and then pulled out her trackpad and tapped at the screen. Soon the clearing was lit by a pink light.

"Eh. Pink? Really?" Darian put her hands on her hips. "I thought I was starting to get used to these aliens being all about the colorfulness, but pink lights? Wow."

"There's a reason for the color choice." Samantha adjusted the setting. "It lights up the area very well if you're close, but from a distance, it's barely visible."

"That's right," Claire said. "They're called watchglows, by the way."

Holly had her notepad ready and jotted down the term. She knew better than to fall into the trap of thinking she would remember. One word soon became ten, or a hundred.

"You take the lead as to how we do this, Claire." Samantha walked over to stand between Holly and Darian.

"All right. I don't know if you've realized this, but my trackpad is a different version from the generic ones. Like Raoul having a medical trackpad, I have an engineering version. I think they're all the generic version until they connect with us, the computer, and our respective NIECs." Claire held up her device. "I'm going to need four of you to stand in each corner of the hatch with your trackpads. Let's see. Samantha, I need you in the southwest corner, facing south. Darian in the northwest corner facing north. Raoul, northeast corner, facing east. Carl, southeast corner, also facing south. I'll be in the center of the hatch."

"What?" Darian stopped as she was circling to the northwest corner. "If you get it to open, you'll fall straight through."

"No. I don't think so. It opened the wrong way because it was done by mistake. It won't happen again." Claire sounded calm.

"Since we don't have a task yet," Holly said, "why not use us as a backup plan? I know you have climbing gear with you, Claire. Let's attach a harness and some rope to you and around a tree. If something goes wrong, we can get to you and pull you up."

Claire seemed to hesitate but then shrugged. "Sure, since I can tell you're going to gang up on me if I refuse. I'm still right though."

"Better safe than sorry," Raoul said.

After Claire had expertly put on her gear, she and Raoul secured the rope around a thick trunk, letting the rope stretch between Carl and Samantha. Holly and Brandon placed themselves on either side of it.

"All right." Claire walked to the center of the rock hatch without hesitation. "I'm going to send a signal to your respective devices.

When you hear it, direct it the way you are facing until you have confirmation on your screens that you connected with the sensors we just found, and the one on the meadows."

"The meadows? The one on the hatch?" Darian asked.

"Precisely. Everyone ready to go?" Claire looked at them one by one. After everyone answered that they were, she began punching in commands on her trackpad. Soon, one by one, the other four devices began to light up. The four of the team at the corners of the hatch raised their arms, pointing in their respective directions. The devices gave muted pings, then changed color.

"Excellent. Now, keep as still as you can." Claire pivoted slowly, holding up her trackpad. "That's it. A little longer." Once she'd made a full turn, a blue glow emanated from her device.

It probably took only a few seconds, but Holly was holding her breath, and perhaps that was why it felt a lot longer. Then a blue light in the shape of a cross appeared under Claire's feet. The lines forming the cross seemed to crawl along the ground to four yellow dots, and when they made contact, the hatch opened. Holly hadn't seen how it opened when Darian fell, but this time, it slid open much the same way the shutter on Holly's camera did. This thought made her realize two things. She should be taking pictures, and—Claire seemed to stand in midair in the middle of the square hole.

Holly pulled the lens cap off and began to photograph the scene. She switched between looking at the screen on the back of her camera and above it.

"You can turn off your trackpads," Claire said. "If you give me a few of those watchglows, Samantha, I can prove that this worked perfectly."

"So we can move?" Darian said, slowly turning around. "Holy crap. You're…floating?"

"Not at all." Claire chuckled, but her voice was not entirely steady. Perhaps she hadn't been as sure as she'd sounded after all.

Samantha had hurried over to her backpack and now tossed Claire a small pouch. Bending, Claire placed a ring of watchglows around her feet, and now they could all see what made her not fall into the hole.

In the center of it, seemingly made from the same charcoal-gray rock, a platform connected to the ground around them and led to a set of stairs winding down into the pitch-black darkness below.

"That's a lot better than just jumping off the edge attached to a rope," Holly said, directing her flashlight into the depth. "I can't judge how deep it is, which means…it's deep." She gazed around the group. "I suppose this makes part of our task easier. Nobody has to feel the need to be an athlete to walk down those stairs. Philber, you and Brandon will be our ground crew, as we planned. The rest of us will descend."

"I'll go first," Darian said. "I have a bit of a bone to pick with this hole, and I'd like to get that chance by tackling it before anyone else." Something in Darian's voice made Holly understand that she was not going to back down from that request.

"All right. I'll be right behind you. The rest of you, space out and allow for the person before you to make a full turn in that spiral staircase. It's damn narrow, which means the steps are treacherous."

After they all strapped on their gear and checked their speakers and walkie-talkies, Darian began her descent, attaching more watchglows along the way down. Holly waited until Darian's head had cleared the first turn and then stepped out on the dais. Claire had removed her rope but kept her harness on. Rolling up the rope, she hung it over her shoulder. "I'll be right behind you, Holly."

Nodding, Holly gripped the center pole of the spiral staircase and carefully walked where the steps were the widest. There was nothing to hold on to on that side of the steps, and one wrong move could make her fall. "Make sure you get a good grip of the center," she called upward. "It's slippery." She moved at the same pace as Darian, grateful for the excellent lighting the watchglows provided. It had been a relief to see how many Samantha had brought. They were going to need them.

"Why couldn't they have installed one of their elevators here as well?" Carl muttered somewhere above Holly. "Slippery is the word."

"Just be careful," Samantha said. "Take your time."

The six of them slowly made their way down. Holly could hear Darian counting the steps and didn't want to interrupt her. When Darian finally said, "Holy crap. Three hundred and sixty and I'm standing in ankle-deep water and it's damn cold! No wonder my legs are like jelly," Holly tried not to think about going back up the same way.

Holly joined Darian at the bottom and found her feet submerged in water. She wore her water-resistant boots, but they quickly flooded, and the water was icy. "Damn." Holly groaned.

"I know. Didn't think to bring rubber boots." Darian grinned. "Here. Help me attach them." She handed Holly a fistful of watchglows. After lining the walls around them with the small squares, Holly looked around and gaped.

"Oh, my God." She waited until the others had joined them, and then they just stood there.

Samantha's speaker buzzed to life. "Philber to Samantha. Everyone okay?"

"We're fine, Philber. Sending you images. To Camilla and Walker too." Samantha used her trackpad to record their surroundings.

Holly regarded the walls that rose more than twenty feet around them. Sparkling veins created beautiful patterns, and the water dripping down along the walls made them look like gold. Nothing was as smooth or glasslike as the walls in the tunnel or in the basement of Brynden 4. Here, they almost looked chiseled by hand. The floor was about eight yards long and three yards wide, Holly surmised. A faint metallic smell tinged the air, perhaps originating from the water.

"There's an opening there. It's not tall, but we'll fit." Carl pointed to the north.

"Then I suggest we waste no more time," Holly said. "Let's keep a few feet between us, and if Darian doesn't mind taking the lead again, we'll stick to the same order that we walked down."

"I'm on it." Darian grinned. "Let's go, folks." She took a few steps toward the oval opening about four yards from the staircase. "I'm setting my trackpad to record and send to the others on the ground."

Holly followed a few steps behind Darian. They both kept placing watchglows to make it easier for the others, and for their return. The chiseled walkway wasn't very wide, perhaps a little more than a yard. Water dripped down the walls, and sometimes the floor dipped, and they were wading through it up to their knees. In retrospect it had been a good call to keep Brandon and Philber up top. If nothing else, their slightly older joints wouldn't have fared well in the freezing water.

"I'm going to relax in a hot tub when I get back to the house," Darian muttered ahead of Holly. "A hundred and six degrees at least. This sucks."

"I hear you." Holly knew morale could easily become an issue, no matter how motivated everyone was. "This reminds me of my father's aunt. She was an avid winter swimmer. Insane, if you ask me."

"And remember, I was brought up in California. Warm. Sunny. And, yes, smoggy." Darian snorted. "That said, I love the fresh air in these parts. I love a lot about Dennamore, actually."

"Just not the freezing water sloshing between your toes." Holly chuckled but was starting to shiver.

"I'm actually not in water right now. We must be at an incline." Darian shone with her flashlight. "And over there...can that be the exit?"

Holly added her beam to Darian's. She saw a rounded opening that looked like a doorway. This was nothing like the roughly chiseled bedrock they'd walked through. This was smoother. Glasslike.

"Wow," Claire said behind them. "Guess we just have to go through and see what we find."

Darian didn't seem to hesitate. She stepped through the opening, and as Holly walked up to follow her, Darian gave another "holy crap" and started laughing. Holly entered the new area, and if they had been amazed by the walkway that led them here, it was nothing compared to this part. They stood in what could only be called a hallway. Nothing was wet here. Oak benches lined the wall, and compartments had been made into the shiny bedrock. A computer console sat dormant on the far wall.

"Goodness." Samantha stood in the center, turning around slowly, as if to take it all in, over and over.

"That's putting it mildly," Claire said and walked over to the console. "I'll see if I can stir this—oh, shit. There it goes, all by itself." The console lit up, the now-familiar, colorful lines and dots ran, much like the water, across the screen.

"You get your wish after all, Carl," Claire said. "There's an elevator at that far wall. All we have to do is punch in the commands here and line up."

Carl walked over to where Claire pointed, examining the wall. "I can barely see the cracks. Can't have been used much. The ones in the tunnel are more worn down."

"Hang on," Raoul said. "We need to report in before we continue."

Samantha quickly spoke to Brandon and Philber, who seemed entirely comfortable as they had put up a tent and crawled into sleeping bags that would keep them warm even if a blizzard occurred. Walker and Camilla were up in the library working on the journal and their list of potential recruits. After information had been given and received, Samantha set her trackpad to keep recording.

Holly had taken the chance to set up her tripod and photograph some more. From what she could see on the screen, the photos would be among the best she'd ever taken.

"All right. I'm opening the elevator. It takes all of us, so no one will be kept waiting." Claire ran her fingers along the lines and dots. A hissing sound, followed by a muted thud, made Carl jump.

"Hey, that was fast." He stepped inside the elevator as the large door opened, but then he hesitated. "What if we're in this car, and it opens up to a water-filled room?"

"I thought of that." Claire nodded approvingly. "I've downloaded the elevator controls to my trackpad. That way, once we reach our level, I'll have time to scan what's behind the wall before I allow the door to open."

Relieved at how Claire's mind worked, Holly joined them, and so did the others. As the door closed, a faint light from the ceiling bathed them in turquoise. It seemed to make everyone's teeth stark white, which gave the ride an eerie component.

"Seems to be only one stop," Claire remarked. "And we're going down pretty fast, so hold on, in case there's a jolt." She had barely finished the sentence when the elevator stopped abruptly. "No idea if this compares to the elevators you've already tried, but that was not a smooth ride." She shook her head as she stood closer to the door. Running her device along the door and its edges, she examined the results and then repeated them. "No water. Dry as a desert."

"You're sure?" Samantha said, touching the edges with her fingertips.

"Very sure." Claire held up her trackpad. "Are we all good?"

After a barely noticeable hesitation, Holly answered yes, and so did the other six.

"Fine, then." Claire tapped a quick sequence of commands. "Here we go."

The door slid open, and Holly exhaled. No water, but entirely dark. What was out there? Another pathway? Or had the entire thing caved in? She couldn't see anything.

As if on cue, the six of them in the elevator directed the beam of their flashlights into the void behind the elevator door.

At first, Holly couldn't grasp what she was seeing. She raised her beam a forty-five-degree angle upward. The others followed suit.

Holly's chest ached, and she could barely breathe. She blinked and blinked against the tears that rose in her eyes, but new ones took their place. Now she knew what it was. Now she knew why she was meant to be part of this group. "That's her," she whispered, the rawness in her voice making it sound foreign. "That's her. That's the *Velocity*."

CHAPTER TWELVE

Darian slowly raised her head, allowing herself to take in the closest strut. It was a dizzying experience in two ways. It was tall. Their flickering beams from their flashlights as they moved up the slender column initially gave her vertigo. Perhaps they needed to change the batteries, because it was as if the strut was too tall for the light to reach the ship itself.

Samantha didn't curse often, but now she stood next to Darian, her head tipped back. "Damn. This is the strangest feeling I've ever had."

"How do you mean?" Darian didn't take her eyes off the strut.

"It's so much bigger than I ever could have pictured it, and yet another part of me thinks it's just the right size. Like I know it." She shook her head slowly.

"It's your NIEC. It knows the ship." Darian took a few steps forward, and it was as if that was the sign the rest of them needed to start moving.

"We need more light." Claire walked over to the left of the elevator they had arrived in. "Give me a sec." She placed her trackpad on the much-larger console, compared to the one she'd just used at the other end of the elevator shaft.

Thudding sounds echoed through the large space as one huge light after another switched on. Soon the hangar, because that's what it was, was bathed in bright, warm light. Darian looked up again, and now she saw the full scope of the *Velocity*. She made sure she was transmitting to the ones in their group that weren't present. She was so stunned at the sight of the enormous ship, she barely registered Camilla's excited congratulations.

Six tall struts, each at least twenty-five feet tall, supported the body of the ship. From Darian's point of view, the ship resembled an uneven, slightly bulky rectangle. All kinds of pipes, hatches, vents, and other contraptions adorned the hull, which was almost identical to the charcoal-gray bedrock in the walkway they'd just left. This was clearly made of some metallic alloy, and when Darian placed her hand on the closest strut, she could feel how dry and cold it was.

"Wow. Do that again." Carl pointed to the center of the *Velocity*'s belly. "I saw something move, but then it stopped."

Darian touched the strut again. This time, she didn't let go, despite how cold it felt, and above them, a ramp of sorts lowered from below the ship. When it gave a resounding click, Darian carefully let go, and the ramp remained open.

"I take that as an invitation," Samantha said. "I don't know about you guys, but nothing's going to keep me from going inside."

"In for a penny," Darian said and lengthened her stride to catch up with Samantha. Side by side they walked up the ramp. The surface felt rubbery and made Darian think it could be to keep people or goods from slipping off, as the ramp was steep. As they neared the narrow, rectangular opening, the lights went on above them.

"Now that we're almost there, I suddenly recall an easier way to enter the ship. The center strut in the front holds an elevator." Samantha chuckled, and her cheeks flushed. "I hope our NIECs will be good to us and not completely overwhelm our senses with information about the ship."

"We may have to ration how much we wear them if they overload us," Raoul said from behind.

Darian stepped into the area above the ramp at the same time as Samantha. Without realizing she already knew, she pointed to a door. "Behind that is one of the weapon storages. Ten of them are scattered throughout the ship."

"Good thing we don't need any. Yet." Carl joined them, and soon all six of them stood in the center of what looked like a large storage facility. "I think we came in the staff entrance. And by that, I mean the ones in charge of loading and off-loading."

"I think you're right. And look here. An orientation board, but missing a large, red dot that says, 'You are here." Darian pointed to the port bulkhead. "Oh. I stand corrected." She tapped the cluster of small green dots with an alien number next to it. The board changed, and they saw the deck they were on as a 3D image. "No crew quarters here. Storage, mainly. The shuttle bay that hosts the speeders. Next level is, let's see, engineering. That's your domain, Claire."

"I'll go there. It'll save time if we don't do the grand tour all at the same time." Claire was already absorbed by her trackpad and heading toward a bright-red spiral staircase.

"I want to go to the bridge," Samantha said. She nodded at Holly. "Would you join me and Darian?

"I was just going to ask you," Holly said, looking surprised.

"Good. I have a feeling that coming with us is the right thing. Also, you can only rely on your walkie-talkie, which might not work well enough aboard the ship," Samantha said, turning to the two men. "Carl, you can go with Raoul to the infirmary until we know your specialty?"

"Sure thing." Carl had his cell phone out, taking pictures. "And no, I'm not going to post this on Facebook." He grinned broadly.

"Cute." Darian tapped the orientation board, and eight decks above them a large, triangular area in the center of the ship appeared. "There it is. The bridge where the chief helmsman and chief of security have their duty stations. An elevator should lead directly to it from over there." She pointed toward the center bulkhead across from the opening they'd just come through.

Samantha nodded. "That's the one." She ran her finger over her speaker. "All hands, this is Samantha. Alert the rest of us on your speaker if you run into anything that looks like trouble."

"Aya, ma'am," Carl said from where he stood by the board. "We just found sickbay. Deck five, section four. It looks huge."

"Good luck exploring. Be safe." Darian waved as she stepped into the circular elevator with Samantha and Holly. "Now, am I the only one who hopes we find some crew quarters with dry socks and boots? My feet are like ice."

"We may have made an error in judgment by wearing our own clothes. We would have done better in our uniforms." Samantha shook her head. "Live and learn."

"Uniforms. That's something I have yet to see." Holly supported herself against the wall and gripped Samantha's arm as the elevator came to an abrupt stop. "That'll take some getting used to."

"That was fast." Darian waited until the door slid open, not with the hissing sound that she'd heard in movies and TV shows, which suggested a hydraulic system, but rather a soft whisper. She stepped outside, moving slowly since the area was dark with only the light from inside the elevator lighting up the immediate vicinity. As soon as Darian set foot on the deck, lights went on and put the bridge on display.

"Oh, my God." Holly gasped behind Darian. "That's...I couldn't even dream up something like this if I tried."

"It's enormous," Samantha whispered.

They had entered the bridge at the middle, and it obviously stretched along an entire section, as tall as two decks.

"That's the helm," Samantha said weakly and pointed at the semicircular console that faced the front of the bridge. The bridge was shaped like a rounded, blunt triangle, with one large screen facing toward the stern, which in turn was surrounded by eight smaller ones. The pilot could choose between using the main screen or one of the five curved ones following the outline of their station.

Behind the helm, an elevated chair with built-in screens on both sides showed this was the captain's seat. To the left of it, a massive station with a multitude of consoles—Darian counted eighteen—turned out to be her station. In charge of security and anything to do with the ship's weapons' array and general armament, she could keep track of everything in real time from this station. She climbed the two steps to her chair and sat down.

Immediately, the chair molded itself to her form, and not only that, but it also began to warm her legs and back. "Take your seat, Samantha. This is one way to get warm." She grinned as Samantha slid into her even plusher seat. All the seats, even at the smaller stations behind them that had been placed in a horseshoe formation, at four levels, had impressive chairs.

"Mm. Nice." Samantha swiveled her chair and nodded approvingly. "Why don't you try the captain's chair, Holly? You need to rest your legs as well, after all."

Holly looked incredulous. "Are you sure? I may end up causing damage since I'm not one of you."

"Hey, don't worry about that. Just sit down and enjoy it. That chair looks amazing." Darian waved her hand toward the captain's chair. "When Brandon tried a NIEC, it just stayed limp and dormant. Come on. It'd be cool to see what it will look like to have a captain sit there once we get that far with our recruitment process."

Something that looked a lot like pain ghosted across Holly's features, and Darian wondered if she and Samantha had put both feet in it and accidentally hurt Holly's feelings. Before she could take her words back and apologize for being clumsy, Holly gripped the handle next to the chair and pulled herself up. She agilely slipped into the seat and seemed to hold her breath.

"Anything?" Samantha asked.

"No. I'm fine. Chair's just keeping still, like a good chair should. I see some objects here on the right armrest that you could perhaps examine later." Holly lifted a long, metal bar and held it up for them to see.

Darian craned her neck, but before she got a good look at it, Holly cried out and jerked backward.

Holly stared down at the metal bar that had wrapped around her left wrist. It wasn't constricting her blood flow, but it sat firmly, as if glued to her skin. Her heart pounded so hard, her ribs hurt. Her right hand trembled as she pushed at the band, but it didn't budge. She just hurt her skin.

Darian reached her only a moment later, and Samantha took the two steps up to the dais holding the captain's chair.

"What the hell happened?" Darian placed her hand on Holly's shoulder. "You're pale."

"Remove that thing," she said stiffly, her teeth beginning to clatter, pointing at the metal bar. "It...it attached itself. I can't get it off!"

"What?" Darian reached for Holly's hand and raised it carefully, examining the metal object. "What the hell's that? It has some alien text on it."

"Darian? Do you see that?" Holly watched Samantha's eyes grow bigger as she ran her finger along some of the symbols. Darian rounded the chair and looked at the metal object from Samantha's angle.

"This is called an information bank. Is that something the captain uses? Or are there information banks around for the entire crew?"

Holly tried to speak, wanting to remind them that she needed them, the descendants of the aliens, to remove the damn thing, but it was as if her tongue had swelled up. She swallowed against the sudden dryness in her mouth. "Uhh…"

Samantha's head snapped up. "Holly? Damn it, Darian. She's not looking well." She touched Holly's forehead. "She's burning up!"

Holly felt her eyes close, and, in her mind, images and symbols spun in a flurry that made her nauseous and dizzy. "N-no." Not just her teeth, but her entire body was shaking now.

"Darian to Raoul. We have a medical emergency on the bridge. It's Holly."

Holly tried to say she probably only needed to get the damn thing off her wrist, but she seemed to fade.

"On my way," Raoul said.

"I heard. Me too," a female voice said. Claire? Holly wanted to ask, but the heat in her body increased, and she began to slip into a strange, soft kind of darkness.

"What happened?" Samantha was relieved to hear Raoul call out as he ran toward them, with Carl right behind.

"This metallic bracelet attached to her. See?" Darian pointed.

Samantha was holding Holly propped up against the backrest of the captain's chair, but now Raoul motioned for them to pull her down onto the deck. He slipped a blood-pressure cuff around Holly's arm and inflated it. "140/90. Heart rate 95. Breathing frequency normal. She's affected, but not enough to worry me—yet."

"But she's got this thing on her, and she's not from Dennamore." Samantha pushed the light-brown hair from Holly's damp, hot forehead. "She's adopted." Her eyes snapped up to Darian's. "Wait. That can be it. She's *adopted*. We don't know where she's from. Her mother or father, or both, could have alien genes, for all she, or we, know. She was adopted from Albany."

Darian gazed at Samantha and then back at Holly. "And we never even tried a NIEC on her. It didn't occur to me."

Samantha gripped Holly's hand harder. She was still so hot. Her eyelashes lay in full, black semicircles against her flushed skin.

Darian touched Samantha's arm. "Here's Claire." Quickly explaining what had just happened, Darian moved to let Claire examine the band around Holly's arm.

"This is an information bank." Claire began scanning the device while Raoul used his medical scanner on Holly. "Normally only the captain uses it, according to my trackpad. And you put it on after the NIEC, as it needs information from the personal device, or it won't work properly. No doubt it's flooding her brain with scattered, uncategorized information that it doesn't know what to do with."

"And we didn't bring any NIECs. I mean, why would we?" Samantha tried not to panic as she felt the overwhelming burden of being responsible for what happened to every one of her team members. And Holly, as well as Brandon, had the disadvantage of not being hooked up and thus monitored, like the rest of them.

"That thing looks like the mother of all NIECs," Carl said and pointed to the right armrest.

Samantha stood and joined Carl by the captain's chair. In a form-fitted indentation sat what looked like an egg-shaped NIEC. It was a third larger than the ones they had found in the Town Hall archives.

"Let me see." Claire joined them and scanned it. "Yup. The captain's NIEC, which needed to go on first. But I thought you determined that Holly isn't compatible. Like Brandon."

"We didn't determine anything, which is my fault," Samantha said. "Holly surmised that since she's always felt like an outsider, she doesn't have any alien DNA."

"Not just your fault," Darian said from the floor, where she held Holly's hand while Raoul got an IV going.

"Just saline with some added glucose." He scanned her again. "She's still unconscious, and her vital signs are the same."

"We should attach the NIEC." Claire sounded certain. "As she accidentally had it happen the wrong way, it might be the only way to rectify the information that's kicking up a storm in her brain."

"Are you sure?" Samantha looked down at Holly. "Raoul? Dar?"

"I haven't been able to pry the damn thing off her, and until I do, it seems we're out of options." Darian ran her fingertips along Holly's cheeks. "We can't let her lie here like this and just hope it will dislodge on its own."

"But we don't know what allowing this NIEC to attach will do to her either." Samantha shoved her fingers through her hair. "Raoul?"

"Let's wait a little longer. If her vital signs don't improve, or if they deteriorate, it's really our only option."

"No, it's not." Samantha clenched her hands into fists. "To begin with, why don't we take her to the infirmary? You were just there. Is it operational at all?"

"Actually, it's pristine, and as soon as I entered, it sensed my NIEC and came alive, so to speak."

Raoul turned to Carl. "I can't leave Holly. Can you find your way back and fetch one of the gurneys?"

"Absolutely. I'll be right back." Carl started toward where he and Raoul had come from.

Darian rounded the captain's chair. "I'll come with you." She squeezed Samantha's shoulder when she passed her. "We'll be quick."

Samantha shifted to get closer to Holly. Raoul was still scanning her, and Claire was examining the large NIEC and the area around the chair. Holly was still flushed. Leaning forward, Samantha took out her flashlight and directed it toward Holly's face. Her almond-shaped eyes were closed, but behind her eyelids, her eyes were moving as if she was in the REM cycle of sleep. "Have you seen that?" Samantha indicated Holly's eyes to Raoul.

"Yes. It's not REM sleep, but something similar. She's not asleep or in a coma. Her brain's just…busy, for lack of a better term." He adjusted the infusion. "Better not let it go in too fast."

"Anything new about the NIEC?" Samantha asked Claire. She admired the woman for being so calm amid all that was going on. Only a few days ago, Claire had been completely oblivious to all this, and now, as the chief engineer, she was one of the most valuable members of their group.

"I still maintain that we have to attach the captain's NIEC when we get Holly to sickbay. Whether she's meant to wear it or not, it has to be able to organize the information flooding her brain. Think of it as a fragmented hard drive where the computer is struggling to sort through the data. That's what's going on right now."

"I hear you—and it makes sense. It's just, I'm worried we might end up making things even worse for her. It was a big mistake to let someone not equipped like the rest of us go near equipment and not even consider that something might happen." Samantha massaged Holly's hand. "Come on, Holly. Try to push through the information influx."

"Nothing could have stopped her." Raoul spoke quietly. "Surely you've seen her take charge more than once. Normally, when you're new in a group, you take a backseat and study the group dynamic before you barge in. I know I did when you recruited me. I didn't want to just assume I knew anything when I didn't. But Holly, she knew when to listen and learn, and when she needed to take charge. And I could tell the difference in you, Samantha, the relief of having someone else step in as leader, NIEC or not."

Samantha sighed and held Holly's hot hand against her cheek. "I know. Part of me felt selfish for it, but it was such a nice feeling to be able to count on her. She actually captured the sensor we sent to investigate her on the meadows in flight. Did you know that?"

Raoul smiled. "I know. She's carried it in her pocket every day since then. Like a reminder that she hasn't dreamed this up."

Quick steps approached, and Samantha turned her head. Darian and Carl were pushing a gurney that hovered between them. Multicolored lights lit up the sides of it, and at the head, a bulkier console hummed discreetly. "We're here. Not sure why, but when Darian put her hands on the gurney and said, 'We have an emergency,' it popped off its tether on the wall and began to hover. All we had to do was push it here."

"Excellent. A grade-one gurney. The most advanced. Help me lift Holly." Raoul stood and handed the infusion bag over to Samantha. Carl and he pushed their hands under Holly while Darian maneuvered the gurney. A few moments later, they had strapped Holly to it and attached the infusion to an extendable pole on the left side of her head. Raoul worked the built-in console for a few moments before he redirected his focus to them. "Let's go. Bring the technology, Claire."

"Already packed it up." Claire patted the side pockets on her pants. "Let's get her over there."

Samantha and Darian walked on either side of the gurney as Carl pulled it along behind him, as he knew the way best, having been back and forth twice. Raoul didn't take his eyes off Holly and the console screen.

"Her condition is status quo. What worries me is that she's started to frown. She may be in pain." Raoul tapped in commands to the gurney console. "Once I've hooked her up to the more-advanced system in the infirmary, we need to make a quick decision about the captain's NIEC."

Dread filled every vein in Samantha. No matter how many times the others insisted they were in this together on equal terms, she somehow knew the buck stopped with her. The only one who could have relieved her of some of the pressure was also the one unconscious on the gurney.

The infirmary was nothing like Samantha could have imagined. A bed sat center stage, and everything around it blinked as if on standby. Twelve screens were attached to it, and row after row of small infusion apparatuses sat on grids around the bed.

"There." Raoul nodded, and they maneuvered the gurney to align it with the bed. "This is called a remedial bed. There are four in here, but this is the most advanced one."

Samantha quickly gazed around the infirmary while following the others' example and pushing off her backpack. She counted twenty beds, some appearing more advanced than others. Returning her focus to Holly, she saw that Raoul was easing her out of her wet clothes, with Darian's help, and then he pulled down a screen that emanated warmth.

"We're not going to cook her, but even if her temperature is slightly elevated, I don't want to risk her developing hypothermia later." Raoul connected small dots to Holly's temples, the middle of her ribcage, her ribs and ankles. "Now she's connected to the medical surveillance equipment." He studied the readings, tapped in commands, and then looked marginally relieved. "She's not in distress physically, but the NIEC needs to go on now." His unwavering gaze went from Samantha to the others, one by one. "Claire?"

"I agree. I can't come up with any other way. She's been in the information storm too long already. We can't wait." She walked over to Samantha, who stood at the foot of the remedial bed. "It has to be unanimous though. Samantha?"

Samantha looked at Darian, who nodded without hesitation. "All right. If it's our only viable plan, let's do it." She shuddered. If something happened to Holly, injury, or worse, she would never forgive herself.

Darian joined her on her other side, while Claire took the NIEC from a pouch in her pocket. She adjusted the filaments with their small, circular, metal "feet," and Samantha counted at least ten of them.

"Carl, Raoul, I need you to roll her onto her side." Claire walked to the side of the bed that would give her access to the back of Holly's neck. "Darian, would you part her hair in the center?"

"Sure thing." Darian inched in between Claire and the closest rack of infusion material. "Like this?" She had created a parting with her fingertip and now pushed the light-brown hair out of the way.

Claire held the NIEC between her thumb, index finger, and middle finger. It looked too big, but as soon as it neared the back of Holly's head, the filaments began swaying, then stretching. "Damn. This thing feels alive." Claire's fingers grew white as she gripped the NIEC harder. "I'm just going to—whoa!" She stared at the NIEC that had left her hand and slammed itself onto Holly. Aligning perfectly, it seemed to wriggle into place, sending its filaments into her thick hair.

"Hey. She needs to sit up. Raise the backrest of the bed," Claire called out. "Something's happening."

Samantha joined Carl on the other side of the bed and helped guide the head of the bed in a semi-reclining angle. Raoul held Holly's head and kept it from resting against the mattress.

"What's going on?" Darian asked, sounding out of breath.

"Look at the NIEC." Claire pointed, and the fact that her hand was trembling made Samantha's stomach clench. "It's growing."

"The filaments are finding their spots," Carl said, his voice half an octave higher than usual.

"No, that's not it. The NIEC's expanding." Claire pointed at the back of Holly's head. Samantha leaned in to see, but nothing could have prepared her for what was taking place before their widening eyes. The metal that the NIEC was made from was expanding. Whereas the narrow part of the egg-shaped device easily settled into the nape of Holly's neck, its broader end appeared to grow, moving through Holly's hair and finally settling after enlarging at least six inches on either side. It created a curve from the nape to the back of Holly's ears, slinging around them and ending up with two coin-like ends against her temples.

"Shit," Carl whispered. "Did anyone know this was going to happen?"

"I should've known, but all my NIEC showed me was more filaments. This…" Claire cleared her throat. "This was unexpected."

Raoul was staring at the monitors while tapping his trackpad.

"Raoul?"

"Wait." He frowned and walked over to yet another console by the wall behind the head of the remedial bed. "Just a sec." He moved his hands, cursing under his breath long enough to scare Samantha.

"Um. Guys. She's opening her eyes." Carl placed a gentle hand on Holly's shoulder. "Holly?"

Samantha's heart thudded so hard, she was afraid she might pass out. "Holly, can you hear us?"

"Mm—uh-huh…" Holly sounded as if she was half under water.

"Raoul!" Darian called out. "What's going on?"

"Her brainwaves are settling down. Her temperature is almost normal." Raoul rounded the bed. "I'm going to perform some old-fashioned neurological tests. Just to be sure." He shone with a penlight into Holly's half-open eyes. "Good. Excellent. Equal and responsive." After testing Holly's reflexes with a small stainless-steel instrument, he pushed his finger through his dark hair. "She's getting there. I suppose the NIEC has a lot to deal with."

"Sch-sure does," Holly said. "That band i-sch a damn library, Schamantha."

Samantha snorted softly at Holly's words, but if Darian hadn't been right next to her, she might have fainted after all. "You can tell me about it when you feel better."

Holly nodded and closed her eyes. "Tired."

"I'll say." Darian ran her hand along Holly's leg. "Just take your time. You've been through the wringer."

"More like a…centrifuge." Holly's voice was growing increasingly clearer.

Samantha looked around them while gripping the foot of the bed harder.

"What's up?" Darian murmured. "You're pale."

"I need a stool or something." Samantha briefly closed her eyes. "And a power bar."

"We all do." Darian pulled a matte-gray stool over and gently nudged Samantha to sit down. The others grabbed stools of their own, while Darian fetched a container from her backpack. "I have power bars and dextrose, and you guys have your own water. Let's just take a moment while Holly recuperates and eat something."

"Good plan." Raoul nodded approvingly. "It's that, or I'm going to hook us all up after all this stress. We must have burned through a lot of glucose." He smiled as he looked down at Holly. "Normal color." After a glance toward the screens, his smile turned into a relieved grin. "And normal vital signs."

"Thank God," Samantha said after swallowing her first bite of the bar.

"No kidding." Holly opened her eyes again. "I feel a lot better. I could hear you, but your words were garbled, and my brain was full of noise. It's calmer now."

"I'm so relieved to hear that." Samantha patted Holly's foot.

"I hope you still think so after what I've learned." Holly shifted on the bed and located the sensors that raised the head with ease. "What's really strange is that it's as if I always knew, which seems ridiculous."

"What are you talking about?" Carl appeared concerned at Holly's words.

Holly looked only at Samantha, her gaze resolute. "I don't know how this happened—honestly, I have no clue." She smiled gently but also raised her chin in somewhat of a challenge. "I'm the captain of the *Velocity*."

CHAPTER THIRTEEN

Holly sat up on the bed. Not sure if she was shocked at how settled everything felt inside or if the obviousness of her revelation made her regard her crewmembers with a calm curiosity, she waited for their reaction. Mostly, she kept her gaze on Samantha, who stood at the foot of the remedial bed with Darian next to her. Holly realized that she just referred to the people around her as her crewmembers. Not "the group," or "friends"—but actual crewmembers that she now had the ultimate responsibility for.

"That's one fucking development, but I'm not all that surprised," Darian said.

Holly nodded. She felt the same way. "And?"

"And thank God," Samantha said, closing her eyes briefly. "This development has been on my wish list for so long. Finding a captain. Finding you." Samantha stepped closer. "And how do you feel?"

"I'm in the right place. Somehow, after I spotted you and found the hatch in the meadows, I've known that wasn't mere chance. I...I just couldn't figure out how to bypass the fact that I'm adopted and not truly a Dennamore inhabitant."

Raoul rested his hip against the bed's console. "I've studied the genetic markers for the group—"

"Crew," Holly said firmly. "We're not a group. You're my crew."

Raoul blinked. "Ah. Of course." He seemed to need a second to gather his thoughts. "I have studied the crew's genetic makeup, and after my NIEC unlocked the alien knowledge of medicine and the medical equipment, it's become easier. If you allow it, I'll add your DNA to this small database that I hope will grow. Doctor/patient confidentiality applies, of course."

"Go ahead." Holly eased herself onto the deck, making sure her legs would carry her. She raised her hands to her head and felt how the captain's NIEC hugged the back of her head all the way to her temples. "I have to admit I didn't see this coming." She ran her fingertips along the device. "Now that it's lodged on me, the information stored in the bracelet makes sense. At some moments earlier I thought I was going insane." She shook her head.

"You look a lot better," Darian said.

"Thank you. I feel all right." She checked the time. "We need to inform Camilla and Walker about the latest developments and that we're doing all right, Darian. Until we have a counselor, I need you, as chief of security, to take care of notifications like that."

Darian opened her mouth, closed it again, but then said, "Aye, Captain."

"I suppose we better stand on formality," Samantha said, "or we'll have a problem with the command structure in the future."

"Exactly." Holly put on her jacket that had been pulled off her when she was unconscious. "You are all members of the senior crew. Apart from a counselor, we also need an ops officer, and if you had been a little older, Carl, a bit more seasoned, you would have been the obvious choice. Thankfully, the most important positions have been filled by all of you. I'm going to need a first officer, though—the sooner the better."

"What's your plan for the immediate future, as in now, Captain?" Samantha asked, the title crossing her lips easily. She truly seemed relieved to be able to focus on being the chief pilot and navigator.

"I want to go back to the bridge and see what wearing the NIEC and bracelet does. After that, it's time to go home, get some much-deserved sleep, and then document everything. I also want to look at the list of people in Dennamore that Camilla and Walker think are good candidates. We need sixty-seven more to wear the NIECs, but also people who are willing to join us on this adventure without them. Although this ship needs a skeletal crew of seventy-seven hands to function, ideally the crew manifest should consist of a hundred and twenty." Holly saw that this was news to the others for about half a minute, but then it was as if their NIECs caught up with what they'd learned. It was quite the thing to see the information dawn on them. It literally made their eyes sparkle.

"I'll just report to the other four." Darian engaged her speaker. "We're all doing well. We have had a development that we're looking forward to sharing with you, but for now, we're going to check out the bridge one more time before we head back."

"Why can't you tell us right away?" Philber said, sounding frustrated.

"There's a lot to explain and discuss, Philber. Once we're by the water-tower site, we'll return to Brynden 4 and brief the four of you. Darian out." Darian tapped her speaker and made a wry face. "That felt kind of rude. I suppose it'll go easier when everyone's fully informed."

"It will." Holly knew she couldn't expect everyone to slip seamlessly into the chain of command and act correctly. It was, however, part of her job to make sure they knew how things would work from now on. They'd still jointly reach their conclusions on what to do and when, but no matter the outcome, she would be responsible.

The bridge had been lit by only a few red-tinted spotlights when they were there before. Now when they stepped off the elevator and entered the tall, triangular space, it was fully illuminated, and all the screens and consoles were on standby mode.

"Damn," Claire said. "This is what happened in engineering when I stepped inside. This, though, is...majestic."

Holly agreed. The workstations behind the captain's chair made the bridge look like an amphitheater. After she walked over to the captain's chair and sat down, it seemed to mold itself around her, and the screens at her personal disposal all came alive. Placing her hands in the indentations made for that purpose, she sensed a low-grade hum against her palms. She pressed her fingertips in different patterns, and the main screen woke up and showed the cave around the ship. With slight manual adjustments, she shifted between cameras in the stern, aft, and belly of the ship. Other cameras to port and starboard displayed their images on smaller panels on either side of the main screen.

Samantha had taken her seat at the helm, and Darian did the same at the tactical station on Holly's left. Claire climbed one row up, ending to Holly's right.

"These are the bridge engineering stations. This is mine, and there are two more for my second and third in command." Claire sounded awestruck, and who could blame her? "Just the fact that I know this setup as well as I know how to repair a Volvo is still crazy."

"There's a medical station too," Raoul said. "It's mainly for scanning alien planets, etcetera. I'll do most of my work in the infirmary."

"We have a lot to learn, a lot to do. This won't be a secret for very much longer," Holly said. "Once we have enough crewmembers to get her out of here, the *Velocity* needs to leave the cave." She frowned. "It doesn't sit well with me that I don't know why, exactly."

"I've felt that time's running out for a while now," Samantha said and swiveled her chair to look at the others. "Finding our captain is a huge step in the right direction."

Holly nodded, glad she wasn't the only one sensing the urgency. "Time to get back. It's going to be tough on us to wade through the icy water again. Next time we utilize our uniforms. They're made to sustain a lot worse than this."

As they left the bridge, hoisting backpacks and, in Holly's case, photographing a few different angles, the lights went back to the former muted red. This time, they took the elevator to deck six, where they entered the elevator that sent them down one of the struts. After yet another elevator ride, they braved the cold water, but it was clearly almost too much for Holly and Samantha. Claire pushed her shoulder in under Holly's arm, and Darian did the same with Samantha, while the guys took care of their bags.

Holly felt as if the return walk was twice as long, but eventually they reached the spiral staircase. Darian had alerted the two men above, and Holly could have wept with relief when warm, strong hands guided her up the last few steps. She was shivering so badly now, she was unable to thank Brandon, but he seemed more concerned with warming her. He wrapped her in his arms, tugging a nylon survival blanket around them both.

"Shared bodily warmth," he said calmly. "We'll have you nice and toasty in no time."

"Get her into the tent," Holly heard Raoul say behind her, sounding concerned. "I'll warm an IV."

Samantha was white and had stopped shivering. Holly wanted to break free from Brandon's strong grip, but he held her back. "They've got her. Let's get you into the tent. Philber is on his way with one of the cars. Screw the fact that you're not allowed to drive here."

Wrapped in a sleeping bag and clutching a mug of hot tea, Holly started to slowly feel human again. Brandon and Claire had tugged off her wet boots and tied someone's sweatshirt around her icy feet. On the other side of the four-person, lightweight tent, Darian had crawled into the same sleeping bag as Samantha. The men wrapped more survival blankets around them. Raoul opened his alien medical kit and pulled out a large ampoule, then pressed it into what Holly now knew was an intravenous infuser. As he broke the seal, she knew it reached normal body temperature within seconds. Pressing it against Samantha's jugular vein, he tapped the instrument, and a faint hiss proved it was working.

"I added an extra thermal agent," Raoul said. "It's protocol for this kind of situation."

"Please, Samantha. Can you look at me?" Darian said, hugging the pale woman in her arms tighter. "Samantha…"

Carl poked his head into the tent. "Philber's down by the lake path now, but that's as far as he can go with the car."

"We can carry her," Raoul said. "Captain, what about you? Are you able to walk?"

Brandon looked from Raoul to Holly, his eyes widening. "Captain?"

"We'll explain when we reach Brynden 4," Holly said. "And yes, I can walk, but my boots are soaked."

"I brought some regular rubber boots that were in the trunk." Carl held up a pair of large men's boots. "Better than barefoot."

"Good thinking." Holly pushed the sweatshirt away from her feet and stuck them into the cold boots. She winced but managed to get to her feet, with the help of Claire and Brandon. "We have to tear the tent down in record time. We can't leave it behind."

"I'll do it," Carl said, "and then someone can swing back and pick me up once you and Samantha are warm and snug at Brynden 4."

Holly placed a hand on Carl's shoulder. "But what about your feet?"

"All-weather boots. I'm fine." He grinned.

And young and strong. Holly nodded. "All right. Good job, Ensign."

Carl had begun to roll up a sleeping bag but stopped. "Ensign?" He blinked.

"You heard me. See you at Camilla's." Holly shuffled out of the tent, holding on to the nearest tree. It was even colder than before.

"Better get a head start toward the car. They're bringing Samantha out now. She's looking better, but she's slurring her words." Claire wrapped her arm around Holly's waist. "Lean on me, Captain."

Brandon didn't comment on the use of rank, but Holly felt his gaze on her. She felt ridiculous ambling toward the car and was grateful it was only a short distance. Philber opened the front passenger door as they reached the path, ushering Holly inside.

"How did you manage to turn the car here?" she asked, wrapping the nylon blanket closer around her. The heater in the car hadn't caught up yet. This was when she realized that she hadn't been cold once aboard the *Velocity*. It was as if the heat had followed them around the ship, because the vessel couldn't have wasted energy century after century when no one was there.

"I backed in," Philber said, sounding affronted. "Regardless of what others may think, I'm an excellent driver."

"But of course." Holly decided not to bring up how many times the belligerent and distracted man had hit poles and fences in Dennamore, though luckily no living creatures. It was impressive to back up along the narrow lake path in the dark.

They placed Samantha in the backseat, her head in Darian's lap. To her relief, Holly heard Samantha talk, and the fact that Darian was wiping away tears confirmed again how close those two were. Perhaps, as captain, she should have seen this as potential future fraternization, but it was ridiculous to take the command-structure rules that far.

Philber offered to go help Carl break camp, and Raoul took the wheel while Claire and Brandon squeezed in among the bags in the SUV's back compartment. As Raoul drove toward Brynden 4, Holly closed her eyes and allowed the tremors to return. She was warmer now, which made her think this shaking was more to do with the events earlier than with hypothermia.

She couldn't wait to get indoors and perhaps persuade Camilla to let her start a fire in the impressive open fireplace in the parlor. She only meant to close her eyes briefly, but it took mere seconds for her to fall asleep.

Gran sat in her electric wheelchair in the parlor at Brynden 4, her back straight and with her hands folded in her lap. Her blue eyes were unreadable as she took in the sight of the tired, tousled group of people that had just changed into dry clothes borrowed from Brandon and Darian. Darian tried to guess what was going on in her grandmother's mind, but it was impossible.

"Gran?" she asked carefully.

"I'm no fool. I realize this mission we all embarked on, each after their own ability, could, and would, be dangerous. However, you can't expect me to just take it in stride when it endangered someone who, for all we knew, was the most vulnerable tonight. Holly, from what I see, you seem all right, but the fact that you're still wearing your knitted cap concerns me."

"It's because we wanted to explain about Holly and her experience tonight to the rest of you when we're all together." Darian was sitting with Samantha on the same settee as they had occupied before they went on their late-evening mission. Samantha was sipping from a mug of Brandon's homemade chicken soup that Camilla and Walker had taken out of the freezer when they learned of Holly's and Samantha's hypothermia. "We reached a crossroads tonight." Darian drew a deep breath. "Remove your hat, Captain?"

Holly pulled off the cap, and the sight of the captain's NIEC adorning her head, much like a crown, made everyone gasp, including the ones that already knew. The ambiance in the parlor became instantly electric, and Darian could have sworn she felt the air sizzle. Holly sat, regally, wearing the large NIEC as if it had been attached to her head much longer than it had.

"What?" Gran whispered, raising an unsteady hand to her mouth. "What on earth is that on your head? Is that a—a—"

"The captain's NIEC," Holly said, regarding them with an even gaze.

"I'll be damned," Philber said, his voice gruff. "Sure didn't see that coming, and I'm usually ahead of the game."

"Not to mention humble," Gran said. "But—are you all right, Holly?"

"I am now, thanks to my crew and Brandon's soup." She gave a faint smile. "Camilla, are *you* all right?"

"Yes. Yes, of course, I am." Gran pushed the joystick of her chair and wheeled over to Holly. She gripped Holly's chin with her thumb and index finger, turning her head from one side to the other. "Now that's impressive. I know it's probably a ridiculous question, but... does it hurt?"

"Not in the least. How it'll feel to remove it, I have no idea." Holly took Gran's hand between hers. "I'm truly fine. I started feeling all right as soon as the NIEC attached. If it hadn't been for misjudging what footwear to use, I wouldn't have had any residual effects from our mission at all."

"You're the captain." Brandon shook his head slowly. "You have alien DNA after all."

Darian wondered how this felt for Brandon, to be the only one, so far, to not have the marker. She hoped he realized they couldn't do without him.

"I do," Holly now said, answering Brandon's probably rhetorical question. "I know how I felt when I thought I didn't. I hope you aren't as silly as I was and instead know how invaluable you are to the crew. And that you're part of it."

Brandon opened his mouth as if to speak but closed it again and just shook his head. Holly merely nodded and then let go of Gran's hand. "Same goes for you, Camilla."

"I'll say," Gran said, sounding more like her usual assertive self.

Walker had been quiet, but now he leaned forward and took Holly's hands. "Not such an outside after all."

"No." Holly blinked. "I suppose I'm not. Somehow my parents adopted me back to Dennamore, or, at least back to where one or both of my birth parents originated. What are the odds?"

"And as unfathomable as that is, that's not all," Darian said. "You're our captain, and I, for one, couldn't be happier."

"Hear, hear," Samantha said, and the look of utter relief on her face as she met Darian's gaze showed openly how much she had hoped for this day.

"All right," Gran said. "Now that the cat's out of the bag, in a manner of speaking, what's next? I know we have a lot to plan and discuss, not least how it all came about, but I want to know when I'll be able to see the ship."

"God, Gran. You can't make your way there through that water-filled tunnel. At least not until we've figured out a way to modify one of your wheelchairs to make the trip underground." Darian groaned. "As for what comes next...what do you say, Captain?"

"Don't you have a doctor's appointment aboard *Speeder One* tomorrow, Camilla?" Holly ran her finger along a glowing yellow line on her alien bracelet. "We have recruiting to do, so I'll need that list, Walker.'"

"You'll have it, Captain." The title seemed to come naturally to him, but Darian knew he was used to working in a command structure, much like herself.

"If I may add something," Claire said and looked up from her computer. "I've just sent you full specs of the *Velocity*. Once I opened my computer, my NIEC had unlocked the blueprints, and all of you should have them. Let me pull the blinds. Hang tight." Claire got up, and it didn't escape Darian how Holly followed her movements. Only a few days ago, they had been strangers, and now they held two of the most vital positions on the *Velocity*. Claire lowered the blinds and turned off the ceiling light in the parlor. She then lined up her computer on the table and directed a light toward the center of the room. "Here. Let me show you." She flickered her fingertips over the lines and symbols.

A blue shimmer trembled for a fraction of a second, and then a 3D image of the mothership floated between them, four feet above the floor.

"Obi-Wan Kenobi. You're my only hope," Carl murmured.

"I know, right?" Claire grinned, but then she grew serious. "Here's our ship. It's the next best I can do for you, Camilla, and the rest of you who didn't get to go down. And when it comes to the blueprints, here they are." She moved her fingers against the computer again, and the ship's hull became transparent. "What I found most interesting at this point is that there's room for a lot more people than we first thought. A hundred and eighty, to be exact." Claire pointed to decks four, six, and seven. "These decks are crew quarters. And when you look at the specs for this deck," she said, directing their attention to deck two, "see this area? Common rooms, that's to be expected, but these two are meant for education. Schools. For children. Either we haven't realized that some of them had kids, or if they planned to be able to have families."

"Can the *Velocity* be a generational ship?" Darian asked.

"Or they just wanted to cover all their bases," Claire said.

"We haven't found that anyone brought children, but we really don't know when exactly they left Dwynna Major." Gran paled a little. "What if they did have children, and they were traveling for so long that they grew up? Bech'taia writes about the unmatched crewmembers living in special dwellings in Dennamore. And she mentions how she and Gai'usto hope to have a family of their own. What...oh, God...what if she was a child, or at least very young, when they left their home world?"

A strange sort of silence spread as everyone seemed to think about what repercussions this possibility had for them. "Pity the NIECs don't keep some of the previous owners' memories," Carl said.

"Are you kidding?" Claire circled the 3D holographic model. "I have enough memories to not want someone else's to barge in. Trust me, I don't have space for that."

Darian agreed. It was one thing to learn the ins and outs of the technology. "Split personalities with my great-great-great-great-great-whatever? Nah. Not my cup of tea."

"This might actually aid us when it comes to recruiting." Holly stood. "If they can bring their closest family members, I mean."

"Now there's a thought." Darian snorted. "We might need daycare, school, and, oh God, a pediatrician." She met Samantha's glance. "This situation just got a lot more complicated…eh, who am I kidding? It was always complicated."

"Regrets?" Samantha murmured, and her paleness made Darian's concern escalate.

"Not in a million years." Turning back to the others, she said, "Give us our tasks for tomorrow, please, Captain. I'm starting to fade."

"She actually means me," Samantha said, leaning against Darian.

"We're all feeling the long hours," Holly said. "All right. Gran, Brandon, and Darian, you have a date with Raoul aboard *Speeder One*. I know Samantha has to put in her hours at work. I have to teach a class at ten a.m., but after that, I plan to work on the recruitment lists. Walker, are you available?"

"I am, as long as nothing happens with Camilla that I need to help out with." Walker raised one of Gran's hands to his lips.

"Good. Philber, I need you to continue the work on Bech'taia's journal, if Camilla allows it. I'm aware that this journal is your private property," Holly said.

"As long as nobody except the people in this room sees it, I'm fine with that." Gran maneuvered her wheelchair back to Walker.

Philber nodded. "My legs can do with a day of sitting still."

"Carl, I know you have school. Afterward, if your homework situation doesn't take too long, I want you to join Samantha for a mission down into the archives. Go in via the tunnel after hours."

"I'll be on it."

Holly turned to Claire. "I need you to work on what it will take to get the *Velocity* out from under the lake. The procedure. The minimum crew required. I want to be prepared as soon as possible. I can't shake the feeling that we are working on borrowed time."

"It's not the first time you've said so, and Samantha expressed something similar. I should have paid more attention to your intuition at the time—but I am now," Darian said.

"It is a concern." Holly nodded. "That's why we need to keep things happening. And now to my last point. Yes, I'm the captain, though it doesn't mean I don't want suggestions, thoughts, and so on. But we also have to be clear that the buck stops with me. I'm responsible for what we choose to do, or not do, and when it comes to decision-making, the last word is mine. This is how this works."

Darian watched the other crewmembers intently. Holly's words didn't leave any room for interpretation, and in Darian's mind, their captain was right. If they didn't agree with this point, what was the use of having a captain in the first place?

"Hear, hear," Samantha said weakly.

The others joined in, and Darian saw Holly's shoulders lose some of their tension. She stood and met their eyes intently. "All right." A faint smile flickered over her lips. "Dismissed."

Samantha woke up, pain coursing through her legs. Her heart pounded hard and fast, and the room was dark, but she still knew she wasn't in her own bedroom. A strong arm rested on her hip, and the warmth behind her was familiar. Darian.

Shifting, Samantha stretched her legs and couldn't hold back a moan. They felt rigid, like someone had poured concrete into her veins. She really hadn't tolerated the cold water last night. Warming up pretty fast after sitting by the fireplace with the others and having chicken soup, she had thought she was over the worst of it. Had she sustained more damage than they first thought? Reaching down, she touched her legs. They were warm on the outside. Huh. This was weird. They felt a lot colder on the inside.

"What's up?" Darian murmured and got up on her elbow. "Your legs?"

"Just stiff." Samantha didn't want Darian to worry. She had vivid memories of the fear in Darian's voice from when they'd put her in the sleeping bag.

"May I see?" Darian switched on the nightstand lamp.

"All right." Dreading what she might find, Samantha pushed the covers off. To her surprise, and relief, her legs looked all right, if a bit pale.

Darian ran her hands over her feet and up her shins. Cupping Samantha's calves, she squeezed gently, immediately frowning when Samantha whimpered. "You're in pain."

"Just sore. It can be exercise pain. Don't you think?" Samantha studied her legs. "I mean, I can move them at least, even if they feel a bit rigid."

"We should page Raoul." Darian reached for her speaker, but Samantha stopped her.

"Wait. Let's don't panic now. I'll just grab a few acetaminophens first. I really didn't take any painkillers before we went to bed, which was foolish, of course. Let's try that first, before we ask the guy with all the medical toys."

Darian studied her closely but then slowly nodded. "I'll get them for you. You're not putting weight on your legs yet."

"All right." Relieved, Samantha nodded at her backpack. "I have some—"

"So do I. Right here." Darian opened a drawer in her nightstand and took out a small bottle. "Full dosage." She tapped the bottle, and two pills landed in Samantha's hand. Handing over one of the water bottles sitting on the nightstand next to her, Darian watched intently as Samantha swallowed the pills.

"There." Handing the bottle back, Samantha lay down again. "Half an hour and I'll be able to go back to sleep, I'm sure."

"Oh, yeah. And how should we entertain ourselves in the meantime?" Darian had relaxed a bit more now and was smiling down at her.

The question was half said in jest, but it also made Samantha's heart rate go up again. "Um. Entertain ourselves?" She saw Darian's amber eyes darken.

"I had thought of something a lot more innocent, but if you insist on speaking in that tone, with that voice, my mind goes somewhere completely different." Darian pushed a lock of hair from Samantha's forehead.

"What tone? And what's wrong with my voice?" Samantha gripped the slightly wrinkled bedsheet under her hard with both hands. There was definitely something in Darian's voice that wasn't there a few seconds ago.

"All throaty. And suggestive." Darian slid down onto her elbow again, placing her free hand just below Samantha's rib cage.

"Now that's a first. 'Throaty and suggestive.'" Samantha managed only a whisper.

"You can add 'husky whisper' to that," Darian said, her own voice definitely a purr.

"You should talk." Running her curled index finger along Darian's cheek, Samantha blinked slowly. Apparently, this too had affected Darian, because she closed her eyes hard for a few moments.

"You're too beautiful." Pressing her lips to Samantha's forehead, Darian then let them travel down her temple, follow the curve of her cheekbone, and track her jawline. "And you smell far too good for my sanity."

"It's your shower cream," Samantha whispered and hooked an arm around Darian's neck.

"Its scent is different on you. Mesmerizing. Intoxicating." Dipping her head again, Darian kissed Samantha's lips lightly.

Samantha parted her lips and pulled Darian closer, then slid her tongue along the fullness of Darian's lips. "I've missed this. I haven't allowed this, us, as I've truly wanted. Every waking moment, our mission, our discoveries, took over, when all I wanted was to scream for it all to stop, to put it on pause." Samantha felt tears run down her temples and back into her hair.

"Hey. I was just as wrapped up in everything as you were. And don't forget, you were *it*, for months." Darian returned the caress with her own tongue. "And I had Gran. The house. It has been a lot."

"It has."

"But now we have a captain. And here we are." Darian slid down and kissed Samantha's neck.

Samantha arched against Darian, pushing the back of her head into the pillows, wanting to give Darian better access. The heat from the damp kisses, the gentle nips, and the soothing tongue made Samantha groan and tug at Darian's T-shirt for her to come closer.

"Shh. Easy, Samantha. I'm right here." Unfastening the top two buttons of the borrowed flannel pajama jacket, Darian trailed more kisses down between Samantha's breasts.

"God…" Samantha pushed her fingers into Darian's hair, gently holding her in place. "Amazing."

"Mm. Agreed," Darian murmured against Samantha's skin.

Long, slow caresses, open-mouth kisses across heated skin, and Samantha knew she was more aflame than she'd been in her life. Normally shy, she didn't recognize herself with Darian, especially not like this when she was ready to tear off her clothes and have Darian claim every inch of her.

Instead, the caresses slowed until they became a molten, slow-flowing river that ran around them and occasionally washed over them. Somewhere, Samantha knew this was Darian's way of showing how much she cared, but a small part of her wanted to make love to Darian so badly.

"I want you, Dar," she said, needing for Darian to know.

"I'm trying to be good here. You must know I want you more than I've ever wanted anyone, or anything." Darian rolled over onto her back and pulled Samantha with her. "I could devour you all night, and it wouldn't be nearly enough. I just want you to feel better first. If I accidentally made you worse, or hurt you, I wouldn't forgive myself." Darian kissed Samantha again, this time not keeping it light or soft. "Like this," she murmured against Samantha's lips. "Just like this." She slipped her tongue inside Samantha's mouth, caressed her, gave of her own taste, and all Samantha could do was hold on in the vortex it created inside her. She clung to Darian and returned the kiss with all the pent-up emotions she had struggled to keep on the back burner for so long. Feeling free to express how much she wanted this woman, how much she cared about her, beyond cared, she let her mouth and body show it.

Finally, they both needed to breathe, and they parted enough to gasp for air.

"God." Darian moaned against the skin just below Samantha's ear. "If this is how you kiss when you're not entirely a hundred percent, heaven help me."

Chuckling under her breath, Samantha pressed closer to Darian and ran her fingertips across her lips. "And when you know I'm not in need of 'protection,' heaven help me?"

"Precisely." Darian reached out and switched off the light. Pulling Samantha closer, she kissed her temple. "Let's try to go back to sleep—if it's humanly possible."

Samantha adjusted her shoulder and dragged the pillow in under her head, not wanting to hurt Darian's shoulder, but not wanting to pull back either. She settled down, the scent of Darian—and yes, the shower cream did smell different on her too—surrounding her. It took her a while to realize that the pain in her legs was almost gone. If it was because of the acetaminophen or Darian's kisses—Samantha didn't have to guess.

In this moment, it was all about Darian.

CHAPTER FOURTEEN

Darian operated the winch that pulled her grandmother's wheelchair up along the ramp to *Speeder One*. She could have probably pushed Gran up, but she had to admit she was still sore and tired from last night. When she woke up this morning and found Samantha sitting up in bed, nursing a cup of coffee, and scrolling on a regular tablet, Darian had been content to just lie there, studying the woman she'd cradled most of the night. Samantha had finally raised her gaze from the tablet and noticed that Darian was looking at her, but she'd only smiled and returned her focus to her work. Now, Samantha was at the library at Town Hall and wouldn't be available until six in the evening. She was also planning to go into the old archives with Carl late in the afternoon.

"I'm still so awestruck when I enter this vessel," Gran said, sitting regally in her chair. "It's unfathomable that this technology is centuries old...perhaps even older, as we don't know when it was invented on Dwynna Major."

"Yeah. There's a lot we don't know, Gran." Darian sometimes found it quite daunting, albeit also very interesting, when she thought of how little they most likely knew about their ancestors. The mere hypothesis that the alien settlers had been the good people Bech'taia described was a huge assumption.

"Let me help you, Camilla," Brandon said and assisted the frail woman out of her chair and onto the LSC bed. "How's that?"

"Quite comfortable. It molds around my body, kind of like a memory-foam mattress, but better." Gran wriggled into a comfortable position. "And there's Raoul. Hello, there."

"Camilla. Looking radiant as always," Raoul said as he stepped out of the aft area of the shuttle. "I've prepared the wands and different possible treatments, after putting my NIEC to good use. And don't worry. We're not doing anything crazy. We have to be very careful with you."

"Yes, yes." Gran waved her hand dismissively. "I'm having a particularly horrible day, so if you can do something about the pain in my hands, I'd be forever in your debt."

Darian's heart clenched as looked closer look at the red, swollen joints of Gran's hands. She hated that her grandmother experienced so much as a minute of pain. Yes, she was nervous about Gran receiving untested treatments—well, not counting her own broken clavicle and torn ligaments and muscle tissue. But Darian was also eager for something to work effectively against the rheumatoid arthritis.

"Brandon, I'm placing you at the nurses' station, and I'll show you what to look for on the monitors. It's quite self-explanatory, but it does use alien symbols." Raoul pointed to the screens, and Darian listened too as Brandon learned how to keep an eye on Gran's vital signs. To Darian it seemed easy, but she could see how Brandon pulled out a notebook and jotted down a few things. Good for him.

"You ready, Gran? No second thoughts?" Darian sat on a seat that folded from the side of the LSC bed, keeping her hand lightly on her grandmother's leg.

"I am more than ready. Get on with it, Raoul, if you please. I'm sure Brandon will notice if I so much as hiccup." Gran chuckled, but Darian could see the tension in the thin skin around her eyes. She really was in pain.

"And you've taken no medication this morning at all, like we talked about?" Raoul joined them and lowered the tray of instruments and infusers.

"Not a thing. That's part of the problem right now. I did bring some in case the alien methods do nothing for me." Gran smiled at Raoul, but Darian guessed he didn't buy the bravado.

"All right. We'll start with your non-dominant hand. Left, correct?"

"Correct." Gran leaned back against the raised backrest of the bed.

"This will create warmth, but it shouldn't hurt," Raoul said. "If it does, don't grin and bear it. All right?"

"Raoul has you pegged, Gran." Darian wiggled her eyebrows at her grandmother.

"I have no idea what you're talking about." Crinkling her nose at Darian, Gran took a deep breath. "I won't play brave. Do your damndest, young man."

Raoul engaged the wand, an eleven-inch, matte rod with a crisp, white glowing light along half its length. Directing the light toward Gran's left hand, he ran it back and forth in a way familiar to Darian. She had felt a warmth that bordered on too hot a few times, but it also had a soothing effect. Studying Gran's face, Darian looked for any sign of discomfort, but, if anything, she looked pensive.

After running the wand for a few minutes, Raoul paused and turned to Brandon. "Any changes in her vital signs, even miniscule?"

"Heart rate is eighty-four, but everything else is unchanged." Brandon gave a thumbs-up.

"Excellent. Now it's time for the small wand," Raoul said and plucked a pencil-sized, matte-black wand. The light came out of the top end of this one. As soon as Raoul engaged it, a faint scent filled the air that reminded Darian of warm soil in a greenhouse. "What's this one for?" she asked.

"This will treat the inflammation on a deeper level. We should see a remarkable change." Raoul met Gran's gaze. "Ready?"

"In a minute. I think I need a blanket. Not sure if it's an onset of nerves or a reaction to the treatment, but I'm cold," Gran said.

"On it." Darian hurried over to the storage area and found a package labeled thermal body cover. She opened it, and a large blanket unfolded and inflated until it was an inch thick. "Now we're talking," Darian said as she returned and spread the body cover over Gran's thin form. "Better?"

"Oh, my. I have to get me one of these." Gran squirmed, and after she and Raoul had rearranged her arm, he began running the black wand over her hand and wrist. "Oh, Darian...I can feel it happening." Gran's eyes grew huge as she stared at Darian. "It feels like bubbles, or like someone carbonated my blood."

"Painful?" Darian sat down on the stool that was attached to the bed and took Gran's right hand between hers under the blanket.

"No. Just strange." Gran smiled with pale lips.

Raoul kept working, and before their eyes, Gran's swollen joints reduced in size and assumed the same color as the surrounding skin. Giving a muted sob when Raoul put the wand back on the tray, she withdrew the hand Darian held and covered her eyes.

"Gran." Feeling helpless at this rare display of tears and emotions, Darian wished she could have crawled into the LCS bed with Gran and held onto her like she had when she was little and spent all the nights of the first six months after her parents' deaths in Gran's bed. Instead, she had to settle for merely stroking Gran's leg, which felt entirely inadequate.

"It's a normal reaction," Raoul murmured. "It's to be expected when someone who's been in pain for so many years finally experiences some relief."

"It's not *some* relief we're talking about," Gran said, her voice stronger. "It's a miracle, from my point of view. I was ready to say screw it and take my pills before we came down into the tunnel. My hand was on fire, and now—it's not."

"How does it feel?" Darian bent to kiss her grandmother's cheek. "You look less tense."

"That's nothing compared to what I'll look like when Raoul's done the other hand and my knees and hips." She cleared her throat. "So, to answer your question, it feels wonderful. I'm sore, and my blood still 'carbonates,' but the searing, all-too-familiar pain is gone. Completely gone." She met Darian's gaze. "Now, now. Don't cry, Darian."

Darian wiped at her wet eyelashes. "You're one to talk." She shifted her focus to Brandon, mouthing, "Wow." He gave another thumbs-up.

"I'll wait for a little while to make sure you don't have any immediate side effects to deal with." Raoul hesitated. "Then I want to do your right hand and your leg joints. Hips, knees, ankles. A couple of toes. And if you can tolerate that like you do right now, we can begin discussing another treatment that will actually cure you, rather than mitigate the pain like today."

"Why not discuss this subject now?" Gran drilled her gaze into Raoul's, in a way Darian could still feel what it was like to be on the receiving end. Whenever she had screwed up as a kid, Gran had looked at her like that, but her voice and hands had been soft and loving. Darian had always hated to disappoint Gran rather than make her angry. Not that Gran had ever been very demonstrative, but she certainly could get under your skin if she wanted to. And in Darian's mid-teens, Gran had wanted to a few times.

"It's an effective treatment that heals on a cellular level, a well-tested method from an alien point of view and will keep the illness from recurring." Raoul shifted and looked uncomfortable. "There's one snag, though."

"Snag? What do you mean?" Darian blinked as she tried to fathom what was going on.

"To administer the start of a new, more advanced treatment, you need to be fitted with a NIEC, as it has to do its part." Raoul stopped talking and studied Gran and then Darian. "I know you're against it, I mean the NIEC, Darian, but ultimately it is Camilla's choice."

"And I want that. I want *exactly* that. A chance for a healthier body. I'm seventy-five. Geoff is seventy. If we're lucky, we may have quite a few years together. If it takes a NIEC, I'm not going to chicken out." Gran quieted and then gripped Darian's hand again, now with her left, quite-strong one. To feel her grandmother be able to use her hand like that after suffering from arthritis so many years made Darian hesitate. "And there is something else you might not have thought about, sweetheart."

"What's that?" Darian wiped at her eyes again.

"When you, Samantha, and the rest of the crew, take off toward outer space…if I'm not in better shape, there's no way you can justify bringing me along. Resources will be rationed aboard a ship, no matter how advanced. And the idea of being left behind, of Geoff sacrificing his chance in order to remain behind with me, which I know he would, is unbearable." Cupping Darian's chin, she smiled tremulously. "Surely you can see this is my only chance?"

Darian capitulated without a moment's reluctance. She truly hadn't thought of it this way. In fact, she hadn't thought about it at all. Gran had been so involved from the beginning, so Darian had just taken for granted that this was enough for her to qualify—when it might not be. If any other frail seventy-five-year-old had expressed an interest in joining the crew, they would have been denied in the politest of ways.

"I'm sorry for hovering, Gran," Darian said. "I know you hate that."

"It comes from love, in your case, sweetheart." Gran ran her thumb across Darian's cheekbone.

"Whatever you choose to do, I'm behind you a hundred percent. When it comes to Walker, I would recommend letting him in more on what you want and why. If I've been in denial about the repercussions, so has he," Darian said.

"Then we'll do all the treatments today that Raoul finds advisable, and when I get back to the house, I'll inform Geoff."

"All right. Sounds good." Darian watched Raoul reach for the larger wand again.

Gran caressed the shape of Darian's right ear, a touch that sent her back in time to her childhood. "And yes, you can tell Samantha. She deserves to know." Gran smiled broadly and winked. "After all, she's family."

Samantha had walked into her office in the Town Hall library, distractedly taking her seat behind the old oak desk, when a voice she knew only too well made her snap her head up.

"Working overtime, Ms. Pike? Again?" Desmond Miller, chairman of the Elder Council, stood in the doorway. Dressed in a gray, three-piece suit and a crisp white shirt, he held his hand primly clasped in front of him. The way the man tilted his head when delivering stealthy criticisms had always irked Samantha.

"Just about to leave, actually, Chairman Miller." Samantha had tried to be on a first-name basis with Miller, and he had called her Samantha a few times, but mostly he addressed her as Ms. Pike, which forced her to return to calling him Chairman Miller. It was obvious that he enjoyed their little game. Miller loved running Dennamore, and the other council members were in his pockets, except for a few of them. Samantha had overheard him go at the people on the council as a complete megalomaniac would, and she suspected the council members were divided into complete Miller devotees and the ones who still maintained a mind of their own.

"I'm glad I caught you then. I would imagine you'd keep the door to the library locked after closing hours though. We wouldn't want anyone to sneak in, would we?" Miller walked into her office and sat down in the visitors' chair.

"What can I do for you, *Desmond*?" Samantha had had enough of this man a long time ago, and her patience for his power games had diminished during the last few months.

Miller blinked. "I wanted to inform you of the latest decision of the Elder Council, as it affects you directly."

"Me? Personally?" Samantha squared her shoulders and raised her chin.

"In a manner of speaking. We're putting together a group of unbiased members to conduct a full inventory of the archives. While this activity is in progress, nobody will be allowed there or be able to use any of the books and items for their research. This rule even goes for Phileas Beresford."

"An inventory? But I've worked on cataloguing the archive for years. Why is this responsibility being outsourced?" Samantha was furious but also sure something else was brewing.

"We've been too cavalier with the precious artifacts and books in the archives. Our ancestors placed them in that room for a reason, and just like your predecessor, you've been too lenient when it comes to allowing people to take things out of storage and even leave this very building with them." Miller had the audacity to wiggle an index finger at her.

Furious now, Samantha leaned forward so fast, he pressed back in his chair before he caught himself. "Are you accusing me of criminal conduct? Or my aunt, who had this job before me?"

"Criminal? Far from it." Desmond pinched the knife-sharp creases in his trousers. "As I said, we suspect too much leniency, a 'let go' attitude we can ill afford. For a long time, I've wanted to create a museum to show off the objects that are the most spectacular. I think we can use some of the meadows to showcase such a building museum."

And no doubt name it after Miller. Why were some politicians hell-bent on getting their name on a plaque or a statue?

"An interesting thought," Samantha said slowly. "And as it's taken me years to catalogue about twenty percent of the objects and books, how long will this group keep the basement off-limits?"

"Oh, not that long. I'm sure a group of ten people can work through the rest in a few months." Miller flicked his pale fingers dismissively.

"Months." Shaking her head, Samantha had to reel herself in. "You're not serious?"

"I am. I calculated the square footage and shelf space down there, and it was simple arithmetic after that. Four months at the most, I'd say."

"I don't mean to be rude, but you have no idea what you're talking about," Samantha said, her voice hitting a low register that got through to the most obnoxious person. "The archives are massive. The items need not just cataloguing, but research and evaluation! You can't just find ten random people who muddle through this by just counting them and giving them a designation. If I'd settled for that, I'd have been done my first year as head librarian."

Desmond changed into an even pastier pale. "No need to get all up in arms. If anyone, I'm the affronted one in this equation. You have had too much freedom to come and go as you please among our people's prized possessions."

"What do you mean with 'our people,' exactly?" Samantha forced herself to remain seated. She wanted to jump across the desk and throttle Miller, and this was so unlike her, she barely recognized herself. Perhaps her suddenly more assertive persona was just as much of a shock for Miller, as he pushed his chair back from the desk. To have a clear escape route?

"Our people, the true Dennamore inhabitants who are direct descendants of the settlers who came over from Europe." Miller straightened his tie. "Those people are the only ones with a say-so when it comes to our archives."

"Well, I think all the people of Dennamore, despite their heritage, should know the truth and have access to these items. I can see where a museum might serve this purpose, I'll give you that. However, locking me, or my colleagues, out is untenable. What will the public think when they learn of this decision? We might lose all credibility."

Miller shrugged, and perhaps he had recovered from his onset of nerves just now, judging from his smug expression. "That is something you should have thought of before you gave special treatment to people like Beresford and snotty high school kids claiming to need access because of some self-important schoolwork assignment." He spat the words, obviously not impressed by the local, well-renowned high school.

"When will this new policy commence?" Samantha thought fast. She wouldn't be able to stop Miller and the council, but if it weren't effective immediately, *Velocity*'s crew might have a valuable window of opportunity. "I'll need time to get the items and books on loan returned, or your ten people won't be able to catalogue anything with accuracy, which will shine a bad light on the council's decision." Samantha eyed Miller stealthily. Two could play this political game, and she could see how he calculated the pros and cons.

"Four days. That gives you until Saturday." Miller stood. "I'll expect you to leave your access card to the archives with security when you exit the building after work."

"Of course. Anything to work in compliance with the Elder Council." Clenching her teeth, Samantha gave Miller a sweet smile. Apparently, her fangs still showed, as he quickly stood and moved behind the visitors' chair.

"Very well, then. Glad we could settle this situation amicably." He walked out the door a little too fast to maintain his arrogance. "Good evening."

Samantha remained in her chair for another minute, fuming, but also thinking of what they needed to do to work around this new development. She was about to page Holly, when a thought she felt wasn't as paranoid as it would have seemed just yesterday made her decide to wait until she was in the car.

After leaving the building, and surrendering the archive access card, she got into her car and attached her speaker to her lapel. "Samantha to Holly. Are you available?"

"I am. What's up?" Holly sounded calm.

"We have a situation at Town Hall that means we need to move up our plans for the archive. Everything needs to happen a lot faster because the chairman wants to send in a team to start cataloguing. There's no way we can hide that we've emptied several shelves."

"I see. Are you still meeting Carl to go into the archives?"

"Yes. I need to page him. He's probably waiting in the tunnel, expecting me to come down via the elevator to get him. Miller had me give up my access card, which meant I had to leave through the front door."

"I'm going to join you. If Darian is available and Camilla is still all right, she might be able to help us as well." Holly was clearly on the move already, as Samantha could hear her footsteps hurrying across a creaking floor.

"I'll page both of them," Samantha said. "It'll be my pleasure to finally show you the archive, Captain, no matter the circumstances."

"I look forward to it. See you in the tunnel. Crowe out."

Samantha knew they hadn't fully got the hang of it when it came to titles and how to sign on and off the speakers in a professional way, but they were going to have to learn fast. Things were moving with increasing speed when it came to discoveries and risks, and if they didn't get it right, they could lose everything they were working for.

Holly saw the other three waiting for her at the end of the long tunnel that stretched for miles under Dennamore. She had entered the tunnel via Philber's basement and found one of the haulers sitting conveniently by the access point. After slipping into the seat, she took off down the wide tunnel, and once past *Speeder One*, she reached Samantha, Darian, and Carl within minutes.

"Report," Holly said as she jumped off the hauler. She could tell from Samantha's thinly pressed lips that they had no time to waste.

Samantha gave her a brief account of what Desmond Miller had said in her office only a short while ago. Taking stock, she thought fast about what they needed to do most urgently. "He always was a weasel," she said slowly, while her mind worked the problem. "Even when he played golf with my father and a few others, he was a backstabber. That's what Dad said, anyway, and normally he never spoke ill about another single soul." She looked back at the hauler. "In the back of the hauler are containers on wheels. Four of us are here tonight, but we can make a few runs, I believe."

"Excuse me? Runs?" Samantha asked.

"We all realize that we have to get as much out from under Miller's nose as possible before he sends his damn posse in." She raised a hand. "I know, I know, it's not their fault, but they're going to do his bidding since he's their boss. We will take shifts, collect everything directly related to the settlers and the *Velocity*, and take it to the mothership. Anything from the time after our ancestors buried the ship and put the speeders in the underground shuttle bay stays." Holly couldn't help noticing how using the words "our ancestors" still made everything inside her tingle.

"Most of what's relevant for us is located in the oldest part of the archive, at the back of the larger room." Samantha seemed to understand now. "We're looking for anything that documents the landing, technology, and so on."

"And you're sure we can get in without your access card?" Holly asked.

"Absolutely." Samantha walked over to the back of the hauler. "We better get started."

Darian had stood silently but now began pulling the metal containers off the back of the hauler, with Carl's help. She was still subdued, and Holly chastised herself. Why hadn't she asked about Camilla right away? Granted, Holly had a way of developing laser focus when she had an assignment, but she still had time to show an interest.

"How's Camilla doing?" Hoping her question didn't sound too much like an afterthought, she studied Darian's expression as each of them hauled a large container toward the smaller elevator at the end of the tunnel under Town Hall.

"I'm still not sure how to feel. She's doing wonderfully. Her pain is at a one or two on the scale. She even wanted to walk up the stairs to Brynden 4 herself, but Raoul put a stop to that, as she must develop her muscles more before she makes such an attempt. For the first time since I can remember, she's not in agony—and she hasn't had to take a single painkiller. Raoul says she'll need more treatments, but after she undergoes the procedure that includes wearing a NIEC, her body will do the rest. She'll be...well." Darian's voice trembled, and she cleared her throat.

"That's wonderful news, but I can tell that you're torn." Holly spoke quietly as they stopped by the elevator console, absentmindedly running her fingertips in the pattern that would summon the elevator.

"I am. It'll be invasive in a way that rivals going under the knife at our hospitals. Raoul and Gran are confident, but...she's my gran."

"And that makes you nervous." Samantha touched Darian's arm briefly. "And that's perfectly natural."

Darian nodded, but as the elevator door slid open, it was obvious that her focus shifted, and she stepped into her role as chief of security. It didn't surprise Holly that Darian was armed. A sidearm sat strapped in its harness on her right hip, and Holly's NIEC identified it as a low-grade dazer—non-lethal but packing enough power to incapacitate a person from thirty feet.

They entered the elevator, somewhat cramped because of the containers, even if they stacked them two and two. As they reached the level of the Town Hall basement, Darian scanned the door and what was behind it.

"No life signs detected," she said quietly. "Let me go first, just to be sure."

The door slid open, not making more than a whisper, and Darian glanced outside and then stepped out, giving the others a signal to follow her. Carl quietly placed the containers on the basement floor. The wheels were made of something resembling rubber and rolled effortlessly on the floor.

Samantha hurried over to the corner of the basement, where a small slot opened as she approached. Holly had never been in the Town Hall basement, and her NIEC had no information stored about the location of this secret entrance to the archive. A part of the bedrock swiveled open, and this time it made a crunching sound as it moved inward. Holly winced. "Damn, that's too loud." She hissed the words and cast a glance toward the staircase at the far end of the basement. "Hurry. Get inside."

They pressed through the narrow opening. The containers fit as if they'd been made for this purpose, leaving only half an inch on either side.

Holly stopped after taking a few steps inside the archive, the bedrock opening closing behind them. They had to be in the newer section, as it was enormous. Row after row of books, maps, magazines, papers, and—kept in acrylic boxes—art objects filled the space.

"That's amazing. I don't know what I expected, but this is…" Holly didn't have enough words."

"And you still haven't seen the best part," Darian said, smiling. She motioned toward the far end of the archive. "Come on. We better hurry. There's no way of knowing if Miller won't find it in his shriveled little heart to do a little cataloguing of his own."

Holly followed Darian along one of the aisles, pulling her container behind her. They reached a low, very old, oak door.

"Samantha, you need your access card for this room." Carl groaned.

"No, she doesn't." Darian pulled out her trackpad and ran it over the lock. The digits lit up and then started flickering in a random pattern. "This lock isn't monitored on any intranet, as the computers down here aren't connected other than among themselves. So, no little alert will go off on the security monitors." She slid her fingertips along the trackpad, and the lock clicked open.

"Well, that's handy," Carl said, grinning. He lifted his container and was literally bouncing to get inside.

"When we collect items, we need to be consistent," Holly said. "If we find something we know belongs on the *Velocity*, we take everything in that category."

"Makes sense," Samantha said. "I'm going down to the far-end wall. I know we collected all the NIECs, but I want to start there and go through the shelves from that area."

"Good idea." Holly nodded. "Carl, you start to the left, Darian to the right, and I'll go from here. Keep your voices low, even if I doubt anyone will hear you in here. If you're in trouble, tap your speaker twice. Any questions?"

"Got it, Captain," Carl said and even saluted before he hurried to the left of the room. Samantha and Darian moved in their directions, and Holly decided to start in the center aisle and work her way from there.

It didn't take her long to find a flat metal box, about eight by eleven inches, boasting the alien symbol for Insignias. Holly pulled it to her and ran her finger along the faint green ridge on the front of it. The lid flipped open, and she looked down at row after row of rank insignias, in two layers. She closed it and tucked it in under her arm. Perhaps this was the last thing the crew gave up after the Elders on the *Velocity* decided they weren't going back to their home world. She kept perusing the shelves, one by one, sometimes pulling one of the ladders attached to them with her, to reach the top shelves. It was when she climbed up at the far end of the second row of shelves that she found a large crate of the same metal alloy, but this one was too large and too heavy for her to manage on her own.

"Hey, Carl," she whispered, not daring to raise her voice. "I need a hand."

"Coming!" He was closer than she realized and rounded the corner of a bookcase two aisles away. "I haven't found anything that looks remotely alien. What did you discover, Captain?"

"Can you grab one of the ladders on the other side, and I'll show you." Holly pointed across the aisle they were in.

Carl quickly hooked another sliding ladder next to hers and climbed up beside her. His eyes grew bright when he saw the crate. "Hey, that looks promising and heavy."

"It is. It might just barely fit into one of our containers. On three?" Holly counted, and they pulled the crate toward them. "There are indentations on the side. Hold on so we don't fall and break our necks when we take it down."

"I'll catch you," Darian said and showed up below them. Samantha joined her, and with their combined efforts, they managed to lower the box.

"I have two things so far," Holly said as she stepped off the ladder. She pointed to the smaller box. "That contains rank insignias for the crew. And this…" She paused and drew a deep breath. "Let's open it and see."

Samantha slid her finger along the now-familiar ridge-opening mechanism. Nothing happened. "Hm. Now what?" She tried again, but still nothing. "I have no idea what I'm doing wrong."

"We don't have time to experiment here," Holly said. "We'll take it to *Speeder One* to begin with." She looked at the others. "I know Carl came up short. Did you two find anything we need to lay our hands on?"

"These things. Small scrolls without boxes attached to them." Darian walked to the end of the shelf unit and returned with four glass-like containers. Holly quickly counted thirty-six scrolls in each, placed standing up in six rows of six. "More to research." She loved the research part of these discoveries, but the sense of urgency about what they were doing made it impossible to truly look forward to it.

"I found a shelf with some crates I need help with." Samantha motioned behind her. "Not all of them are heavy, but two of them weigh a ton."

It took them another forty-five minutes to secure their finds in the containers they brought with them. The largest crate fit its container as if it were made for it.

"Carl," Samantha said, "you're young and strong. Take a quick walk along the bookcases and just do a last once-over. If we miss something important…" Her voice broke. She cleared her throat and shook her head. "We might have a few more days, but we also may not set foot in this basement for a very long time, if ever again, if they can prove we stole any items." She blinked rapidly a few times.

"On it," Carl said and began walking briskly through the aisles.

"Samantha." Darian took her hand. "We'll be back. More important, you'll return and finish the cataloguing the right way. That idiot Miller won't be in power forever, and not all the councilmembers are horrible people."

"I know. I know." Samantha gave Darian a soft smile, making Holly feel she was intruding on something far too private.

"Sorry about that," Samantha said, letting go of Darian's hand. "Didn't mean to get all emotional."

"I don't blame you," Holly said and then turned her head as Carl returned. "Anything?"

"Just this. Glad I got to find something, at least." He handed over what looked like a glass ball with a high-viscosity liquid inside that seemed to float. "My NIEC knows nada what this is."

Holly took it, and her NIEC nearly made her topple over as it sent the knowledge forward so fast, it hurt. "Goddamn it! It's a grenade." She held it carefully.

"Fuck!" Darian pushed Samantha behind her and stepped away from Holly.

"Don't worry. It's not armed. I can't believe they stored a single grenade under their Town Hall." Holly groaned, and then she pulled off her hoodie and placed the beautiful, but lethal, object in the hood, wrapping the entire fabric around it. She tucked it in among some of the other items, making sure it couldn't dislodge. "Carl. When your NIEC doesn't know, just assume it's dangerous, all right?"

"Ah. Um. Yeah. Absolutely." Carl was pale and stuttered a bit, but he still reached for the crate with the grenade when it was time for them to leave. The young man had guts.

They made it to the hidden door, and Holly and Darian both listened before Darian opened it via the small console. She poked her head out, and after a few moments, she carefully pulled her container through. One by one, they followed her, and Holly prayed that the heavy cargo wouldn't make the wheels squeak. Thankfully, the aliens made durable objects, and the containers slid along the floor almost silently.

After opening the elevator door, they pushed the containers in first, and this time, they couldn't stack them two and two. They were too heavy to lift, which meant they would have to go down to the tunnel twice.

"Darian and I will stay behind. Samantha, you and Carl go down and send the elevator back up for us. Don't worry about removing the containers. It'll take the two of you too long. It's vital to get out of here fast."

"Yes, Captain," Samantha said. She and Carl pressed themselves into the elevator, Samantha half-sitting on the large crate. The door closed, and just as it did, Holly heard voices.

CHAPTER FIFTEEN

Darian nudged Holly toward the staircase that she knew had a crawl space underneath. They ran as quickly and quietly as they could over to the darker end of the basement hallway. Pushing at Holly to go under the stairs first, Darian pulled out her stunner and slipped in after her.

"Any guesses?" Holly breathed the question into Darian's ear.

"Sounds like more than two people. Not sure." Darian made sure her stunner was set on the lowest grade. She really didn't want to shoot anyone, especially as she had no idea if this weapon handled like a taser. Her NIEC showed her how it was done but didn't provide details.

The voices grew louder, and Darian recognized Miller's voice as one of them.

"Miller," Holly murmured.

Darian squeezed Holly's arm as a warning. Now she could make out what the council chairman was saying. "You should have seen Ms. Pike's face when I gave her the news today. She has run that library, not to mention the valuable archive, with full autonomy far too long. Just because her old aunt was considered a saint, this woman isn't above the rules and regulations of our town."

Darian clenched her teeth, wishing she could stab the despicable man straight through the steps between them.

"I can see that you engaged us just in time," a female said in a prim voice. "She's popular and, I suppose, good at what she does from a country-librarian point of view. This is why I suggested that

Mr. Green here take over the cataloguing. That way, Ms. Pike can dedicate her hours doing what she's good at—handing over books and receiving returns." The woman gave a snickering kind of laughter that ended in a giggle.

"Oh, God. I know this woman," Holly whispered. "She's the wife of one of the other elders."

"I'm happy to put my services to your disposal, Chairman Miller. I will again emphasize that I won't tolerate interference by someone less qualified than my own staff."

"Don't worry. We have confiscated the access cards. If anyone were to enter this door, it'd show up on the guard's monitors right away. Just wait until you see what treasures you will have at your very fingertips, Mr. Green." Miller chuckled, and now Darian could see him as he walked over to the main entrance to the archive. He produced the large key and an access card and opened it. "Voilà!" he said with a terrible American pronunciation that made the word sound more like "voyilla" and, with a sweeping gesture, showed his guests in.

When all three had stepped inside, Darian slipped out from under the stairs. Holly was right behind her as they ran toward the other end of the basement hallway. Darian had the elevator door open when Holly caught up with her, and she shoved the captain inside. She glanced behind her, saw that the door to the archive was still closed, and pressed herself in and to the side, relieved when the door closed with a muted hiss.

"Damn it, that was close," Holly said darkly. "I have to say Samantha knows how this man operates. I never liked him but honestly didn't care much one way or the other. I regret that now."

"And the way he spoke about her—" Darian stopped talking as the elevator door opened and two frantic-looking faces glared at them.

"What happened?" Samantha barked. "You took forever!"

"We had company." Darian stepped out, followed by Holly.

Samantha grabbed Darian by the shoulders, looking intently into her eyes. "And?"

"We're fine." She gave Samantha and Carl a rundown on what had just happened. She didn't sugarcoat what had been said about Samantha but kept her voice matter-of-fact.

Carl reacted stronger than Samantha did. His dark eyes turned to narrow slits, and he spoke with an underlying growl. "They don't know what they're talking about. They have no fucking clue."

"They don't matter, Carl," Samantha said and put a hand on his arm. Her expression was stoic, and the way she raised her chin told Darian that Miller better keep away from her in the imminent future.

"We have to take our containers to *Speeder One* and store them in the cargo area." Holly pointed at the hauler. "There should be a crane at the back to load them."

Carl and Darian hurried over and deployed the sleek-looking metal crane. It effortlessly hoisted the crates onto the back of the hauler, and when Darian returned to the front, Samantha was at the controls.

"Ready," Darian said after checking that Carl and Holly were in their seats.

Samantha tore down the tunnel toward *Speeder One*, her lips pressed to a fine line. Her hands flew over the controls, and Darian knew that compared to flying the speeder, driving the hauler was nothing, but they were going very fast.

"Why not take your foot off the gas just a tad?" Darian murmured.

"What? Oh. Of course." She slid her finger back marginally along the blue line on the small console and flexed the fingers of her other hand a few times. "I swear I'm not losing it, but...I don't know. I just had this awful feeling."

"I know what you mean. I felt like that when you suffered from hypothermia. We're going to have to learn to deal with the fact that we'll both possibly be in danger on and off in the future. It doesn't make it easier, but perhaps it is a little bit more of a familiar feeling to me, as a cop."

"True." Samantha shook her head. "And we'll get the hang of it, I'm sure."

Darian thought of her own dread when Samantha had collapsed. "We will. The real difference is that we, um, care about each other. That's what can throw a wrench in the wheel. We're both good at what we do, and I plan to start training the crew in combat skills as soon as we have recruited a large-enough group."

"I'm the first to sign up."

Now Samantha gave a real smile and less of a feral grin.

"Me too," Holly said from behind.

"And me. I have zero fighting skills," Carl added.

"Well, then. Sooner or later you'll be all mine," Darian said and chuckled, glad they could at least attempt lighthearted conversation.

❖

After summoning the group to *Speeder One*, Carl and Walker changed the configuration of the crew seats. Instead of rows, they folded some seats into the floor and changed the others to a square formation, facing each other, the large crate in the middle.

"Here's the stubborn thing that won't open," Darian said, looking around at the crewmembers.

Holly studied her find, trying to figure out what she was missing. "It has more options when it comes to the ridges and indentation. None of them are lit up by the different colors we've become accustomed to, though. Thoughts?"

"I assume you have tried tons of combinations?" Walker rubbed his chin. "And the fact that it seems dormant...could it be out of power?"

"I suppose so," Claire said. "But at the same time, nothing else is. And bringing it aboard the speeder was the right thing to do. If it had been depleted of power, it should have started a new charge while in here." She slipped off her seat and knelt next to the crate. "With all these markings, it's as if they've given us too many options."

"A puzzle?" Holly crouched next to Claire. "That seems farfetched."

"Not a puzzle. Code. For only the person, or persons, who locked it to open it." Claire gestured to the crate. "For some reason, this was stored in the old archives, not aboard any of the speeders, and not aboard the *Velocity*. That fact has to be significant, right?" She looked around at the others.

"That's a really good deduction," Samantha said slowly. "But why? What could they need off the ship so badly?"

After a prolonged silence, Claire and Holly retook their seats.

"Either way, I think we should keep it here for now," Holly stated. "I'm not comfortable having it where we can't reach it if we need to take off with the shuttle."

"Agreed." Darian nodded. "I'll put it in secure storage in the back until we figure out what it is and what to do with it."

"I'm just going to take a picture of it and share it with all of you," Holly said and did so, using her trackpad to document all sides of the crate, even underneath. "There. If you would, I'd like everyone to spend some time trying to solve this code. Not only is it in an alien language, but it's not presented like any of their regular texts."

After Darian had stowed the crate, they continued the meeting. Darian briefed the others in more detail about their heist at the archives.

"I suppose this is burning another bridge of sorts," Camilla said calmly. "It was unavoidable, but surely this puts pressure on the timeline we have left to recruit more crew."

"It does." Holly wanted to stand, to pace, as that sometimes helped her think faster and better, but the limited space available in the speeder didn't allow for much pacing. "And I've pondered it, even more so after hiding under the staircase with Darian. Let me bring up a few points." She mentally placed her ideas into mental compartments, which was her way of remaining focused.

"We need sixty-six crewmembers, willing to carry NIECs. Camilla and Walker have gone over all the suggestions you've come up with, and we're close. Apart from that, we need at *least* twenty more, and that's pushing it. Forty more would be better, and that still leaves room for passengers." Holly stopped talking as something inside her clicked into place with an almost audible snap.

"Holly?" Claire touched her lower arm briefly.

"What? Oh. I apologize. My NIEC…it seems to do things more quickly than I would prefer. Give me a moment." Thinking faster than she ever had before, she closed her eyes to avoid the distraction of nine concerned faces around her. She rubbed her damp palms along her thighs and then continued. "We haven't spoken a lot about why we're doing all this. Why we're trying to gather a crew, find all the technology, get the speeders and the *Velocity* ready. We just assume this is what we're meant to do, and we haven't voiced what we're going to do *exactly*, after we've met all those goals."

"Aren't we going to Dwynna Major?" Samantha asked slowly. "Isn't that the purpose?"

"It's part of it, but it can't be just about curiosity, or a desire for adventure. It has something to do with this yearning most of you have felt, that I moved back in time not to experience, or Claire, who never moved away. The same urgency. We want to go to Dwynna Major—"

"Because we've inherited the longing for home that our ancestors felt after the Elders on the ship trapped them here." Camilla nodded. "I've read so much of Bech'taia's texts, and even if she and Gai'usto settled and had children, it was a hard life that didn't resemble anything they were used to, full of the challenges, dangers, diseases, and prejudice that came with that time. We can't know if they originated from an enlightened society, but they still yearned for home."

Holly nodded slowly. "And that's why we're risking everything, including our lives, to make that return journey. We have no idea why they came to Earth. Natural resources? First wave of an invasion that went awry? Curiosity? Were they explorers or colonizers?"

"If they were, they must have learned quickly that we were tossing out the British and claiming autonomy." Darian snorted. "I just don't get that feeling from the journal. They don't seem hostile. If they were, would they bring their matched and coupled mates with them? That doesn't make sense."

"Agreed," Holly said. "Just throwing it out there. Either way, the point is, we've done a lot we never thought we'd ever be part of, and we're doing it for the yearning to take the *Velocity* back to Dwynna Major. Also, we don't have weeks or, worse, months to vet potential crewmembers. We have to make this recruitment an event."

"What do you mean?" Samantha looked startled.

"Did any of you ever truly consider turning this opportunity down?" Holly answered with a question of her own.

Everyone shook their heads an emphatic no.

"Then neither will those crewmembers who see the *Velocity* set down on the meadows." Holly held her breath as she watched the others catch on. One by one, they blinked in surprise and then looked back and forth at each other—and finally at her.

"Are you crazy?" Philber asked, scratching his beard.

"Not at all." Holly waited for more questions or statements.

"You mean to take the *Velocity* up and land her, and when people rush to see what's going on, *then* ask them to join up?" Darian gaped.

"Something like that. I estimate we'll have to keep her cloaking off-line for only an hour or two."

"And the military planes that will arrive with bombs to drop on our heads?" This time Raoul incredulously stared at her.

"Claire. If we remain between the mountains, will the various radar systems available on Earth be able to detect us?" Holly asked.

"Um. No, Captain. Until we take off. Unless we're cloaked, of course."

Holly smiled. "Of course."

"What about all the yahoos that will take pictures and send photos to the FBI, CIA, NSA, the military, and God knows where?" Philber waved his hands in the air, obviously flustered.

"Claire, I have to ask you something else." Holly checked the imaginary boxes in her mind. "Can you erect a shield that prevents that from happening?"

"Yes. Using the prism-shields. You can walk right through it, but if someone directs an imaging device of any kind, it'll just bounce off." Claire was taking notes on her computer.

"Well, that sounds reassuring. How about anyone calling said agencies," Walker asked quietly.

"Claire?" Holly said.

Snapping her head up, Claire nodded absentmindedly. "Scrambling. We know how to do that on Earth already, but with a few well-placed antennas from any of the speeders, they won't be able to call out until we've left."

"Wow." Darian grinned at Holly. "If I wasn't already so glad you're the captain, I'd be celebrating now. It's obvious why you were chosen."

"Thank you, but honestly, this isn't about me so much as what you and the future crew will be able to do. This time, Claire had the information I needed. You're the experts in your respective areas."

"Hm. I almost buy that," Darian said, smirking. "But it takes an agile mind to put the pieces together and form a plan. And that mind is yours."

"As much as this society for mutual admiration is lovely, what do you suggest, I mean, in detail?" Philber asked acerbically.

Holly merely glanced at him through narrowed eyes, and he had the good sense to lean back in his seat.

"We have to work out a doable timeline. Before we can take the mothership out from under the lake, we have to recruit at least twenty people, and the top choices on Camilla and Walker's list are a good place to start. Considering what might be happening in the library right this minute, we must do this tomorrow. Should we gamble on bringing all of them down here at the same time and then show off *Speeder One,* or should we talk to them, say, five at a time?"

Camilla raised her hand. "All at once. Rip off the bandage, if you will. We can inform people and talk about our findings until we're asphyxiated, but nobody will believe us unless they have some sort of tangible proof. Just think of how you and Claire were roped in. You found us, Holly, and Claire was present in her clearing when you located the sensors in the rock. You saw physical, tangible proof."

Holly nodded. "A valid point." She looked down at the copy of the list in her hand. "I know three of these people. I'll invite them. Walker, there are three police officers, so they're yours to approach. Samantha and Raoul. Between the two of you, I'd say you know the rest. Can you divide them between you? If you're unfamiliar with anyone, perhaps Claire can step in?"

"If they have a car, I'm probably acquainted with them." Claire nodded. "We'll get them here. When?"

"Tomorrow evening at eight." Holly watched the others nod. "All right. It's getting late, and I have work to do, both with this," she said and waved the list, "and my day job."

"And we're all hungry." Camilla stood and then stopped in midmotion. "What?" She looked around the crew, and Holly could tell that she had no idea why they were gaping at her.

"Gran," Darian whispered as tears began to fall down her cheeks. "You jumped up like you were twenty years old."

If the situation hadn't been so poignant, Holly would have laughed at the otherwise so put-together woman's expression. Camilla looked down at herself, standing in the center of them all, back straight and joints moving smoothly.

"Well, now. I didn't even think about it. I just...got up. It's been so long since I could do that, but still I just rose as if it were 1985 again." She covered her mouth with a trembling hand, but Holly knew the tremors stemmed from emotions rather than arthritic pain. The finger joints and knuckles weren't swollen anymore.

Darian flew out of her chair and embraced her grandmother. One by one the others joined in until only Holly and Claire were left. That didn't last long. Walker reached out and gripped Holly's hand and pulled her into the celebratory embrace, and another arm, Holly wasn't sure whose, did the same with Claire. It was a brief but heartfelt group hug, and this was the first time since Frances died that Holly felt she truly belonged with other people.

CHAPTER SIXTEEN

Darian stood next to Gran, who was sitting in her favorite armchair in the parlor, with Walker on the other side. Brandon was hovering in the doorway to the kitchen area. Sitting on a dining-room chair in front of Gran, Raoul was pulling out his medical equipment of both the alien and human variety.

"Are you sure we shouldn't do this in the speeder?" Walker asked. He looked worried, and Darian couldn't blame him.

"I have everything I need. And honestly, I don't foresee any problems. If there's an adverse effect despite my conviction of the contrary, then we'll pull the NIEC off." Raoul looked pointedly at Gran. "Now, I want to know once and for all that you're doing this, knowing that it might not work out for you."

"I realize this. I want to do it." Gran regarded him calmly and then took Walker's hand. "I better hold on to this one, or he might faint on top of me."

"Camilla." Walker sighed, but Darian saw that he squeezed her hand. Just a few days ago, he couldn't have done that, because of her swollen joints.

"All right. The time is seven a.m., and we're doing our first attempt to pair a NIEC with Camilla Tennen." Raoul pulled the NIEC out of the box and gave it to Camilla. "There you go."

"Thank you, dear." Gran held the small metal oval with a steady hand. "And I just push it against the base of my skull?" She glanced at Darian.

"That's right."

Gran moved without hesitation and pushed the oval in under her elegant updo. The NIEC immediately lodged onto her scalp, and Darian observed the now-so-familiar sight of the filaments with their little metal "feet" disappear into Gran's hair. It took a good five seconds, which felt long enough for Darian to fear it might not work for her grandmother, before Camilla closed her eyes and clung to Walker's hand.

"Camilla?" Walker said huskily.

"Give her time," Raoul said. "Remember, it takes a while. From what I've seen, the older the person is, the longer it takes for them to snap out of the initial vertigo and nausea."

"Not nauseous, just dizzy," Gran murmured. "I'm all right."

Darian dared to relax some, but until Gran opened her eyes and seemed like herself, she would be on edge.

It took ten minutes before that happened. Her eyes huge and sparkling like sapphires, Gran locked her eyes on Darian first. "That was some trip, sweetheart." She was a pale around the lips, but other than that, she seemed all right.

"And now?" Darian asked, crouching next to Gran's armchair.

"I need a nap to digest everything my NIEC is filling my mind with." Gran stood, but only after she let go of Walker's hand. "Give me an hour, and I should be able to let you all know what my expertise will be." She rose on her toes and placed a kiss on Walker's cheek. After doing the same with Darian and Raoul, she walked over to Brandon. "Dearest friend. You can breathe now." She cupped his cheek, her fingers pale against his olive-tinted skin. "I promise."

"All right, Camilla." Brandon exhaled audibly. "That's the second time you Tennen women have decided to shave of a few years off my lifespan." He closed his eyes hard. "Want me to escort you?"

"Yes, actually. I may be doing a thousand percent better, but I'm still a little dizzy." She looked over her shoulder as she stuck her arm under Brandon's. "I know the rest of you are busy with preparations today. Please. Brandon will check on me, mainly to keep you all from worrying."

"All right," Walker muttered. "I'll swing by around lunch."

"Me too," Darian said. "I'll be down in the shuttle preparing packages for our presumptive recruits. Just page me and I'll be up here in minutes. All right?"

Gran promised after rolling her eyes and then left the parlor with Brandon.

"Thank God," Walker said. "This...took a toll."

"Sure did." Darian crossed the room to him and gave him a brief hug. "What do you say? Should we get some coffee to go in the kitchen and sort out those welcome packages?"

"I need the distraction so I'm game." Walker patted her shoulder as they made their way into Brandon's domains.

"We could also look at some of the items we haven't categorized yet. I mean, from the heist yesterday." Darian poured coffee into two thermo mugs.

"I'd like that." Walker lit up. "I have mostly done paperwork with Camilla, but I'd love to get my hands on some of the technology. That might help my NIEC show me more clearly where my own expertise lies."

Darian thought about Walker's words as they made their way down the steep staircase to the tunnel. She had been so wrapped up in her own duties, Samantha, and the frantic search for the entrance to the *Velocity* over the last few months, she hadn't thought of Walker's status.

"I'm sorry, Geoff," Darian said, deliberately using his first name as they jumped into the hauler at Brynden 4's access point. "We've ignored you that way. And Carl."

"Hey, don't think of it like that. Maybe the NIECs need a larger selection before the computer can make a reasonable estimation." Walker grinned. "I certainly haven't felt slighted in the least. And young Carl is going to become a great all-around crewmember until he gets older, if you ask me."

Relieved, Darian nodded. "You're right."

They entered the shuttle and began pulling uniforms from the storage. Darian placed them on twenty of the seats together with scroll boxes containing NIECs, speakers, and computers. It took them an hour to make sure they didn't forget anything, but then they moved into the larger area in the back where what Darian called the loot from the previous evening sat in crates.

"I'm not even going to attempt the code on the big one." Darian glared at the offending locked crate by the port bulkhead. "That's going to be a job for Holly, Claire, or Samantha."

"All right." Tapping in commands on a console, Walker engaged a table and two stools to appear out of the floor. Opening the container holding the miscellaneous things Samantha had found, he hoisted an oval metal box onto the table between them. "Heavy enough." He examined the lid and dragged his index finger along the opening mechanism. The lid flipped open toward Darian, and Walker turned the box so she could see the contents.

It took Darian a few moments before her NIEC had identified the objects. Walker's NIEC worked at the same pace as he snapped his fingers only a second afterward.

"These are ration coins." He took one of the round, filigreed coins and held it up. "You register it with your trackpad, and it will be good for a certain amount of foodstuff in the reproducers." He frowned. "Reproducer units are located in all quarters and in the mess halls aboard the *Velocity*," he said.

"Yes." Darian could picture the blueprint of them, even if the technology was beyond her. Claire would know exactly how they worked, though. "You slide the coin in, and depending on how much you've used at any given time, you can ask for special things. The reproducers will always give basic food, but…if you want something else, it is withdrawn from your, well, account, I suppose, that's stored in your coin."

"Why not just keep tabs on it in the trackpads?" Walker held the coin up toward the light. "It's beautiful."

"Maybe not everyone has the trackpads. Family members. Those in the crew without NIECs." Darian watched Walker put the coin back and close the box. She made note of it on her computer, and then they moved on to the next box. Most of the items were spare parts, which they tagged and put into one of the storage bins attached to the bulkheads.

After two hours when they were almost done, Darian stretched her arms over her head, while Walker placed the last box on the table.

It turned out to be a forty- by twenty-inch box that contained another box. The second one had markings that made both Darian and Walker push back from the table.

"What the hell?" Darian bent forward and read the alien text again. "Does that really mean poison?" she asked, her heart beating faster. "Why would they keep poison around?"

"No, not poison. It says venom." Walker ran his finger along the ridge, but nothing happened.

"Oh, don't tell me it's another puzzle box." Darian groaned. She repeated the maneuver, and to her surprise, the lock snapped open, but the lid remained almost closed. "Huh."

"You're the chief of security. Makes sense that probably just you and the captain can open this." Walker nodded thoughtfully.

"Okay. Perhaps we shouldn't open it without protection. Like in a lab." Darian leaned over to the side and peered into the crack created by the barely open lid. "Then again, if something in there was broken, we'd be toast already."

"Agreed."

Carefully, using the tip of her nail, Darian poked the lid open a few inches. "Can you use your flashlight and shine a light under the lid?" she asked.

"I didn't bring a flashlight," Walker said apologetically.

"On your cell phone." Darian grinned at him.

"Ah. I keep forgetting about that one. It's not that I have my cell surgically attached like your generation does." Sheepishly, Walker returned her smile as he fumbled with his cell. "There."

The LED light revealed row after row of narrow glass-like vials, about two inches long and half an inch wide. They were deeply set in a foam material, meant to keep them from breaking. Darian counted ninety vials. As she lowered the lid carefully, her NIEC caught up, but she also knew she couldn't share everything it told her brain with Walker. "This is part of a weapons' system," she said. "We have to store it in a secure lockbox."

Walker studied her for a moment, but then seemed to decide he needed to take her words at face value. "There are several at aft bulkhead." He carried it over to the lockboxes, and Darian opened the largest one. Walker slid the flat box onto the bottom shelf and drew a deep breath when she closed and locked it.

Darian peered up at him. "Why don't we poke our heads in at Brynden 4 and check on—"

"All hands, this is Samantha. All hell's breaking loose at Town Hall. We need to call our recruits in ASAP." Samantha's voice was low and noncommittal. Darian slapped her speaker in her haste to answer.

"Are you all right?"

"So far. Miller is here with Chief Billings and two of his officers. So far, Miller's just grandstanding and hasn't directed any accusations against me, or—I have to go." Darian's speaker went silent.

"I have to get to Town Hall." Darian hurried toward the hatch.

"I'm coming with you. I know Billings. He's a good man." Walker was right behind her.

Darian knew Samantha's voice so well, it was obvious that she was in more trouble than she let on. She tapped her speaker as they jumped into the hauler with Walker at the controls. "Darian to Holly. Captain, did you get that?"

"I did. I'm getting together the recruits along with the others. You go to Samantha."

"Walker's with me."

"Good. Holly out."

As if he'd read Darian's mind, Walker didn't bother to go by Brynden 4. Instead, he drove to the Town Hall end of the tunnel. Darian already had her plan ready. They would sneak in the back way and, if need be, remove Samantha the same way. No way Miller was getting his hands on the woman she loved.

Samantha kept in the background, observing Desmond Miller, who held court in the hallway just outside the entrance to the library. The ten citizens who had been browsing the shelves inside when Miller showed up had just been escorted out of Town Hall by a couple of police officers and asked to return another day. Samantha and her two colleagues stood together, merely observing the drama.

"What's he talking about?" Beatrice, the youngest of the librarians, asked. "I've never had to go down into the basement more than twice in the last six months."

"He's not talking about either of you. I'm not sure who he suspects of wrongdoing, but I'm ultimately responsible," Samantha said, absentmindedly patting Beatrice's shoulder.

"Her! That woman." Miller snarled, his face so red, it hinted toward blue. Was the man working up to a heart attack? Then Samantha realized that Miller was pointing at her with a stabbing index finger. "Samantha Pike," he spat.

The man who was trying to keep up with Miller's tirades, Chief Billings, looked over at her, a surprised expression on his narrow face, filled out only by his impressive beard. Tall and gangly, he towered over the diminutive Miller.

"Let me get this straight. Are you accusing Ms. Pike, who is the head librarian and has worked here for years, of stealing?"

"The people in this town may consider her flawless, but the last few months, I've noticed a lot of coming and going. She, and that other woman she socializes with, Tennen, are here together too much. Their behavior is suspicious."

Chief Billings waved Samantha over. "Ms. Pike? Can you shed some light on Chairman Miller's accusations?"

"I know that Mr. Miller thinks very little of me, but I assure you, Chief Billings, that I'm not a criminal. I know the difference between what belongs to me and what doesn't." Samantha was stunned at how calm she sounded. Inside, she was trembling and certain that Miller would convince Billings to cuff her and perp-walk her out to his police cruiser.

"It's *Chairman* Miller to you, *Ms.* Pike," Miller said, his voice a growl.

"Let's try and calm down here, sir." Billings frowned. "And I have to say that I expect you to provide me with substantial evidence for these serious theft allegations, Chairman Miller."

"All you have to do is come down to the archive and see how much is missing from the shelves. I have no idea what items were stolen, but no doubt they'll garner a pretty sum when changing hands. Who knows? She might be selling them on eBay as we speak."

Chief Billings blinked, and Samantha had to hide a smile at how ridiculous that last sentence sounded.

"Um, Desmond, that theory sounds farfetched. eBay?" Chief Billings exchanged a glance with Samantha that spoke of how unhinged he thought Miller was getting.

"It was an example." Miller pointed down the stairs. "You have to come check out the scene of the crime. That's what you do, right? Unless being a small-town cop makes you too soft and weak." Miller was so wrapped up in his ire, he didn't seem to notice that his scornful remarks didn't sit well with the burly, tall man who had taken over after Walker.

"Let's go downstairs. Would you come with us and unlock the door to the archive?" Chief Billings motioned toward the stairs.

"Certainly." As they walked down the stairs, Samantha turned to Chief Billings. She refused to engage Miller in conversation unless she was forced to. "When did the theft take place?"

"Sometime last night. Miller was here during the evening, and between then and half an hour ago, someone apparently removed some objects from the premises. Do you know who might have access apart from yourself?" Chief Billing asked.

"But I don't have access. I mean, as of yesterday, I handed in my access cards to the guard in the lobby when I went home. If you check the logs, you'll find that I left the building around six p.m." Samantha was glad that the facts were correct, albeit incomplete. She stealthily regarded her small bracelet watch. Darian was on her way. Soon she wouldn't feel so exposed and put on the spot.

They reached the basement, and Desmond hurried toward the open door to the archive, where a group of eight people stood, clearly waiting for him to return.

"These are my scholars, who are about to start cataloguing," Miller stated pompously.

"I see." Chief Billings nodded at the poshly clad men and women. Samantha thought they looked more corporate than scholarly, but who was she to judge? "Folks, you have to remain out here, or up in the lobby, where you can get quite decent coffee from the vending machine." He turned to Samantha. "Ms. Pike, would you show me around in there? You are the expert on this archive as I understand it."

"Of course." Samantha walked inside, starting the tour in the outer area. She could tell that Miller was impatiently waiting for her to reach the older archives.

"I had no idea it was this big. I've been down here a few times, but only to get some blueprints, and I never ventured this far inside." Chief Billings motioned at the long aisles. From what I've seen so far, nothing has been disturbed."

"Not here. In there." Desmond, who was stalking like an irritable panther behind them, pointed to the open door to the old archive. "That's where the oldest, most coveted items are or, should I say *were*, located."

Samantha braced herself and raised her chin, knowing she might not be able to maintain an impassive expression when they walked inside. So much was missing from in there, it would become obvious that whoever had taken the items on the different shelves, and, she realized, made footprints in the dust on the floor, had done so for a lot longer than last night.

"Samantha!" Darian's voice from behind her nearly had her doubling over.

"Walker. What brings you here?" Chief Billings looked confused, which was a new expression for most who knew him.

"I just wanted to make sure that Miller's vendetta against Ms. Pike didn't cause her unnecessary pain." Walker walked over to Samantha's other side.

"Vendetta?" His expression darkening, the chief looked over at Miller. "What is your response to that?"

"They're lying. All of them! That woman," Miller said, indicating Darian, is one of the latest returnees. She's with her grandmother, who's treated as if she's damn royalty. I've seen how people recognize her."

"Grandmother?" Chief Billings glanced at Darian. "Can you shed some light on this situation, because I'm losing track here."

"Sir, I'm Detective Darian Tennen, on leave from LAPD. I came with my grandmother to help her get settled at Brynden 4. We have both become good friends with Samantha and Chief Walker and have been down here together because we needed copies of the old blueprints from the archive."

How easily Darian spoke, and even if all that were true, a lot was left out, obviously.

"Detective? Are you a returnee as well or really planning to return to LA?" Chief Billings rubbed his chin and placed the other hand on his hip."

"Looks like I might stick around, Chief," Darian said.

"If you do and you need a job, come see me," Chief Billing said and nodded.

"Are you insane? You can't employ that woman—they're in this together! I'm not surprised how they've managed to wrap Walker around their little fingers, or, rather, this grandmother has."

"Wait. Brynden 4." Chief Billings held up a hand again to quiet Miller. "Brynden 4. The old Wells house?"

"Camilla Tennen, born Wells, yes." Walker's features looked chiseled in the same bedrock as the basement walls. "And before you open your mouth again, Miller, I suggest you consider your intended words a few more times." He snarled the words, which made Billings hold up a hand for the third time.

"Calm down. I'm going to go into the old archive, and you need to go with me, Chairman, as you seem hellbent on getting on these people's nerves." He rolled his eyes and motioned toward the door. As he walked behind Miller, he looked back over his shoulder. "I need you to wait here. All right?"

"Sure," Walker said amicably. "We'll be around."

This remark seemed to give Chief Billings pause, but he still walked into the old archive after Miller.

"Quick," Darian said. "The basement hallway was empty when we got here. Let's go. We can't be here once Billing sees the empty shelves."

"Not to mention our footprints," Samantha said and strode among the shelves to the door.

"If this had been LA I would have put an officer in charge of us until I returned, but clearly you do things a bit more loosy-goosy in Dennamore," Darian said, which made Walker huff.

"I suppose," he grumbled. "Not the same crimes, or perhaps the same, but not as much of it."

Samantha poked her head outside the door, and the basement was still empty. The voices filtering down the staircase from above suggested that the scholars were helping themselves to the delights in the vending machine. "Come on!" She ran on her high heels over to the hidden elevator and entered the command to open the door, and they all threw themselves inside. Only when the door closed again was she able to draw a full, deep breath. "Oh, God." She slumped against the elevator wall.

"I've got you." Darian wrapped an arm around her waist. "I'm so sorry it got so ugly, but you're out of there now."

"Yes. But—" Samantha looked over at Walker, who nodded slowly. "You've burned your bridges. And, I believe, so have I."

Samantha swallowed hard against the bile that rose in her throat. "We…we knew it might come to this. That it would most likely be the outcome. Our jobs. Our homes."

"Yes, but not like this. Miller forced our hands yesterday." Darian pulled Samantha closer as the door whispered open, and they saw several people standing outside.

"Who…Ho—Captain?" Samantha stared at their captain, who stood at the front of at least twenty people, half belonging to their group. Half were strangers, well, not all of them. Some she recognized as library patrons.

"Glad you're here." Holly nodded. Motioning behind her, she indicated the newcomers. "It's not all twenty of them, there wasn't time for that, but eleven isn't bad. It'll have to do."

"We're on borrowed time," Walker said after nodding at the group of people who, in all honesty, looked quite dazed. Who could blame them? "Billings is with Miller in the archive. He knows that Darian and I are on Samantha's side, and now that the three of us clearly have vanished into thin air, we don't have a lot of time."

"I've gathered that." Holly started walking toward two haulers that sat ready to go.

"Where's Camilla?" Walker asked.

"By *Speeder One*," Holly said shortly. "We figured the only ones they're not going to approach are Philber, Carl, and Raoul. Brynden 4 will get a visit, and so will Walker's house. Mine won't, nor Claire's, but that's of no use to us. Camilla and Brandon brought the bags he has kept packed for the three of you, in case of a development such as this."

"Bags?" Darian frowned. "Like go-bags?"

"Exactly. I don't need one, as I have my computers, human and alien version, and that's all I need."

"What about you?" Darian asked, turning to Samantha as they climbed into the hauler.

"I have everything I want here." Samantha took Darian's hand. "But how did you get the recruiters so fast?"

"As it turned out, Brandon and Camilla had called these eleven and set things in motion already, for later today. When they reached out again, they just showed up on the doorstep of Brynden 4." Holly shrugged. "I heard a few of them talk about a similar sensation as the yearning."

"Huh." Darian looked over her shoulder. "I hope they snap out of that foggy look ASAP."

"Give them time. This is a shock. We took them down into the tunnel and then sealed all access points. Only the senior crew can open them." Holly pulled up to the speeder, where Camilla stood in the hatch opening, waiting for them.

Holly jumped off the hauler and walked over to the other one, where the recruits sat, wide-eyed but remarkably calm. The age span seemed to vary between twenty-five to fifty-five, but one woman looked older than that. "You are all going to be all right. Though we have to be down here for a bit, you haven't committed to anything you may regret later. Do you understand?"

A few said, "Yes, Captain," and others merely nodded.

"Good. Now, walk up the ramp, and you'll get a seat and a welcome package. Don't try to open anything before you're instructed how to. Just relax, and we'll get you something to drink and try to answer your questions."

As the recruits passed them and entered the speeder, Samantha could hear ohs, ahs, and wows. Yes, that was to be expected. She remembered when she first set foot in it. "What's next, Captain?"

Holly pinched the bridge of her nose. "We have to bring *Speeder Two* down, but I'm going to have Darian and Claire fetch it." She shook her head. "You're the chief pilot, but the engineer and the chief of security know how to maneuver the shuttles as well. In the meantime, we have to figure out how to get to the *Velocity*. She needs to launch. Today."

Samantha could see where Holly was coming from. They were out of time, and if they didn't show the inhabitants of Dennamore what they'd been literally sitting on for centuries, they wouldn't be able to recruit enough hands to maneuver the mothership. They couldn't approach groups of individuals like they had today before Miller, and also Billings, called in the cavalry, as in the military and every agency known to mankind. If they could show the people of Dennamore the ship, prove in one shocking event that they were not crazy, that this was true, Samantha knew, and she wasn't sure how she was so certain, that the same instinct that induced the yearning would bring them their crew. It was essential that they did—it was what they were meant to do, and that in turn meant that failure was not an option.

The senior crew was divided into four groups. Camilla, Walker, and Raoul held the introduction for the recruits. Philber and Carl served as their eyes to the world, at least until they had time to launch probes. Darian and Claire had taken the smaller of the haulers to the other end of the tunnel, where *Speeder Two* was kept. Holly knew they could taxi it to meet up with *Speeder One*, but it was still an unknown variable, as they had only started it up before, not actually flown it.

Beside Holly in the aft cargo and lab area of *Speeder One*, Samantha was changing into her uniform, her expression pensive.

"What are you thinking?" Holly said and closed her own uniform. It was snug but comfortable. She opened the flat box containing the rank insignias and attached the captain's pin to her collar. The speaker fused easily with the uniform material. She ran her fingertip along the insignias until she found the one for the chief pilot and navigator. Realizing that she hadn't received an answer, she held it in her hand and turned around. "Samantha?"

"Excuse me? Oh, sorry. I'm afraid I'm a bit scattered all over the place, trying to think up plausible scenarios how to pull all of this off." Samantha's gaze fell upon the insignia. "What's that...oh!"

Holly attached the pin and watched Samantha move her speaker to the uniform, looking like it was an everyday task. "There. All set."

"Thank you." Craning her neck, Samantha peered through the frosted material in the hatch leading to midship. "Wonder how things are going?"

"I don't hear cries of horror, laughter, or throwing up." Holly's attempt to be facetious seemed to relax Samantha marginally. She leaned against the aft bulkhead but then suddenly lost all color and pivoted.

"What?" Holly took Samantha by the shoulders and felt her tremble. "What's wrong?"

"What the hell?" Samantha shoved her fingers through her immaculate blond hair, disheveling it completely. Neither the cursing nor the tousled appearance was like the always well-put-together Samantha Pike. "I felt something. Right here." She pressed her hand against the bulkhead. "No. Wait. Not here." She lowered her gaze. "There. That." She pointed at the big crate Holly had located in the old archive, the one they couldn't open.

"That crate?" Crouching next to it, Holly found herself unceremoniously shoved aside when Samantha knelt on the deck and ran her hands over it. "Yes. Yes!"

"What's going on?" Raoul appeared behind them. "I just want to report that we have eleven volunteers, and three are now getting used to the NIECs...excuse me?"

"Wait," Samantha said slowly. "I mean, that's fantastic, but... this crate. I think I can open it."

Holly had looked at Raoul as he spoke, but now she snapped her head around and took in Samantha's rapt expression. "Are you sure?"

"Sure? No. But fairly confident." Samantha ran her hands in a few different patterns over the lid, but nothing happened. "No. Not like that. Not just with my hands."

"*Speeder Two* present and accounted for, Captain," Claire said from the door, but neither Holly nor Raoul turned around.

"So much for 'yay, you piloted a spaceship for the first time, whoo-hoo'," Claire said and sighed. She paused, but then Holly heard her call Darian over. "Darian, Samantha's up to something with the crate."

Holly could feel the others stare intently at what was going on, but all she could focus on was Samantha's efforts. Then a buzzing feeling in the back of her head traveled through her shoulder and down her left arm, to the bracelet. Images flickered through her mind, and she knew, from one moment to the next, what to do. "Samantha. It has to be both of us."

Samantha stopped her attempts. Holly could tell that Samantha's movements had been right, but they weren't enough. Gripping Samantha's hand, she nodded. "Do it again.

Their hands clasped, Samantha moved in the same pattern she had attempted several times. When she was done, a soft whirring sound came from inside the crate, and then the lid opened with a muted hiss. Looking inside, Holly tried to understand what she was staring at, and what it might be for.

"This," Samantha said and turned to the others, her eyes shining. "This is how we get the *Velocity* out from under the lake."

CHAPTER SEVENTEEN

Samantha stood behind the aft door, watching Holly prepare herself to address the crew. She stood with her back against the helm of *Speeder One* studying the people in the crew seats. For the first time since she and Darian found some pieces of alien technology, Samantha was calm and knew exactly what her task was.

Holly looked formidable in her uniform. Blue, formfitting, with gold and black stripes adorning it in the same pattern, it was recognizable from the computer consoles. Sweeping lines and dots were woven into the material that wasn't quite fabric but looked like it. It was programmable to sustain them outside the ship in space, along with one of the helmets.

"Crew of the *Velocity*." Holly spoke with confidence, and Samantha's heart swelled with pride as she regarded their captain. How Holly had found her way to them was a miracle, and Samantha doubted it could be all chance. The same for Claire, standing on Holly's left, who was the perfect woman for the position of chief engineer. On Holly's right stood Darian, the woman who had started it all, as far as Samantha was concerned. Darian, who held her heart so firmly. Darian, whom she loved.

"To the eleven of you who are new, thank you for coming here in the first place—but most of all, we're grateful that you're staying," Holly said. "For you, the process has been much too fast. You haven't been given the time that some of the senior crew was allowed, which must feel daunting. I want to give all of you another opportunity to change your mind."

Samantha couldn't see the crew's expression, but several heads were shaking, and then a male voice called out, "I'm sure I'm breaking protocol, but there's no way in hell you're getting rid of me now. This is where I have to be."

That summed up what Samantha had felt ever since she put on her NIEC for the first time. Other voices among the new recruits voiced their agreement.

"That's good to hear." Holly raised her hand to quiet the crew. "We're facing a bit of a standoff with Chairman Miller, as you may have gathered, hence the rush to get as many of you here as possible. We still weren't fast enough, as our contact in town tells us Billings is on the lookout for some of us. This means we can't get to the *Velocity* via ground level."

"But what other way is there?" Camilla asked. "And where's Samantha?"

"That's just it, Camilla." Holly clasped her hands behind her back. "Samantha's the solution to getting the mothership from under the lake." She nodded back at Samantha, who knew this was her cue.

She opened the door and walked down the aisle between the rows of crew seats. Both the old and the new crew looked at her with astonishment.

"What is she wearing?" Raoul murmured.

Samantha didn't answer until she was standing next to Darian. "I'm wearing a device that Holly and I found in a large crate with a code lock. This attachment to my uniform will allow me to remotely operate the *Velocity* and then dock with her in orbit, even if her cloaking device is engaged." She shifted the impressive bright-red helmet to her other arm. What looked like a metal backpack made of the same material as the helmet was strapped to her back. The harness keeping it in place reminded Samantha of what bungee jumpers wore when leaping off bridges and cliffs. She didn't want to think of how the harness was already chafing her inner thighs.

"In orbit?" Darian whispered.

"If need be," Samantha said quietly. "I hope to dock with her when she's still on the ground. That'd be easier."

"Well, duh." Darian shook her head.

Holly once again quieted the crew by raising her hand. "We will have to hurry. We have to get three pivotal moments right to fulfill our mission of paying our ancestors' home planet, Dwynna Major, a visit.

One. We can't allow the mothership to remain decloaked long enough for the military or any agency to discover her. Two. This may seem like a contradiction to moment one, but we must keep her decloaked long enough to spark this second yearning in order to recruit enough new crewmembers. Three. Once we cloak her, we take her into orbit, and this will take major cooperation among everyone present here. We haven't even taken *Speeder One* that far up yet, so we'll learn as we go. I have full faith in our respective NIECS to guide us."

It was so quiet in the shuttle-crew section, Samantha felt she was getting tinnitus.

"Any questions?" Holly asked.

Walker raised his hand. "How will we get Samantha topside without Billings sweeping in and arresting her?"

"We're going to fly both shuttles up through the chute and cloak them. There's a protocol for how this is done from a shuttle, and it means opening the aft loading ramp," Samantha said. "Once I have the *Velocity* under control, I'll take off and dock with her. In the meantime, you'll set down together with *Speeder Two*, between my landing site and town. That's crucial moment one, you could say."

"And when the townspeople see the mothership, supposedly a spark will go off in the right ones?" A man Samantha had seen in a police uniform before he changed to his crew uniform asked the question. "I'm Nate, by the way."

"Nate." Samantha tilted her head. "Are you comfortable going against everything you learned—and your boss?"

"No, but I don't have a choice. You're right about the yearning. This is the second time I've felt it, and the last time was when I graduated from college in Rhode Island. And besides, my first chief is here." He nodded at Walker, who returned the gesture.

"To answer your question very briefly. Yes. That's the plan. We need a skeletal crew of seventy-seven, just for the basic maintenance of *Velocity*. We have to have twice that number to not burn ourselves out on the way to Dwynna Major."

A few minor questions found their answers, and then Claire looked over at Darian. "Guess it's time for us to return to *Speeder Two*. We'll be ready to follow you up the chute when you give the word, Captain."

"I'll be piloting *Speeder One*," Holly said. "I want Walker by my side." She motioned for him to take the co-pilot seat, which he did after kissing Camilla's temple.

Darian turned to Samantha. "Don't fall out of the sky," she said, only the faintest of tremors present in her voice.

"I don't plan to." Samantha put the helmet down on an empty seat, wrapped her arms around Darian, and hugged her close. After kissing her tenderly on the mouth, she grabbed her helmet again. "Better get going."

"All right. See you aboard the mothership." Darian shot her a last look and then exited *Speeder One*.

Samantha walked back down to the aft area, and this time Raoul and Camilla joined her. "You don't have to be here. I know what to do." Samantha was focused on her mission, but part of her was still amazed at seeing Camilla not only wearing a uniform, but also moving so effortlessly on steady feet. It was a miraculous recovery, going from having to use a wheelchair and increasing medication regularly—to this. Samantha didn't dare hope it would be permanent, but she knew Darian would be crushed if it wasn't. Perhaps Camilla's NIEC made her seem to take her improvement in stride, but, then again, Samantha knew this woman had always possessed a strength that was next level, from what Darian had told her. Samantha broke out of her reverie when Raoul grabbed her wrist.

"That's where you're wrong. You're going to wear a monitor, and we're going to make sure you're not jeopardizing yourself." Raoul attached a small device the size of a lump of white sugar on the inside of Samantha's wrist. Then he clasped it shut with three filaments. "There."

"I'm wearing one too, twenty-four seven." Camilla pulled up her sleeve and showed her monitor. "Actually, it makes me feel safe."

"All right. No problem." Samantha folded out three extra crew seats. "Better buckle up. Holly's going through our preflight status check."

Camilla and Raoul took the two other seats, and they all strapped in.

"Not my first flight," Camilla said, "but my first while wearing my NIEC."

Samantha took Camilla's hand, reveling in how the joints were smooth and not swollen and painful. "Holly will do great. She's our captain."

As if on cue, *Speeder One* was hovering in the tunnel. Holly's voice came over the intercom system. "*Speeder Two* is hovering as well. We're going to perform the turning maneuver, and then we're off into the chute. To new crewmembers, it won't be worse than your average roller-coaster ride."

A slight understatement, but Samantha agreed with Holly. Then she realized that this was Holly's first time in a shuttle, and she was at the controls. She didn't point out that fact to Camilla and Raoul, who both had their eyes closed. What was the point?

Speeder One lurched and then hurtled through the chute. The hatch in the ground at the meadows opened, and they shot through at a perfect angle. As the only one before today who knew how much it took to fly the speeders, Samantha was impressed. Holly clearly didn't fight her NIEC but allowed the information to filter in at the right pace.

"Remain in your seats with your harnesses on." Samantha unbuckled and stood. "I'm going to open the aft loading hatch as Holly is positioning us the right way with our aft toward the lake." She walked over to the control console and gave the command to open the hatch.

The sound of the wind was deafening at first when Samantha let it slide open. When the opening was large enough not to trap the wind in a huge whistle, it became more bearable. Putting on her helmet, she walked back to the other two and crouched in front of them. "Double-check the fastening, please."

Four hands felt around Samantha's neck, and eventually Camilla gave her a thumbs-up. "You're good to go."

"Thanks. Now, just remain here unless something goes awry." Samantha hoped they realized she outranked them both—at least until they'd received their insignia from Holly.

"Be careful," Camilla called out. "If something happens to you, Darian will never forgive me."

"I'm going to tether myself until it's time to take off." Samantha walked over to the ramp and the open hatch, slipping a hook from her belt into a hoop attached to the bulkhead. She held on to a long pipe by the hatch, watching the ground streak by.

It wouldn't be long now.

❖

Holly set the controls to hover. *Speeder One* was positioned with its aft section directed toward the lake, half a mile from its shore. Samantha was going to need room to maneuver the *Velocity*, and Holly set the proximity warning to have *Speeder One* move out of the way should something go wrong. A cold sensation rippled down her spine. The worst-case scenario—no—disastrous scenario, would be if the mothership crashed into the residential area four kilometers away. Holly pushed the thought away.

"There she is!" Walker pointed at the viewscreen where the video feed from the aft sensors was shown. As the video was crystal clear, it was easy to see the small figure moving swiftly through the air, away from *Speeder One*. Somewhere to their port side, *Speeder Two* was cloaked, helping them monitor the situation.

"Darian to *Speeder One*. See her?" Darian's tense voice came over the shuttle speaker.

"We do," Holly said. "She's on a steady trajectory."

The afternoon sun made the helmet and hover-pack glimmer like red gold. Samantha circled the lake and then took up a position halfway between the shuttles and the water. Holly looked back at the crew. Enthralled, some were standing up.

"Holly to Carl. What's your status?" Waiting and hoping that Carl hadn't been made as one of Samantha and Darian's friends, she was flooded with relief when he answered.

"I'm on my bike at the edge of the meadows. I saw what looked like a freaking superhero shoot out of nothing and begin hovering toward the lake."

"It's Samantha. Maintain your distance. Anyone there with you?" Holly asked.

"Four more recruits from the list. One is my math teacher, Ms. Komarov."

"I'll let you know where to bring them once Samantha's done," Holly said.

"Done with what?" Carl asked.

"Look toward the lake. You can't miss it."

Carl gasped. "She's bringing up the *Velocity*!"

"Stay alert. We don't know how much Miller and Billings have figured out. Crowe out."

"Look!" Walker pointed to the screen. "The water."

Holly had already seen the shift in the water. Rippling, it cascaded in toward the center of the lake, only to seemingly vanish off to the sides when the waves returned to shore. She kept her eye on the chronometer at the bottom of the screen. One minute. Two. After four minutes, the lake was drained. Holly hadn't expected that.

The red glowing figure that was Samantha moved from one side of the lake to the other, as if in a search pattern. Was she in trouble? Didn't she know what to do? Once she was on her way back toward them, she stopped over the center point of the lake. There she moved out to the side and hovered. Another minute passed.

"What's she doing?" Camilla murmured, coming up to stand next to Holly.

"Wait." Holly stood and placed a hand on Camilla's shoulder. "Something's happening."

"Is that the bottom of the lake?" one of the new recruits asked.

Holly took one step closer to the screen. "No." She could barely talk as her mouth was instantly dry. "That, everybody, is the *Velocity*."

Samantha backed up as antennas and other protruding parts of the top of the ship emerged from below the lake. She found herself staring down into the large space where the *Velocity* had rested for centuries, but now emerged like a hibernating prehistoric animal. The sound could only be compared to a roar as the recently dormant propulsion system pushed the ship straight up. She was tapping in commands on the console that had flipped open in the front of her hover-pack. The number of calculations this comparatively small console had to do to control the basic flight commands was impressive. The fact that her NIEC knew how to do it and had her believe she had trained at this feat for years was even more unfathomable.

Now the ship was high enough for Samantha to see the struts. She wasn't going to pull them up into the belly of the ship, as she meant to set it down on the meadows.

Persuading her hands to remain stable, she coaxed the ship forward and hoped the ones piloting the speeders would back off. Samantha didn't dare even glance at the town but assumed that the noise was already drawing attention and that once she had the ship up above the treetops, people would start approaching. This gave her just enough time to set the ship down, and as she would much rather do that from the helm, she maneuvered her hover-pack toward the emergency hatch located closest to the bridge. She slid her fingers against the console and looked for where the hatch might open but couldn't see it.

"Crowe to Samantha. What's going on?" Holly's voice startled her.

"I'm attempting to enter the ship. Can you help me look for a hatch opening on the starboard side, deck three?"

"Both speeders will decloak and move to the *Velocity's* starboard side and help you look," Holly said.

"Darian to Samantha. Claire's pulling up the blueprints. She'll direct you in a moment if you haven't found it."

Moving as close to the hull of the mothership as she could, Samantha set the enormous vessel to hover while she scanned it. She saw so many protrusions, indentations, grids, and patterns, it was impossible to determine which one could host the hatch.

"Claire to Samantha. Got it. Go another fifty yards toward the stern, and then go up six feet." Claire's cheery voice made Samantha feel calmer.

Adjusting her position, she had to spend another half a minute to locate the hatch, which was circular and only five feet across. She pressed the sensor that opened it on her console, and it obediently swung inward. Pushing herself inside, she closed the hatch behind her and checked the pressure in the small area. As she was not in space, it didn't require repressurizing.

"All hands, this is Samantha. I'm in." To the sound of cheering, Samantha pushed off her gear and placed it in an empty bin by the bulkhead, keeping only the console. Opening the inner hatch, which was rectangular and bigger than the first one, she entered a corridor. The inner hatch closed automatically behind her, and she began to run through the hallway. As she entered the bridge, she was momentarily taken aback by how every single instrument and computer console was lit up. She could imagine the aliens who came to Earth sitting behind their screens, working to hide the ship under the lake.

"All hands. I'm at the helm. I'm going to set the *Velocity* down at the coordinates we agreed on." She took in the helm, and it was as if she had done this her entire life. Her hands flew across the controls with the familiarity that comes from long practice. How could her muscle memory so flawlessly operate a spaceship the size of a soccer field? She decided to grow philosophical later and let the ship rise until it cleared the trees with the struts.

"Samantha to Holly. What's going on in town?"

"Hm. A bit of a commotion," Holly replied. "You'll see for yourself when you've landed the ship. See you soon."

It took Samantha ten minutes to get the ship at the perfect angle, with its stern facing the town. Once the struts made contact with the meadows, the automated system took over and secured the vessel. Following the plan, she opened the cargo door and watched *Speeder Two* enter and find its bay. She smiled, relieved, as she knew Darian was piloting it, which meant she would be at her side within minutes. In the meantime, she pulled up the feed from the stern sensors.

And gasped.

Holly set down *Speeder One* in front of the majestic spaceship behind her. She could tell this was going to be a challenge and wished she'd thought to bring a bullhorn. "That's at least half of Dennamore's population." She peered at the screen. "And the other half is probably not far behind, or will be, once everyone gets off work."

"Guess it's time to face the music," Walker said and put his arm around Camilla's shoulders.

"It is." Holly turned to the rest of the crew. "This will be hard for all of us, but it will be extra difficult for those of you who are new. Your family members know nothing about this situation, and you don't know enough yet to answer all their questions. We still must show ourselves, all of us, and we have to move quickly. It won't take people long to call the authorities, even if I doubt that the phrase 'a spaceship came up from the bottom of our lake' will have the military dashing over instantly."

"We're behind you, Captain," Nate said, apparently the spokesperson for the newest crewmembers.

"Very well." Holly opened the hatch and watched the ramp lower itself onto the grass. She stepped outside with the rest of the senior crew behind her, followed by the new recruits. Behind them, the *Velocity* was on standby, its propulsion system now purring rather than roaring like before.

Carl was running toward them with a big grin. Behind him, fifty or so Dennamore inhabitants approached with some trepidation and, farther back, hundreds more.

A vehicle approached, and Holly recognized Chief Billing's SUV. It stopped twenty yards from her, and the others and he stepped outside, followed by Miller and two police officers.

"Ms. Crowe?" Billings frowned. "What—"

"To save time, let me go first," Holly said and walked closer. She noticed the men tensing up and hid a smile. Yes, talking to someone that is backed up by enormous space vessels had to be intimidating. "This is why we removed items from the archive, Chief. Some of us have been working to uncover Dennamore's secret past for months, and Chairman Miller's attempt at shutting us out from the archives forced our hand."

"She confesses," Miller said, but his voice was weak.

"Quiet." Holly glared at the man. "The items we took belong aboard this ship. We are recruiting crewmembers to join us on our voyage to the home world of the people who once founded our town. You're one of their descendants, Chief. So are you, Miller." It pained Holly to say it, but it was the truth.

"I have to come." A woman approached, appearing rapt with awe as she looked up at the *Velocity.* She was in her thirties and was holding a grocery bag.

"That sounds fantastic," Holly said. "I will inform everyone who shows an interest, and from what we've learned, those who are destined to join are the ones who know immediately."

"This is…insane." Billings pushed his cap off and rubbed his scalp vigorously. "This…you can't just take people and fly away."

"Of course not." Holly understood that his shock was talking. "Volunteers only."

"And Nate? What are you doing over there with them?" Billings had found his subordinate among the recruits.

"This is my calling, sir." Nate didn't sound apologetic but regarded his former boss with kindness. "I hope you'll understand one day."

"What about your parents?" Billings was getting worked up, and Holly signaled to Camilla and Walker to start moving back up the ramp again.

"My parents will see me again. I'll talk to them before I go." Nate waved as he reentered *Speeder One*.

"A few of my crew and I will return and talk to the ones who are adamant about going. I'll post on the Town Hall website about where and when later." Holly smiled and waved as she was the last to go aboard. When she turned to step through the hatch, she heard Billings yell behind her.

"Don't move! I'm placing you under arrest, Ms. Crowe."

Turning her head back over her shoulder, Holly saw the man had pulled his sidearm on her. "Really?" She tapped her bracelet and kept walking. If he fired, her personal force field would absorb most of the energy of the bullet.

As it turned out, Chief Billings didn't fire, and the hatch closed behind her. So relieved she felt dizzy, she shook her head.

"Now there's a man who had his view of the world turned around from one minute to the next. Well, I suppose that's true for all of them," Walker said as he sat down by the controls. "Want me to take the speeder into the cargo hold?"

"Go ahead, please." Holly felt a bit nauseous and guessed it had to be from the brief standoff outside. She sat down next to Camilla as Walker maneuvered *Speeder One* around the struts and into *Velocity*'s belly.

"I don't think their initial shock will be as detrimental to them as you seem to fear, Holly," Camilla said.

"What do you mean? Their loved ones will go off on an adventure that they want nothing to do with, or they'll start questioning their faith, or—"

"I have a plan for the first part. One person from our team should remain behind as liaison, someone who keeps their NIEC and will be able to stay in contact for as long as it's technically possible. Perhaps we will even be able to extend the range of the communication array. After all, we're resourceful people."

"I see." Holly wondered what poor soul would be chosen to stay behind. Philber came to mind, as he was the only one from the original group that was still in Dennamore. What would he say to such a suggestion? "And the second part?"

"Regarding faith and so on, I think the ones on the fence could still be swayed either way Those who are devout will remain devout, once they realize that technology isn't necessarily on a collision course with religion. And when people understand we truly aren't alone in the universe, they might just see things in a broader perspective." Camilla gripped Holly's hand when Walker put them down in *Speeder One*'s bay. "Ah, we're here."

Holly wondered if Camilla was trying to encourage her, or if she genuinely believed humanity might respond so favorably to their decision to unearth the ship.

"Hey, look," Walker said. "The lake water's back."

Holly blinked at the screen, and even from the odd angle of the starboard sensors, she could see the water looking like it had before. She had no idea how the aliens had created a way for the water to flow back, but the beautiful sight made tears sting behind her eyelids.

"All right, everyone. Disembark the shuttle and take your duty stations." Holly moved toward the hatch and tapped her speaker. "Captain Crowe to the bridge. Commence launch sequence once sensors show no people are too close. Once that's done, engage cloaking and take us into high orbit, outside the perimeter of satellites, etcetera. We don't want to accidentally wreck something."

"Aye, Captain. Samantha here. Initiating launch sequence."

Under Holly's feet, the deck reverberated as Samantha readied the ship for takeoff. Holly knew it couldn't happen fast enough, as she was sure Dennamore would soon have visitors. All they could hope for was that it all sounded like too much of a stretch for the serious-minded people of the different agencies and military branches. Their recruitment plan depended on it.

CHAPTER EIGHTEEN

Darian stood in the doorway of the quarters that Camilla, in her added duty as temporary quartermaster, had assigned to her once they were in high orbit. Located among the senior officers' corridor, it looked pristine. She walked inside, looked around, and then turned back to Camilla. "It's so big. Much larger than I expected."

"And still, it's part of a duplex, you could say." Camilla pointed at a door Darian hadn't noticed. "That connects this unit to the neighboring one."

"Which apparently is mine." Samantha poked her head in. She looked pale but also relieved.

"Thank God for that," Darian said, her heart beating easier. She had suffered from elevated stress ever since Samantha took off with the hover-pack.

"I'm going to continue with my list. Captain's quarters are next." Camilla winked at them and continued down the corridor.

"Come here." Darian pulled Samantha in for a hug. "You were amazing today. Utterly amazing, and you scared the shit out of me." She buried her face against Samantha's neck.

"And you are quite the pilot yourself," Samantha said, running her fingers through Darian's ponytail. "I was frightened too, as you can imagine. I had visions of letting the *Velocity* plummet on top of people's houses." She shuddered.

"But you didn't. You landed it perfectly on the meadows." Cupping Samantha's cheeks gently, Darian kissed her. It wasn't as much an erotic sort of kiss, more like one of reconnection and gratitude. "So, we'll be neighbors? Or cohabitants?" Darian asked the last part with hope in her heart.

"Cohabitants. Definitely. Should our duty shifts not follow the same pattern, the door might come in handy."

"That would be the only time, I hope." Samantha pressed the sensor that closed the door to the corridor. "I heard voices." She took Darian's hand and pulled her with her. "Come over to the viewport. Have you looked outside since we settled into high orbit?"

"No. I was going through some documents on the computer when Gran came and got me, insisting I learn where my very own quarters are before, as she put it, 'all hell breaks loose.'"

"Then come and see." Samantha tugged at Darian's hand again.

The viewport was really two separate ones. Low and wide, one was placed just above the backrest of a couch and the other at eye level when standing up. As they approached, Darian could tell that they were maintaining a steady position in orbit. Samantha had located the controls to keep the ship from spinning in space. Now they orbited around Earth, and their beautiful blue-and-green planet was staggeringly beautiful.

"It's amazing. It's a sight I never thought possible for me to see in real life." Darian drew a trembling breath. "Seeing it here with you, after everything we've gone through and figured out—it's miraculous."

"It is. And the idea that we and our crew will perhaps be able to see other planets, especially our ancestors' home planet...I can barely wrap my brain around that possibility."

"Has the captain made a decision yet, do you think?" Darian tugged Samantha closer. "How she'll go about getting the crewmembers we need aboard, I mean?"

"I think so. It'll involve compromising. That's all she told me."

Darian nodded slowly. "She's got the brains to pull this off. Thank God, because all I know is how to kick ass." Grinning at Samantha, she was surprised when she saw her serious expression. "What? What's wrong?"

"Nothing." Samantha ran a thumb along Darian's lower lip. "May I finally tell you something I've been working up my courage to share?"

Darian frowned. "Sure. You can tell me anything." She caressed Samantha's back.

"I'm in love with you. I should have told you before we entered separate speeders, but everything was so frantic. So, I'm telling you now—oh…"

Darian pressed her lips to Samantha's, making sure the kiss conveyed her own feelings. Pulling back just enough to be able to speak, she said, "I love you too. It's as if I always have."

"That collision was the start of a lot of things. Dar…" Hugging Darian close, Samantha began to cry. "I'm sorry…I really was so afraid…"

"Shh. It's all right. Just let it out." Darian knew this was another sign of Samantha's feelings, that she could let her guard down enough to cry in her presence. She kept holding Samantha, sitting perfectly still, not rocking or saying anything. This was what Samantha needed, and Darian was the one who could give her that safe harbor. Soon enough they would embark on a no-doubt perilous journey toward an unknown world.

Until then, Darian would make sure Samantha never doubted her love.

Holly stood in her office, which was on the starboard side of the bridge. A small, flat viewport showed her Earth where it spun on its axis, her home, her planet that she was so eager to leave…but also to return to.

She returned to her computer, now docked with all the resources on this amazing ship, which she knew they had only scraped the surface of. It was most likely a dangerous thing to learn on the go, trusting the NIECs to help them, when embarking on a deep-space exploration.

Pulling up the list of the crewmembers aboard the *Velocity* thus far, she read through their brief personnel facts and noticed that their respective NIECs had found them positions already. She saw one obvious choice for a security officer—Nate, the police officer. Three people for engineering, two maintenance officers, two ops officers, two pilots, and one nurse. On the other side of the screen two names, among the ones she already knew, blinked with suggested ranks. Camilla Tennen, chief counselor. Geoff Walker, first officer.

"Those suggestions shouldn't have come as a surprise." Holly leaned back in her chair. It was comfortably cushioned, and the pattern in the leatherlike finish was familiar. She had seen it on the hull of the speeders and the ship. Perhaps she couldn't pinpoint the pattern's significance because more pressing matters were at hand. She pulled the flat box with rank insignias out of the drawer of her desk and selected the ones she required. Camilla and Walker needed to know that she realized what their assignments were going to be.

She exited her office and found every crewmember, except the four that were needed in engineering, present on the bridge. It was still a surprise to see Camilla stand without effort. Holly walked over to her first and stopped in front of her. "I know you've found your calling."

"I have."

"Are you pleased?" Holly studied the stunning face and tried to fathom that this woman was seventy-five years old. Once Raoul had treated the rheumatoid arthritis, it was as if he'd taken fifteen years off Camilla.

"Very pleased."

"Pleased about what?" Darian murmured, who stood just behind Camilla.

"Camilla Tennen, do you accept to serve at the rank as chief counselor aboard the *Velocity*?" Holly held up the rank insignia.

"I do." Camilla smiled brightly, and her eyes had turned a brilliant blue.

"Welcome aboard." Holly pinned the insignia on Camilla's uniform and then turned to Walker. "You know as well, don't you?"

"I do, but the choice is yours, Captain," Walker said calmly.

"An easy choice. Geoff Walker. Do you accept to serve at the rank of first officer aboard the *Velocity*?"

The others gave a collective gasp, but Holly didn't take her eyes off Walker's weathered face.

"I do. I won't let you down, Captain." Walker didn't look as emotional as Camilla but grinned as Holly pinned his insignia on.

"I will hand out more ranks, but these are the most important ones. I'll swing by engineering before I go down to Dennamore and do the same for Claire," Holly said.

"Excuse me? You're going down, Captain?" Walker clearly took his job as first officer serious from the first moment.

"I've given this a lot of thought, and only by compromise can we see our mission through. Going down to Dennamore in a controlled manner will give us our best outcome."

"They can just grab you and throw you in jail, Captain," Carl said.

"They can, but they won't. I'm going to make a few more preparations, and once I'm done, I'll need a pilot and a security officer." Holly turned her attention toward Darian and Samantha.

"We'll be ready, Captain," Samantha said.

"Then follow me into my office. You need to know what's going to happen. For the rest of you, I have left instructions on your computers, which will become available if I have somehow miscalculated the situation." Holly checked the time. "It's seven thirty p.m. now. We have half an hour. Dismissed." She strode back to her office, with Samantha and Darian right behind her.

Samantha took *Speeder One* through the clouds, keeping a close eye on normal air traffic. She was nowhere near any airline corridors, but other aircrafts such as helicopters and private planes could be passing by.

"I want you to put it down on the square. Chief Billings has promised he's going to keep people at a safe distance." Holly stood behind Samantha and Darian. "He thinks he's going to have the upper hand, which is what I want him to believe for another forty-eight hours. I'm pressing the matter tonight only because we *need* at least a skeletal crew right away."

"Right now, we can keep only the most basic functions going, so, yes." Darian turned to look at Holly. "Gran...I'm sorry. It's not professional, but I can't call her Counselor Tennen...is providing food for the others, showing them where to find the reproducers. I just hope that what our ancestors ate is at least palatable."

"I hope so, because that's all we have," Samantha said. "As for the ranks and titles, as long as we use them correctly when addressing each other in front of junior officers, I feel we're all right. Except with you and Commander Walker, Captain."

"Sounds doable." Holly nodded.

"Miller won't know what hit him," Darian said. "He's probably trying to spin this in some way, and if he's not careful, he might just spin himself out of the Elder Council."

"He's not my main concern," Holly said. "Billings, who is in charge of the police, and thus the weapons that come with that job, is. He's always seemed levelheaded and calm, but this is an unprecedented event, and it can mess with the quietest among us."

"And what about Philber? Will he be there?" Samantha said. "Have you talked to him, Captain?"

"I have. He'll be there, but he's not joining us. At least not yet. It all depends on how things work out over the next couple of days."

Samantha moved along the northern part of the East Coast and then over the state of New York. Hurtling toward Dennamore, she began her last descent as she reached the taller mountains, thus prepared to stay under the radar when it was time to decloak. She saw the lights of her hometown appear in the distance as she came in over the meadows. The cloaking device did dampen the sound of the propulsion system, but she knew that the inhabitants would hear them come in.

"Decloak now, Darian," Holly said.

"Aye, Captain." Darian moved her hands over the console, and the faint pinging sound alerted them that it was done.

"How does it look?" Holly asked.

"The square's empty and cordoned off. We'll be able to set down in the center and still have enough space around the speeder to keep it safe," Samantha said.

"Then put us down."

Samantha landed in the center of the square, facing the Town Hall, where she had spent a lot of her childhood and all her professional life. "When you're ready, Samantha, cut the propulsion and open the hatch."

"Cutting propulsion." The sound whirred to a stop.

Standing up, Samantha and Darian moved in behind Holly. Samantha made sure her uniform was correct and that the vest that came with it held the devices she might need, which included a sidearm. Holly and Darian had similar equipment. "When you're ready, Samantha, open the hatch."

Samantha pressed a sensor on a small console on the bulkhead. The hatch opened, and the ramp lowered itself onto the cobblestones. Holly stepped outside, with Samantha and Darian right behind her.

"You did return," Chief Billings said from the outer perimeter. "You owe the people of Dennamore an explanation."

"They owe us more than that!" Chairman Miller appeared a few feet from Billings but kept his distance. "Who are you people really? You're not going to make me believe that you're just regular people who have access to this type of technology."

"Chief Billings," Holly said and walked toward him, stopping when she was ten yards from his position. He was flanked by two police officers, and Samantha guessed others were located around the square.

"Don't worry, Darian murmured. "I have them on my trackpad. They're not approaching. Yet."

"All right." Samantha nodded.

"I have alerted the military, FBI, and naturally, Homeland Security." Billings spoke firmly. "Not sure how you pulled it off, but apparently the clips and photos taken of the ships are not visible online, nor will they go out via text messages. Still, they believed me enough to be on their way here."

"I bet they're not hurrying," Darian murmured.

"Not yet, but they will, once I've contacted them," Holly said in a low voice.

"What?" Darian snapped her head to their captain. "Captain?"

"Trust me. There's no other way." Holly kept her gaze trained on Billings.

Samantha swept her gaze across the people, many of whom she knew well, and when she saw a large group, all with large backpacks or carry-ons, being held back by police officers, she nudged Darian. "That group is our people, Dar."

Darian rounded Samantha. "Sure looks like it. Captain?"

"I see them." Holly took two more steps forward. "Why don't you let the people over there approach us, Chief? They're here because they want to be."

"Are they? I think you've sent some sort of signal that's turned them into mindless robots who can even imagine going aboard that... that ship of yours and not knowing what they're getting themselves into." Billings spat the words, but Samantha could tell that he wasn't as certain about his own opinion as he tried to sound.

"I have done nothing of the sort. I need a crew, that is correct, but I'm not interested in anyone whose heart isn't in it. People who feel something like the yearning, like our returnees feel about Dennamore, a phenomenon you are well aware of, Chief, are very welcome to join, as well as their closest family."

"You're asking them to risk their children?" Miller roared. "Do you hear this, good people of Dennamore? This woman won't even draw the line at endangering children." He pointed more at her, Samantha noticed, than at Holly.

"I will go," a woman called out, "and so will my husband and two sons. You have nothing to say about that, Chief. You're a good man and you mean well, but I know that Ms. Pike and Chief Walker wouldn't be part of this if it wasn't important. And I'm sure this is the right thing for my family." She nudged a very young, peach-fuzz-faced officer out of the way and walked up to Holly hand in hand with her husband and boys, the latter looking to be around ten and twelve.

"Welcome," Holly said. "I'm Captain Crowe."

"My name's Matt, and this is my wife Tricia," the husband said. "I just need to know one thing. Will we return to Dennamore at one point?"

"Yes. That's our goal. This isn't a one-way mission."

"That's good enough for us." Tricia smiled.

"Excellent. If you will step into the speeder, you'll find crew seats waiting. We'll be there shortly."

Tricia, Matt, and their sons walked up the ramp and through the hatch opening. Once they were inside, the dam seemed to break over by the police officers. People pushed them aside and walked up to *Speeder One*, introducing themselves briefly as they passed Holly, then nodding at Samantha and Darian. When thirty individuals had gone on board, Darian held up her hand. "I can see many more of you who want to join us, and we're not saying no to you, but we'll return several more times if you're willing to wait."

"You mean tonight?" a young woman asked.

"Yes. We'll shuttle you up to the mothership until we're done. Once up there, you can ask any questions you want and then make a truly informed decision."

"I already know," the woman said, looking up at the star-filled sky. "And I'll wait right here."

Voices repeated her words in unison. Samantha could barely breathe at the dedication she could detect already in the faces of the people in line for the speeder. They weren't wearing a NIEC or any other device to affect them, but they had inherited their ancestors' deep longing for Dwynna Major, and it showed.

"Just stay back when we take off. Walk over to the perimeter set up by the police. I don't think they'll try to stop you." Holly turned to Billings. "Will you, Chief?"

"Not tonight. I don't want a riot on my hands. You have these people fooled, but the military will deal with you when they get here."

Samantha, who had listened to Holly's strategy, knew he was in for a surprise. She saw no point in trying to convince him of this right now. Instead, she hurried up the ramp with the other two and started the takeoff sequence. Behind her, thirty people who, until this afternoon, had been living their lives as normal, everyday inhabitants of Dennamore, now stood on the threshold of their greatest, most life-altering adventure.

As *Speeder One* hovered above the square and Town Hall, Darian was on the speaker relaying Holly's order for Walker to take *Speeder Two* down to collect the next group of thirty recruits, with the assistance of Carl and a security officer.

"Ready to cloak, Captain," Samantha said, sliding her fingers over the controls.

"Then do so, and set a course toward high orbit," Holly said, glancing back at the passengers. "For the *Velocity*."

EPILOGUE

Camilla stood in her and Geoff's quarters. Beneath the *Velocity*, Earth spun and rushed along its trajectory through space. Soon they would leave the beautiful orb behind, and it was uncertain when they'd see it again. Camilla wasn't worried about that. She had Darian and Brandon here with her. The company that had taken care of Brynden 4 when she lived in LA would continue to do so. Geoff, obviously, was here. Right now, he was making his second round-trip to Dennamore to pick up new potential crewmembers.

No, something else was nagging at her and popping up in the back of her mind, becoming harder to ignore. She knew exactly when it had started—the day Holly had returned with the others from the *Velocity* wearing the captain's NIEC. That was when Camilla had understood how blind she had been regarding the possibility that she might have information about Holly's origin.

She hugged herself. There was a decent chance she could be wrong, but that inner voice insisted she was right. When she learned that Raoul had sampled Holly's DNA to confirm she had the marker for alien ancestry, Camilla had known she must act. If nothing else, she needed to know, and Holly deserved to learn the truth.

No matter the outcome.

About the Author

Gun Brooke, author of more than twenty-five novels, writes her stories surrounded by a loving family and two affectionate dogs. When she isn't writing, she works on her art and her crafts whenever possible—certain that practice pays off. Gun loves being creative, whether using conventional materials or digital art software.

Web site: http://www.gbrooke-fiction.com

Books Available from Bold Strokes Books

#shedeservedit by Greg Herren. When his gay best friend, and high school football star, is murdered, Alex Wheeler is a suspect and must find the truth to clear himself. (978-1-63555-996-5)

Always by Kris Bryant. When a pushy American private investigator shows up demanding to meet the woman in Camila's artwork, instead of introducing her to her great-grandmother, Camila decides to lead her on a wild goose chase all over Italy. (978-1-63679-027-5)

Exes and O's by Joy Argento. Ali and Madison really only have one thing in common. The girl who broke their heart may be the only one who can put it back together. (978-1-63679-017-6)

One Verse Multi by Sander Santiago. Life was good: promotion, friends, falling in love, discovering that the multi-verse is on a fast track to collision—wait, what? Good thing Martin King works for a company that can fix the problem, right...um...right? (978-1-63679-069-5)

Paris Rules by Jaime Maddox. Carly Becker has been searching for the perfect woman all her life, but no one ever seems to be just right until Paige Waterford checks all her boxes, except the most important one—she's married. (978-1-63679-077-0)

Shadow Dancers by Suzie Clarke. In this third and final book in the Moon Shadow series, Rachel must find a way to become the hunter and not the hunted, and this time she will meet Ehsee Yumiko head-on. (978-1-63555-829-6)

The Kiss by C.A. Popovich. When her wife refuses their divorce and begins to stalk her, threatening her life, Kate realizes to protect her new love, Leslie, she has to let her go, even if it breaks her heart. (978-1-63679-079-4)

The Wedding Setup by Charlotte Greene. When Ryann, a big-time New York executive, goes to Colorado to help out with her best friend's wedding, she never expects to fall for the maid of honor. (978-1-63679-033-6)

Velocity by Gun Brooke. Holly and Claire work toward an uncertain future preparing for an alien space mission, and only one thing is for certain, they will have to risk their lives, and their hearts, to discover the truth. (978-1-63555-983-5)

Wildflower Words by Sam Ledel. Lida Jones treks West with her father in search of a better life on the rapidly developing American frontier, but finds home when she meets Hazel Thompson. (978-1-63679-055-8)

A Fairer Tomorrow by Kathleen Knowles. For Maddie Weeks and Gerry Stern, the Second World War brought them together, but the end of the war might rip them apart. (978-1-63555-874-6)

Holiday Hearts by Diana Day-Admire and Lyn Cole. Opposites attract during Christmastime chaos in Kansas City. (978-1-63679-128-9)

Changing Majors by Ana Hartnett Reichardt. Beyond a love, beyond a coming-out, Bailey Sullivan discovers what lies beyond the shame and self-doubt imposed on her by traditional Southern ideals. (978-1-63679-081-7)

Fresh Grave in Grand Canyon by Lee Patton. The age-old Grand Canyon becomes more and more ominous as a group of volunteers fight to survive alone in nature and uncover a murderer among them. (978-1-63679-047-3)

Highland Whirl by Anna Larner. Opposites attract in the Scottish Highlands, when feisty Alice Campbell falls for city-girl-about-town Roxanne Barns. (978-1-63555-892-0)

Humbug by Amanda Radley. With the corporate Christmas party in jeopardy, CEO Rosalind Caldwell hires Christmas Girl Ellie Pearce as her personal assistant. The only problem is, Ellie isn't a PA, has never planned a party, and develops a ridiculous crush on her totally intimidating new boss. (978-1-63555-965-1)

On the Rocks by Georgia Beers. Schoolteacher Vanessa Martini makes no apologies for her dating checklist, and newly single mom Grace Chapman ticks all Vanessa's Do Not Date boxes. Of course, they're never going to fall in love. (978-1-63555-989-7)

Song of Serenity by Brey Willows. Arguing with the Muse of music and justice is complicated, falling in love with her even more so. (978-1-63679-015-2)

The Christmas Proposal by Lisa Moreau. Stranded together in a Christmas village on a snowy mountain, Grace and Bridget face their past and question their dreams for the future. (978-1-63555-648-3)

The Infinite Summer by Morgan Lee Miller. While spending the summer with her dad in a small beach town, Remi Brenner falls for Harper Hebert and accidentally finds herself tangled up in an intense restaurant rivalry between her famous stepmom and her first love. (978-1-63555-969-9)

Wisdom by Jesse J. Thoma. When Sophia and Reggie are chosen for the governor's new community design team and tasked with tackling substance abuse and mental health issues, battle lines are drawn even as sparks fly. (978-1-63555-886-9)

A Convenient Arrangement by Aurora Rey and Jaime Clevenger. Cuffing season has come for lesbians, and for Jess Archer and Cody Dawson, their convenient arrangement becomes anything but. (978-1-63555-818-0)

An Alaskan Wedding by Nance Sparks. The last thing either Andrea or Riley expects is to bump into the one who broke her heart fifteen years ago, but when they meet at the welcome party, their feelings come rushing back. (978-1-63679-053-4)

Beulah Lodge by Cathy Dunnell. It's 1874, and newly engaged Ruth Mallowes is set on marriage and life as a missionary…until she falls in love with the housemaid at Beulah Lodge. (978-1-63679-007-7)

Gia's Gems by Toni Logan. When Lindsey Speyer discovers that popular travel columnist Gia Williams is a complete fake and threatens to expose her, blackmail has never been so sexy. (978-1-63555-917-0)

Holiday Wishes & Mistletoe Kisses by M. Ullrich. Four holidays, four couples, four chances to make their wishes come true. (978-1-63555-760-2)

Love By Proxy by Dena Blake. Tess has a secret crush on her best friend, Sophie, so the last thing she wants is to help Sophie fall in love with someone else, but how can she stand in the way of her happiness? (978-1-63555-973-6)

Loyalty, Love, & Vermouth by Eric Peterson. A comic valentine to a gay man's family of choice, including the ones with cold noses and four paws. (978-1-63555-997-2)

Marry Me by Melissa Brayden. Allison Hale attempts to plan the wedding of the century to a man who could save her family's business, if only she wasn't falling for her wedding planner, Megan Kinkaid. (978-1-63555-932-3)

Pathway to Love by Radclyffe. Courtney Valentine is looking for a woman exactly like Ben—smart, sexy, and not in the market for anything serious. All she has to do is convince Ben that sex-without-strings is the perfect pathway to pleasure. (978-1-63679-110-4)

Sweet Surprise by Jenny Frame. Flora and Mac never thought they'd ever see each other again, but when Mac opens up her barber shop right next to Flora's sweet shop, their connection comes roaring back. (978-1-63679-001-5)

The Edge of Yesterday by CJ Birch. Easton Gray is sent from the future to save humanity from technological disaster. When she's forced to target the woman she's falling in love with, can Easton do what's needed to save humanity? (978-1-63679-025-1)

The Scout and the Scoundrel by Barbara Ann Wright. With unexpected danger surrounding them, Zara and Roni are stuck between duty and survival, with little room for exploring their feelings, especially love. (978-1-63555-978-1)

Bury Me in Shadows by Greg Herren. College student Jake Chapman is forced to spend the summer at his dying grandmother's home and soon finds danger from long-buried family secrets. (978-1-63555-993-4)

Can't Leave Love by Kimberly Cooper Griffin. Sophia and Pru have no intention of falling in love, but sometimes love happens when and where you least expect it. (978-1-636790041-1)

Free Fall at Angel Creek by Julie Tizard. Detective Dee Rawlings and aircraft accident investigator Dr. River Dawson use conflicting methods to find answers when a plane goes missing, while overcoming surprising threats, and discovering an unlikely chance at love. (978-1-63555-884-5)

Love's Compromise by Cass Sellars. For Piper Holthaus and Brook Myers, will professional dreams and past baggage stop two hearts from realizing they are meant for each other? (978-1-63555-942-2)

Not All a Dream by Sophia Kell Hagin. Hester has lost the woman she loved and the world has descended into relentless dark and cold. But giving up will have to wait when she stumbles upon people who help her survive. (978-1-63679-067-1)

Protecting the Lady by Amanda Radley. If Eve Webb had known she'd be protecting royalty, she'd never have taken the job as bodyguard, but as the threat to Lady Katherine's life draws closer, she'll do whatever it takes to save her, and may just lose her heart in the process. (978-1-63679-003-9)

The Secrets of Willowra by Kadyan. A family saga of three women, their homestead called Willowra in the Australian outback, and the secrets that link them all. (978-1-63679-064-0)

Trial by Fire by Carsen Taite. When prosecutor Lennox Roy and public defender Wren Bishop become fierce adversaries in a headline-grabbing arson case, their attraction ignites a passion that leads them both to question their assumptions about the law, the truth, and each other. (978-1-63555-860-9)

Turbulent Waves by Ali Vali. Kai Merlin and Vivien Palmer plan their future together as hostile forces make their own plans to destroy what they have, as well as all those they love. (978-1-63679-011-4)

Unbreakable by Cari Hunter. When Dr. Grace Kendal is forced at gunpoint to help an injured woman, she is dragged into a nightmare where nothing is quite as it seems, and their lives aren't the only ones on the line. (978-1-63555-961-3)

Veterinary Surgeon by Nancy Wheelton. When dangerous drugs are stolen from the veterinary clinic, Mitch investigates and Kay becomes a suspect. As pride and professions clash, love seems impossible. (978-1-63679-043-5)

A Different Man by Andrew L. Huerta. This diverse collection of stories chronicling the challenges of gay life at various ages shines a light on the progress made and the progress still to come. (978-1-63555-977-4)

All That Remains by Sheri Lewis Wohl. Johnnie and Shantel might have to risk their lives—and their love—to stop a werewolf intent on killing. (978-1-63555-949-1)

Beginner's Bet by Fiona Riley. Phenom luxury Realtor Ellison Gamble has everything, except a family to share it with, so when a mix-up brings youthful Katie Crawford into her life, she bets the house on love. (978-1-63555-733-6)

Dangerous Without You by Lexus Grey. Throughout their senior year in high school, Aspen, Remington, Denna, and Raleigh face challenges in life and romance that they never expect. (978-1-63555-947-7)

Desiring More by Raven Sky. In this collection of steamy stories, a rich variety of lovers find themselves desiring more, more from a lover, more from themselves, and more from life. (978-1-63679-037-4)

Jordan's Kiss by Nanisi Barrett D'Arnuck. After losing everything in a fire, Jordan Phelps joins a small lounge band and meets pianist Morgan Sparks, who lights another blaze, this time in Jordan's heart. (978-1-63555-980-4)

Late City Summer by Jeanette Bears. Forced together for her wedding, Emily Stanton and Kate Alessi navigate their lingering passion for one another against the backdrop of New York City and World War II, and a summer romance they left behind. (978-1-63555-968-2)

Love and Lotus Blossoms by Anne Shade. On her path to self-acceptance and true passion, Janesse will risk everything—and possibly everyone—she loves. (978-1-63555-985-9)

Love in the Limelight by Ashley Moore. Marion Hargreaves, the finest actress of her generation, and Jessica Carmichael, the world's biggest pop star, rediscover each other twenty years after an ill-fated affair. (978-1-63679-051-0)

Suspecting Her by Mary P. Burns. Complications ensue when Erin O'Connor falls for top real estate saleswoman Catherine Williams while investigating racism in the real estate industry; the fallout could end their chance at happiness. (978-1-63555-960-6)

Two Winters by Lauren Emily Whalen. A modern YA retelling of Shakespeare's *The Winter's Tale* about birth, death, Catholic school, improv comedy, and the healing nature of time. (978-1-63679-019-0)